A BEWITCHING KISS

"Miss Clayton?" Lord Newlyn's voice sounded from behind her.

His unexpected presence startled her, and she almost tumbled headlong into the bushes. His lordship's strong hands grabbed her about the waist and pulled her back from the brink of an accident. As he pulled her upright, she lost her balance, and both his arms slid around her. She found her body pressed against his. A strange silence seemed to fall over the garden. For just a moment, he held her close in the moonlight's silvery glow. A tremble of something unexpected raced through Naomi as she turned her face up to his, wanting and longing for something that she shouldn't desire.

A magic as strong as any spell she'd ever done seemed to engulf them, and his warm mouth closed over hers. In that instant, as her body trembled from head to toe, she realized that, magic or no, she'd lost her heart to him. . . .

From The Bewitched Baron by Lynn Collum

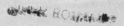

BOOK YOUR PLACE ON OUR WEBSITE AND MAKE THE READING CONNECTION!

We've created a customized website just for our very special readers, where you can get the inside scoop on everything that's going on with Zebra, Pinnacle and Kensington books.

When you come online, you'll have the exciting opportunity to:

- View covers of upcoming books

- Read sample chapters

- Learn about our future publishing schedule (listed by publication month *and author*)

- Find out when your favorite authors will be visiting a city near you

- Search for and order backlist books from our online catalog

- Check out author bios and background information

- Send e-mail to your favorite authors

- Meet the Kensington staff online

- Join us in weekly chats with authors, readers and other guests

- Get writing guidelines

- AND MUCH MORE!

**Visit our website at
http://www.kensingtonbooks.com**

A
BEWITCHING
SEASON

Lynn Collum
Debbie Raleigh
Jeanne Savery

ZEBRA BOOKS
KENSINGTON PUBLISHING CORP.
http://www.kensingtonbooks.com

ZEBRA BOOKS are published by

Kensington Publishing Corp.
850 Third Avenue
New York, NY 10022

All Kensington titles, imprints and distributed lines are available at special quantity discounts for bulk purchases for sales
promotion, premiums, fund-raising, educational or institutional
use.

Special book excerpts or customized printings can also be
created to fit specific needs. For details, write or phone the
office of the Kensington Special Sales Manager: Kensington
Publishing Corp., 850 Third Avenue, New York, NY 10022.
Attn. Special Sales Department. Phone: 1-800-221-2647.

Zebra and the Z logo Reg. U.S. Pat. & TM Off.

First Printing: September 2003
10 9 8 7 6 5 4 3 2 1

Printed in the United States of America

CONTENTS

THE
BEWITCHED
BARON

Lynn Collum

Chapter One

On a chilled September afternoon, the Marlborough stage rumbled to a halt in front of The Block and Barrel Inn. A cloud of dust simultaneously rolled in to announce its arrival. Two chambermaids rushed to the windows of the public room, so rare was the occasion when a stage put down passengers at this remote crossroad in County Wiltshire. To their disappointment, a lone female stepped down, dressed in an unfashionable brown traveling gown. The young lady looked more like a frightened rabbit than bold traveler as she eyed the rather rundown accommodations. The coachman tossed down a portmanteau beside the lady, then tugged his hat before he picked up the reins and shouted, "Walk on." In moments the stagecoach was gone, leaving the young woman to fend for herself.

Losing interest in such a primly dressed female who hadn't even a maid, the serving women returned to the task of clearing tankards and crockery off the tables. In whispered undertones, they questioned whether she was the new governess for Lady Halsham or for the Purvises. Either way they didn't envy her the task.

In front of the inn, Miss Naomi Clayton looked about as a

tremor of uncertainty quaked through her. She had never traveled beyond the borders of her father's parish in the North Riding of Yorkshire in all of her twenty years, and here she was now miles from everyone and everything she'd ever known. It certainly had not been her choice to remain so isolated, for she had longed to come to visit her aunts, who regularly sent her delightful gifts which her father had always refused to allow her to keep. Stranger still, the reverend had been adamant about her never seeing her Aunt Bebe and Aunt Iona. He gave no explanation other than they weren't a proper influence on moral young ladies. But where else was she to go? Papa had died so suddenly, and the new vicar and his family had already taken possession of the vicarage.

Mustering her courage, Naomi picked up her bag and stepped into the darkened hallway of the inn. The innkeeper approached and inquired what he might do for her in an impatient tone. He gave her an assessing look, which clearly found her wanting.

"I should like to hire a gig to take me to Hawthorn Cottage, sir." She smiled politely, with the hope of removing the frosty look in the man's gray eyes.

The rotund old man's brows rose. "Hawthorn? Are ye certain, miss? Don't often get requests to go that far out."

"I am expected, sir." She had sent her aunts a letter two days after her father's passing, and they had immediately sent funds for her to come to Wiltshire.

The old man took a step back with something akin to dread in his dark eyes. Then, after a moment's thought, he shouted for Toby. "I ain't certain any of me lads will want to go, miss, what with all the strange doings out there. But if any will, it'll be Toby, him not knowing what's what."

Before Naomi could question the man, a tall, blond lad in his teens with a dirty shirt and worn buckskins stepped through the rear door. "Aye, Mr. Ferris, was ye wantin' me?"

"Are ye willin' to take the lady out to Hawthorn Cottage at Wood End?"

There was a rather simple look in the lad's face which

made Naomi wonder if the boy was quite right, but when he looked her straight in the eyes, an innocence there made her fears fade. Simple he might be, but there was no wickedness in that face. "Aye, sir. I'll hitch ol' Bess and be right back, miss."

After paying the innkeeper, Naomi waited on a bench in the hall. In the other room, she could hear one little maid berating the old man for sending the beef-witted boy out to "that place." What was wrong with her aunts' cottage? She was tempted to ask, but then she would be there in a short while to see for herself.

Toby soon arrived with the gig. She exited the inn, shoved her portmanteau under the seat, and climbed up. The trip through the Wiltshire countryside was lovely. There had been just enough cool weather to make the leaves turn colors, and the air was heavy with the smell of wild roses and honeysuckle. The young ostler chattered rather inanely about the weather, about one of the maids at the inn who gave him extra biscuits, and he pointed out landmarks of interest.

When they crested the top of one hill, Toby pointed to the left. "There it be, miss. Hawthorn Cottage. Me ma brought me here once when I was just a lad, hopin' the ladies would fix me brain box, but"—the lad chuckled—"the lady said there ain't no fixin' what God intended."

His words sent a feeling of goodwill racing through Naomi. Clearly her aunts did their part to aid and assist the locals who fell ill. She couldn't imagine what the ladies could have done to set her father so against them. Perhaps they were great proponents of Mrs. Wollstonecraft's views about female rights, for her father had very traditional ideas.

In the glen at the bottom of the next hill sat her aunts' small, squat cottage with its gray slate roof. Smoke curled slowly out of the large chimney. The afternoon sun gave the ancient orange brick of the cottage the look of burnished copper. The garden surrounding the house appeared to have had little attention. Hawthorn hedges had been allowed to grow full, with long tendrils extending out, giving the plants a ragged, unkempt look. The weathered front door of the cottage was nearly obscured by the foliage which draped the flagstone walk.

When the carriage drew to a halt, Naomi tipped the lad. She took her portmanteau and entered the garden gate as Toby ordered his horse home. When she approached the house, the scent of lavender overwhelmed her, and she could see the cottage was completely encircled by the silvery bushes full of the tiny purple flower. There was nothing so sweet as the scent of English lavender, but it was quite odd to see it blooming this late in the autumn.

Before Naomi could knock, the door opened and two plump women stepped to the stoop. They were both flamboyantly dressed in vivid reds, purples, and blues, without the least thought to the latest fashion. One was tall and raven-haired, the other short with long tresses the color of a fiery sunset. The taller woman stepped forward and embraced Naomi. "Oh, my dear, we have been waiting for years to see you and here you are all grown-up . . . a pox on Rufus for keeping you from us." She held the girl at arm's length, tears in her eyes. "You look so like your mother, does she not, Bebe?"

Aunt Bebe shook her head even as she took Naomi's hand. "Nonsense, Iona, for she has her father's blue eyes, and Kendra's hair had a hint of red, which Naomi's does not."

Iona sniffed. "Well, let us hope eye color is all she inherited from him."

Naomi began to protest that her father was a good man, but Bebe pushed her demurs aside. "Yes, yes, child I am certain he was very *worthy,* like most vicars." A look passed between the two sisters that Naomi was unable to fathom.

"Now"—Bebe drew her niece into the circle of her arm— "do come in. We have much to tell you, but first tea, for I am certain you are tired after your long journey."

The ladies led her into the front parlor, which was a rather strange room. It was cluttered with a variety of furniture which was quite old, but quite ordinary. It was what else the room held that made Naomi's brows rise. Pots, jugs, and bottles sat on shelves along the walls of the room. An exotic scent hung in the air which she couldn't quite determine, but the aroma wasn't unpleasant. Despite the clutter, it was an inviting environment, done in warm yellows and greens, with a variety of wildflowers stuffed into many of the open containers scattered about the room.

To Naomi's delight, she spied a great black cat curled up on an overstuffed chair. Her father had always forbidden her to keep pets at the vicarage. On seeing her, the sleek animal rose and came to rub himself on Naomi's skirts.

Iona announced, "That is Suma." Then she led her niece to the chair the cat had recently vacated. The large feline climbed on the hearth and sat on his haunches to stare at the guest with his bright golden eyes.

It was soon apparent that the ladies of Hawthorn Cottage had no servants, but they seemed to manage quite well. They took turns going into the kitchen to prepare the refreshments. At last all three were seated before the unlit fireplace. Tea was a lovely affair, with sandwiches, poppy seed cakes, macaroons, and almond biscuits the likes of which Naomi had never before tasted. While they ate, the aunts questioned her about her life at Longbridge Manse. She told them her father had been strict but loving, allowing her little time for social matters. Most of her time had been taken up with helping the needy in the parish. She didn't tell them her father insisted benevolent activities delivered young ladies from sinful acts. Although she hadn't understood what he meant, for there had been no young men interested in a penniless vicar's daughter.

Iona picked up a macaroon, and took a small bite. "So you like helping others, do you?"

"I do." Naomi smoothed the napkin in her lap. "I often wished I could do more than take them calves'-foot jelly and clean linens."

Smiles appeared on both of the old women's faces. "Well, calves'-foot jelly and clean linens are a thing of the past, child. Do you not wish for a bit of excitement and fun?"

Naomi looked from one to the other. "I don't understand."

Bebe rose and went to stand in front of the fireplace. "What did your father tell you of your mother, my dear?"

"Why, very little. In fact, I found he rarely wished to speak of Mother. It seemed a bit too painful. I know that she died very young, but from what, he never said."

Bebe sighed. "Ah, were there two people more poorly suited than Kendra and Rufus? We tried to warn her, my dear. One simply does not marry without telling the groom the truth first. 'Tis my belief she died of a broken heart."

"The truth about what?" Naomi asked, wondering what dark secret her mother might have had. Had there been another man before her father? The very thought shocked Naomi.

"Yes, child. The truth is she should have told him she was a witch." Bebe folded her hands in front of her.

"And"—Iona took the last macaroon—"your father didn't approve."

Naomi stood on hearing the disturbing words. "A-a witch? My mother?" She looked from one aunt to the other, thinking to see some denial, but the old women stared back at her with calm assurance that she would accept this outlandish tale.

"Just as you are, my dear," Bebe added, a twinkle starting in her brown eyes.

Naomi shook her head. So this was what her father had been trying to protect her from. Two demented old women who had delusions about witchcraft. What would she do now that she realized these two old ladies were quite chuckledbrained, to say the least? Where was she to go? Gathering her wits, she calmly announced, "I am no witch, Aunt."

Iona rose and came to her. "But you are, my dear. The power is passed from mother to daughter. Although you have not been trained to use that power you possess, you are in fact a witch."

Naomi began to wonder just how long it would take her to walk back to The Block and Barrel. There would be no way she could make it before nightfall. Perhaps if she went to London, the dowager Lady Newlyn, her father's benefactor, might consent to write a recommendation. Naomi hadn't seen her ladyship in some years, not since the dowager had sent her granddaughter away to school and gone to Bath to be near the girl.

Iona sighed. "She doesn't believe us, sister."

"I see that. So we must show her the truth." Bebe turned her back to the girl and said, *"Susto fogo."*

Naomi stumbled back into her seat when the logs in the fireplace burst into flames. She couldn't believe what had just happened.

Iona eyed Naomi with a grin, then swept her arm and called, *"Troca femme."*

A strange tingle raced over Naomi, and when she looked down, her plain brown gown had been changed into a lovely blue muslin with tiny white stripes in the latest fashion. Her hair was no longer neatly bound at the nape of her neck but hung in curls about her ears. With trembling fingers, she touched the fabric of her dress to make certain it was real.

Naomi couldn't make her mind grasp this strange turn of events. "Witches . . . but—but they are evil, are they not?"

Bebe folded her arms over her ample bosom. "That is your father and his ilk's thinking, but a true witch is whatever is in her heart, my dear. If she is good, then her powers are for good, but if she possesses evil in her soul, then she will go to the dark forces of magic. The very few bad witches have blackened our reputation so we are forced to hide the truth from the world."

"So magic is not evil." Relief raced through Naomi, and at the same time a spark of excitement that she too might one day possess such power.

"Evil? Of course not, child," Bebe said, and stepped forward to take her niece's hand. "But we have a great deal of lost time to make up for since you missed your anointment at sixteen."

Iona hurried to a bookshelf on the far wall and pulled

down an ancient leather-bound volume and brought it to Naomi. "You have a great deal to learn about your heritage. Then we shall begin with the simplest of spells. If you study hard, you will be ready to be inducted into the coven on All Saint's Eve, just over a month away."

Naomi flipped open the large tome to the title page, which read *Necromancy and the Novice*. Did she truly have some untapped power which had yet to be awakened? If so, she had a great deal to learn. The truth was she wanted to believe in the possibilities, as improbable as it seemed.

The two sisters moved to the tea table and began to put everything back on the tray. "We shall leave you to begin, my dear. We will be in the next room if you have any questions." With that, they left Naomi staring into the still blazing fire, utterly befuddled at the strange turn her life had taken.

The room grew quiet and Naomi's thoughts turned to her father. She knew he wouldn't have approved of her studying such things, but she couldn't believe that her mother had been evil, nor her aunts. She would at least study the book to find out the truth.

The black cat stood, drawing Naomi's attention. The animal unhurriedly stretched, arching his back high.

"Well, Suma, I suppose you are magical as well."

The feline stared at her a moment, said, "Decidedly so," then leaped from the hearth, slinking from the room in long fluid strides, leaving Naomi in stunned silence.

"Why am I not surprised to find you here, lurking among your weeds?" The dowager Lady Newlyn stood in the doorway of the conservatory. Her grandson had converted the large space into a plant room to keep the specimens he collected from round the world. Her nose crinkled at the pungent scent of some of the exotic blooms. An elegant woman whose sixty years weighed lightly upon her willowy frame, her only concession to age was a cane with a crystal globe on top on which she leaned. Her deep green morning gown was fashionable without being too youthful, and her white hair was pulled into a regal knot that had been covered by a lovely scrap of ecru Brussels lace.

Her grandson politely rose, his eyes remaining on the notes he was making about a new variety of *chimaphila* he'd acquired from a friend recently returned from San Francisco. Little about the gentleman looked like a proper baron. He stood among the potted plants in his shirt sleeves, wearing a green damask waistcoat, which in his rush that morning he'd partially buttoned, and tan breeches of a superior cut. Yet the negligent way in which he wore them showed he had not the least interest in fashion. His sandy brown hair was overly long for the current mode and brushed his shoulders in soft waves, as if he'd forgotten to summon the barber in the last months, which he had, his thoughts too full of his plants. "Grandmother, is there something I might do for you?"

"You can show as much interest in your sister's well-being as you have this botany nonsense, my boy."

Wyndom Long's, tenth Baron Newlyn's, gaze flew to his grandmother's face. "Is there something wrong with Marion? She was quite well and engaged in drawing a picture of a *rhamnus purshiana* for me in the library when last I saw her this morning."

"Must I remind you that the child turned eighteen three months ago? We have a duty to present her this Season." The lady held up a cluster of invitations clutched in her fingers. "All the noted hostesses have invited her to their daughters' come-out balls, and I cannot delay in responding any longer. They well know we have been in town this past month, since your name has been in the paper on several occasions because of your speeches to this Linen Society."

"Linnean Society, madam, named for noted naturalist Carl von Linne." A frown wrinkled Wyndom's brow. "I cannot think that Marion will wish to go about wasting her time with such nonsense. Moreover, she is far too shy. Why, she stutters whenever she meets anyone new." He picked up a sprig of the plant he'd been studying and eyed it thoughtfully. " 'Tis my belief she is quite content working here with me."

"Do you intend to leave your sister sitting permanently on the shelf? You may be in love with science and content with the cold embrace of plants, but Marion deserves to have a husband, children, all the things young ladies dream about. I had not thought you quite so selfish, Wyndom."

The baron's hand dropped to his side, his gaze returning to his elderly grandparent. "You are being rather melodramatic, Grandmother. Marion is hardly on the shelf at eighteen. Nor am I without prospects. Once Miss Ragsdale comes out of mourning for her father, I have quite decided to make her an offer. It is what her father would have wanted, and I owe him a great deal." He would have stopped then, but, seeing his grandmother's disapproving frown, he added, "Her serious manner suits me."

"Old Ragsdale wanted you to oversee her affairs for her, which doesn't mean you must marry the chit. She hasn't the temperament for being a baron's wife, for she must be a hostess for you, but then what am I saying? The only company she is like to keep married to you would be with the estate's flora and fauna." The old lady ignored her grandson's frown and continued. "All the better for Marion. You will have someone to fill her place and she can do what she should be doing, making her bow to Society."

Wyndom's frown deepened. "Miss Ragsdale hasn't Marion's light touch with a pencil. I cannot—"

"You cannot be so simple as to think I shall allow you to lock that child up when she should be dancing the night away. Marry that prim little widgeon if you must, but Marion must have her Season."

With a sigh, the gentleman came to where his grandmother stood glaring defiantly at him. "I have never locked my sister away from Society. She owns as much interest in botany as I do." He stroked his clean shaven chin as his gaze roved over the billowing plants. "If this is so important to you, then by all means dress her in frills and take her to all the parties, plays, and al fresco picnics. Find her a husband."

Lady Newlyn shook her head, placing her free hand upon one slender hip. "I am not sixteen, dear boy. I am sixty and cannot be burning the candle at both ends."

"Then why are we having this conversation?" Wyndom moved back to the desk where he had been working. "I have no intention of parading before the *ton*'s matchmaking old prunes, even for dear Marion."

A thumping echoed in the glass room as her ladyship made her way down the steps. "Marion is going to have her Season despite your disinterest and my infirmity. The solution is to have someone come who can be her companion at all these affairs."

The baron eyed his grandmother with respect, despite his reluctance to agree with her. She was never one to give up when faced with a problem. "Well, I suppose that no one would take offense if Miss Ragsdale were to—"

"Of course they would take offense. The young woman does not open her mouth except to lecture people on the error of their ways. There would be nothing more certain to dash Marion's chances of marriage than to subject the *ton* to Miss Ragsdale as her companion. Besides, she has two full months before she can put away her mourning gowns, and she would never do anything that wasn't proper."

The baron's face grew grim. "Grandmother, I cannot have you speaking of the woman I intend to marry—"

The sounds of a door closing echoed in the hallway beyond the conservatory, and the pair looked up to see Miss Marion Long approaching, a bundle of paper in her hand. There was little remarkable about the tall and slender young woman. Her hair was mouse brown and pulled into a tight chignon at the base of her neck, which only made her face appear too long. She had a wide mouth but a rather sharp nose which, along with the stark hairstyle, gave her face a somewhat hawkish appearance. Her one fine feature: a pair of emerald green eyes which were thickly lashed.

Miss Long stopped at the top of the small set of steps. "I-is something wrong?"

"No, child." Lady Newlyn moved back to where her granddaughter stood. "I was just explaining to Wyndom that I had invited Miss Clayton to come for the Season."

A smile lit Marion's face, making her appear quite handsome even with her plain features. "Naomi! Why, I should love to have her come. I can take her to the British Museum, to the plays, the opera, and to Astley's Amphitheatre."

The dowager smiled and nodded her head. "If you wish, but you mustn't tire yourselves too much, for the important thing will be the balls and the parties."

Marion's face fell. "Y-you know I—I am not good at p-parties, Grandmama."

The old woman came to the foot of the stairs and put out her hand to the girl, who came down and grasped it like a drowning child. "At first, perhaps, but you will be quite at ease once you have Naomi at your side. Her calm good sense will be all that is needed to put you at ease."

Marion looked doubtfully at her brother, then back to her grandmother. "I always enjoy her company, and I shall do my best to make you proud, but . . ." She hesitated a moment before she added, "Must I stand about to be fitted for gowns and such? I do so detest the dressmakers."

"Of course you must, child. One must look one's best in Society."

The young lady sighed. "Well, I hope you both won't be disappointed if no gentleman makes me an offer."

Wyndom moved to where the two women stood. "Marion, do not allow Grandmother to make you think you are compelled to marry. Know that you will always have a place in my home."

Lady Newlyn's eyes narrowed. "Yes, along with Miss Ragsdale. It seems your brother has decided to make the lady an offer."

There was a slight widening of Marion's eyes, and she looked questioningly at her brother.

"I shall be thirty on my next birthday. Don't you think it time I set up my nursery?" He eyed his sister warily. His grandmother's reaction had made him rather guarded.

The young lady looked to her grandmother, who rolled her eyes, then looked away. "You have my f-felicitations, Wyn."

"Thank you." Wyndom shot his grandmother a smug look, which faded at his sister's next words.

The young lady gripped Lady Newlyn's arm with vise-like fingers. "We must begin my fittings with Madam Celeste . . . at once. Time is wasting."

Lady Newlyn wrapped her arm through Marion's. "My thoughts exactly."

The baron watched the two women disappear back into the hall with mixed feelings. He was glad they were at last gone so he could finish his work on his paper, which was due to be presented by the end of the next week. But the need to convince the ladies they were wrong about Amaryllis Ragsdale almost made him summon them back. He couldn't deny there was some truth to his grandmother's complaint that Amaryllis was a bit severe at times, but no doubt life as the daughter of the world's foremost botanist could not have been easy. As Amos Ragsdale's protégé, it somehow seemed appropriate to Wyndom that he should be the one to marry the young woman. After all, he had been the one to drag the old gentleman down to the West Indies last year on their final plant hunt, where the old man had fallen ill and died. Besides, he certainly didn't want one of those fashionable creatures who needed to be wined and dined at every turn. Amaryllis would never give him a moment's worry on that account.

Confident in his choice of females, Wyn returned to his table and again picked up the small sprig of *chimaphila*. But his thoughts returned to his sister. Perhaps it was for the best that she marry and create a life of her own. Amaryllis did seem to find fault with everything Marion did or said. At least he wouldn't have to worry about the girl's Season. His memory of Miss Clayton was of a dully dutiful daughter of

Longbridge's vicar. Who better to escort his sister about town?

"Try again, my dear." Iona Ware sat perched on a rock beside the lovely pond in the woods behind Hawthorn Cottage, where she watched her niece. Suma was crouched nearby, his eyes tiny slits to exhibit how little he cared about the goings on.

At the water's edge, Naomi closed the spell book and set it aside, then dropped to her knees beside the small fire. From the wooden case beside her, she selected some items. "One leaf from the top of the hawthorn tree." She dropped the leaf into the small cauldron. "Ten drops of myrrh, a pinch of powdered hermit's bone, the scales of a trout, and the petal of a waterlily." She added the ingredients one at a time, then folded her hands together in front of her. She closed her eyes to concentrate. *"Susto cascalho."*

Iona chuckled. "Open your eyes, Naomi."

The girl opened one squinted orb to see her handiwork. She relaxed and opened her other eye when she saw that she had conjured a large green frog on a rock at the water's edge. "I did it." She scrambled to her feet. "Did you see that, Suma? I did it."

The cat yawned and stretched, then settled back on the rock. "Is it time to dine yet?"

Iona slid from the rock. "Remember your manners, Suma, or you might find yourself banished to a land where they dine on cats."

Suma's eyes widened, and he cocked his head. "Jolly good trick, Naomi." Then the feline grinned up at his mistress.

Iona moved to where her niece stood, but before she could critique the spell, a soft breeze whispered through the trees around the pond and Bebe materialized in the nearby clearing. "I'm back from town. Naomi, put away your things. Iona and I will go and prepare the tea."

"But it is early and there is a little problem with Naomi's—" Iona began, but stopped when her sister interrupted.

"There are important matters that have come to my attention." Bebe held up a missive which had the seal broken. The fledgling witch missed the look that passed between the two sisters.

"We will discuss your conjuring later, my dear." Iona joined her sister, and they hurried back toward the cottage.

Naomi sat for a moment eyeing the results of her potion with satisfaction. Then, to her horror, the frog smiled at her with even white teeth that would make any Englishman jealous. She quickly pointed at the large amphibian and called, *"Terminar."* That had been the first thing she had learned from her aunts—how to get rid of a magical accident.

In a puff of sparkling smoke, the frog disappeared and Naomi settled beside her herb box. What had she done wrong? She picked up the spell book and shook her head. Aloud she said, "Too much myrrh?" She closed the book and dejectedly began to put things away. The simplest of things could make a spell go awry. Her aunts kept telling her that things would go more smoothly once she got her confidence, but at present that didn't seem to be happening.

Naomi had been diligently studying the art of witchcraft for over six months, and only recently had her aunts decided that she fully comprehended the rules satisfactorily to allow her to begin doing big spells. It was far more complicated than she had ever thought, but she had mastered many of the simple spells such as levitating objects, making fire, and curing minor illnesses. Yet it all had been quite different from what she had believed about witches.

Her first surprise had been to discover that unless one intended to embrace the dark arts, which she certainly did not, a witch never performed magic for personal gain. Oh, one could conjure a meal or perhaps clothing, but never must one conjure gold or money. It was certainly an unfortunate fact, for her aunts' financial situation was not at all good. Neither having married, they only managed to get by on the meager income they derived from the people who came to them for potions. And there was always the danger that an unsatisfied patron might report them.

For Naomi, there was also the difficulty of remembering the exact portions in brewing potions. Her aunts blamed her late start, for most young witches were inducted into their coven years earlier. She knew it would only require more practice. They often reminded her that patience was a virtue.

Frustrated by her slow progress, Naomi picked up her herb box and spell book and headed back to the cottage. Somehow it seemed strange that despite their powers they were rather at the mercy of fate as far as their lives were concerned.

Inside the cottage, she found the Ware sisters seated at their small table, their heads together as they read the mysterious letter. Iona looked up and gestured for her niece to join them. "My dear, we have what we think is good news."

Leaving her box and spell book on a wooden settle beside the door, Naomi came and sat down. She mentally noted that there had been no preparation for their evening tea, and she was surprisingly sharp set. Their news must be of some import.

Bebe smiled. "Your studies are very important, Naomi, but when opportunities arrive we must take advantage of them."

"Opportunities?" Naomi looked from one lady to the other. Then her gaze dropped to the missive which lay on the table.

Iona tapped the letter. "Lady Newlyn has invited you to London. She wants you to be companion to her granddaughter. Do you remember the girl?"

"Of course I remember Marion. She was a very dear friend before her mother died and she was sent away to school. But surely you cannot want me to go away just as I'm beginning to practice my sorcery."

Bebe and Iona exchanged a look. Iona reached across the table and took her niece's hand. "In a perfect world, no, we wouldn't wish you to leave at this crucial time, but we must face the facts. The Wares are pockets to let. I do not worry about my sister and me, for we manage on what our skills earn, but, my dear, I fear that you must marry—as did your mother."

Naomi's heart plummeted. "Are you saying I must go to London and, to put it vulgarly, marry a rich man?"

Bebe tittered. "Of course not, child. Any man with a modest income can support you."

Iona nudged her sister in warning, then tried to explain their meaning. "My dear, your magic can provide you with a great many things, but you must be careful. People are most curious about a single woman and how she survives without a husband or father. In your case, many will know that your father was a mere vicar. A husband, any husband, can protect you from the imaginations of the ignorant."

"So, I am to go to London and cast a love spell—"

"No!" the aunts shouted in unison.

Bebe shook her finger at Naomi. "No love spells. They are too dangerous even for experienced witches. In fact, I think it best you put your magic aside while in Town." She took her niece's hand. "We are not asking you to marry just anyone. We only want you to have the opportunity to fall in love and marry, which you certainly won't have here at Hawthorn Cottage."

"And, my dear"—Iona winked—"in London there are ever so many handsome wizards." The lady sat back and became dreamy eyed. "Why, that would only make matters perfect if you fell in love with a young man who practiced the arts as well."

"A wizard?" Naomi's face grew wary. "I must marry a wizard?"

Iona bit her lip. "Marrying outside the craft only produces problems, child. Your father never accepted his wife's abilities for what they were. He saw evil where there was none. I think it broke your mother's heart. Most mortal men cannot accept having a witch for a wife. That is why a wizard is best."

"Very well, I accept I must marry a wizard, Aunt Iona. But how would I meet such a man? Do they attend parties and the plays?"

Bebe grinned. "Of course they do, child. Did you think they all had long white beards and odd hats? They blend in with ordinary mortals, just as you must."

Naomi's brow rose. "And how am I to know them? Is there some secret handshake, a magic phrase they recite to everyone they meet, or do sparks fly from their feet as they walk?"

Iona looked at Bebe. "That does present a problem, sister, for she cannot go to the usual places sorcerers meet, not with Miss Marion in tow—and, after all, that is why Lady Newlyn invited her to Town."

Bebe curled one auburn tress round her finger as she pondered the problem. Most witches and wizards instinctively recognized one another on sight by a certain aura, but Naomi was quite inexperienced and might not understand how to home in on her senses just yet. Besides, there could be little doubt she would be tempted to use her newly found powers, and the child had not fully mastered all there was to know. What she needed was a guardian, but one did not send a companion for the companion.

Suddenly Bebe's eyes brightened. "I know what we must do. She needs a Familiar, someone who can alert others in the craft and keep her safe from harm." The Ware sisters turned to Suma, who had curled up in one of the chairs near the hearth.

The black cat's gold-hued eyes opened wide. "Don't look at me. You know I detest London. It's a dangerous place for felines and not a decent climbing tree to be found."

"But, Suma—" Bebe started.

"Don't *but Suma* me." The cat rose and jumped to the floor. "I am content with my humans. If she needs someone to look out for her, send for Audric. I should think he would like nothing better than to be in the thick of things." With that, the cat stalked from the room, as if offended that they would have considered him for the task.

"Audric." Iona's face lit. "Why, we should have thought of him first. Who better to steer our Naomi to the right husband?"

Bebe shook her head. "Sister, we cannot send the child to London with such a scoundrel."

Iona laughed. "He is quite harmless in his present form. Besides, he always had a fondness for our Kendra. He would be honored to be charged with the responsibility of her daughter."

"Who is Audric?" Naomi asked, suddenly uncomfortable with the idea of a stranger involving himself in her life.

But the aunts had already risen and gone to the fireplace. Within minutes they had a fire roaring, and they joined hands. The pair chanted, "From the far corners of the world, through all the war and strife, bring Audric to Naomi to protect her future life."

Naomi looked about and nothing seemed to happen in the room. Then a knock sounded on the front door. The aunts grinned and gestured for her to go welcome their visitor. She moved toward the door and hesitated a moment, fearful of what was behind the portal. At last she reached out a trembling hand and opened the door.

To her utter amazement, there stood a dog the size of a small pony. He was white, with small black spots, and his head was large with ears that pointed upward. She had never seen such a creature. Intimidated by the animal, she stepped back, right into her aunts, who had followed her.

"Audric?" Bebe questioned.

"You were expecting Cerberus who guards Hades?" His voice was deep and husky. "Of course, 'tis I."

"You look quite different since the last time you visited," Iona said, as her gaze roved over the monstrous dog.

"Do you like it? I got quite tired of the little hairy and black incarnation and decided to try something new. Browsed through time for something more interesting, and now I'm a Great Dane."

The three ladies stood and stared for a moment. Bebe at last remarked, "I never knew a Dane, but you are rather great."

Naomi whispered into Iona's ear. "I cannot take such a creature to London. Everyone would run from me in fright."

"London?" Audric's ears perked up. "You want me to go to Town? Ah, to once again be among the beautiful ladies, the plays, the French chefs." He licked his chops.

Bebe shook her head. "Naomi's right. This Great Dane breed simply will not do, Audric."

"Oh, very well." There was a puff of smoke, and where the Great Dane had stood was a small black Aberdeen terrier. "Is this better?" It was clear by his tone that he didn't wish to be a lap dog, for his voice remained just as deep and resonant. Ironically, his long muzzle was bearded, and he possessed tufts of fur over each eye which quite gave him the look of a wise old man in canine form.

"Much better! Do come in and meet your cousin."

Naomi's eyes widened as the little dog trotted into the cottage and jumped up on a chair. "H-he is a relation? How is it he's, well, not in human form?"

Bebe closed the door. "It's a long story."

Audric looked at Naomi. "Not so long. The moral of my tale is never dally with the daughter of a netherworld wizard unless you are content to spent the next hundred years as someone's faithful companion. Now, about this trip to Town." He looked from one lady to another.

Iona quickly explained their dilemma with Naomi and what they required.

"I'm your man." Audric guffawed loudly. "You know what I mean. I shall sniff out all the best wizards who are presently in London and watch over Naomi until she is safely wed. Is this baron a gourmand?"

Iona frowned. "This is no time to be thinking of your stomach."

Audric sighed. "Food has become my one pleasure in this form, cousin."

"Naomi will see you are properly fed." Bebe smiled at her niece.

"Promise?" Audric raised one black tuft above his dark eyes.

"I promise." Naomi eyed her new cousin with awe.

That settled, it was soon agreed that Naomi and Audric would leave for London as soon as Lady Newlyn sent a carriage. Bebe and Iona then hurried to the kitchen to prepare the long delayed tea. But Bebe's worries were not completely allayed. "Are you certain we can trust Audric?"

Iona set the plates upon the tray. "Good heavens, my dear. What is it you think he will do? After all, the women of Town are safe from his charms in his present form."

Bebe shook her head. "I cannot think that a man who has lived his life ruled by his baser instincts is the best person to watch over Naomi and guide her through the pitfalls of Society."

"Good heavens, sister, there is none better. A libertine would recognize the same qualities in others far quicker than you or I. He will watch out for her and find her a handsome wizard to marry."

"And if she falls in love with a mortal?"

"I am certain Audric will nip such foolishness in the bud. We needn't worry."

Chapter Two

Audric jumped up and put his feet on the windowsill of the carriage as the vehicle moved slowly through the crush of traffic in Mayfair. The time was half past three, but the normal flow of carriages was slowed by the sheer volume of travelers coming to Town for the opening of Parliament. "Do you think this baron fellow will have a garden with his town house?"

"I cannot say. I have never been to Town before." Naomi's nose was nearly pressed to the glass as she took in the sights of London—the fashionable women strolling with gentlemen, the shops, and the cart vendors. She had not fully embraced this journey in the beginning. The idea of coming in search of a husband did not suit her, but then she remembered that most females of good birth did much the same. Once her aunts had conjured her a new wardrobe and she'd set out, excitement became her constant companion, for there was so much new to see.

As to the wardrobe, there was nothing too fashionable in the array of gowns in the trunk. After all, how would she explain to Lady Newlyn arriving in the latest gowns when her father had been a penniless vicar? Yet for a girl who'd been restricted to somber colors and three gowns, the simple yet fashionable gowns of yellow silks, pink satins, and blue muslins were a delight. Until they reached London, she had given little thought to the task she was to perform—escorting Marion. Had her old friend changed much since her time at school? She had been rather shy and retiring, with little conversation for strangers. That might prove a difficulty during the Season, when one was expected to charm the eligible gentlemen.

The carriage drew to a halt in front of Newlyn House. A footman in green and gold livery hurried out and opened the carriage door. His eyes widened at the sight of the small black dog who bounded down the carriage stairs and dashed straight into the foyer.

Naomi stepped down. "Come back here, Audric." She gave the footman a sheepish smile. "The trip was rather long." She hurried after the dog and found herself in a well-appointed hall with white marble floors, black lacquered tables, and old family portraits. Audric sat beside a large potted plant, staring at her with unnerving intensity.

The lone footman closed the door, then took her bonnet and cape. "Welcome to Newlyn House, Miss Clayton. The ladies are resting at present, but I shall go and see if Miss Marion is awake."

The servant had scarcely disappeared up the curved set of stairs before Audric said, "We must find me a garden, Naomi, or I shall climb into that potted palm to do my business."

Perplexed a moment, Naomi's eyes widened when she took his meaning. She looked about at the closed doors and hesitated. "The footman should be back any minute. Can you not wait?"

"Now, child, or have the decency to turn your back." The terrier danced about in circles.

Clearly the matter was most urgent. But which door led outside? she wondered. She had seen no garden on either side of the town house, which was a part of a row, so she de-

cided to try one of the doors at the back of the hall. The door
she chose opened into what looked like a conservatory, but
she had never seen a room quite so full of plants. The dog
raced past her toward the end of the room, where a garden
was visible through the glass.

"Wait, I must open . . ." but her voice trailed off as a gentleman stood and stared at her from among the plants.

"May I help you, madam?" His tone was cool.

It took a moment for her to recognize Marion's brother, it
having been some eight years or more since they had encountered each other. Gone was the willowy frame of a
young man recently finished with Oxford, replaced by the
firm, broad physique of a man fully grown. His face, now
leaned to sharp, angular planes, would never be called handsome, with its deep-set green eyes and rather thin lips, but
there was something about him so very masculine that her
stomach behaved in a rather strange manner. Then she remembered her manners.

"I do apologize for intruding, Lord Newlyn. I am Naomi
Clayton, Marion's friend, newly arrived from Wiltshire."

"The vicar's daughter?" His gaze swept her up and down,
while disbelief etched his face.

Naomi suddenly worried that her aunts had gone too far
by putting her hair up in fashionable curls and dressing her
in the elegant blue gown. She resisted the urge to tug at the
bodice, which was lower than she'd ever worn. "The very
one, sir."

The flicker of surprise in his eyes disappeared. Then he
bowed and politely smiled. It was an amazing moment, for
his face was transformed. His countenance, which had seemed
quite plain to her at first sight, now appeared utterly fascinating. Was it possible to be bewitched by an agreeable
smile?

"Forgive me, Miss Clayton. I fear I didn't recognize you,
but then it has been years, has it not?" He moved to shake
her hand. "Welcome to Newlyn House. I hope your journey

was uneventful. Marion has been eagerly awaiting your arrival."

"I am looking forward to seeing her, sir." Naomi felt strangely shy. She searched for something to say and her gaze fell on the plants surrounding them. "This is a remarkable room." She reached out and touched the magenta-colored flower of a nearby plant. "Is this *apocynaneae?* I didn't think it grew in England."

His eyes widened. "Do you know plants?"

Naomi realized she must be careful. A woman rarely exhibited much knowledge about anything but the feminine arts. She mustn't draw too much attention to her magical arts, which involved the study of plants and herbs. "Oh, my aunts use herbs for healing, and I have taken an interest in such things."

Just then Audric barked to remind her he was waiting. Naomi edged past the gentleman. "Is there a door to the garden? My dog needs his walk."

"This way." The gentleman led her to the end of the room and opened the door, where Audric waited with fevered impatience. When the door was open, the dog disappeared into the rear of a beautiful little garden.

"Has my sister been informed of your arrival, Miss Clayton?" his lordship asked as he frowned after the dog.

Uncertain what had displeased him, she decided it was her presumption in having brought the animal with her without permission. "I believe the footman went to see if she'd risen from her afternoon rest. Sir, about my dog. I hope you have no objection that he is with me. He is well mannered, and I own a great affection for him."

" 'Tis the ladies I worry about, Miss Clayton. Not everyone has a love of animals. I do not think we have ever had a pet in the house. I assume he is housebroken?"

"Of course."

Audric trotted back up the flagstone path, drawing both their attention. On arriving back at the door, the terrier sat down to stare back at the pair with eyes that glittered with intensity and made Naomi nervous. Then she reminded herself that to the rest of the world he was a mere dog.

Still, the gentleman stared at Audric, a thoughtful expression on his face. At last he smiled at the lady, which made her sigh with appreciation. Such a smile could certainly melt one's resolve. "Miss Clayton, I am also concerned for the animal's safety. I have many plants in here that are lethal if eaten, and I know canines are rather indiscriminate about what they consume."

A strange sound somewhere between a gurgle and a growl sounded from the terrier. Naomi hurried to cover the dog's vocal display. "Oh, I do assure you that Audric would never do anything so foolish, sir. He is quite the smartest dog I have ever seen."

"Still, I think it best that he not come into the conservatory unaccompanied. I shall speak to Cook and see if she can provide him with an adequate supply of bones to keep him amused. Or perhaps you could set him to catching rats in the mews to keep him occupied."

Audric's head swivelled to look at Naomi. She wasn't certain a dog could show indignation, but every hair on the terrier seemed to shake with outrage. He barked once and positively skulked back into the conservatory, going all the way to the opposite door, where he sat with his back to the baron.

Lord Newlyn chuckled. "One would almost swear he understood what we were saying."

Naomi managed a forced laugh. "Just one of Audric's odd fits and starts. I do promise he won't be a bother, sir. I must go back and see if the footman has returned."

The gentleman bowed. "I shall see you at dinner, Miss Clayton."

She curtsied, then hurried back to where Audric awaited her. She opened the door that led to the rear hall. The door had scarcely closed to the conservatory when Naomi's companion vented his spleen.

"Do I look like a cursed cat? Chase rats, indeed!"

"He was only concerned for your well-being, Audric. A real dog might accidently eat a fallen leaf in there and be hideously ill."

"As if I would eat flowers and leaves when there is"—the dog sniffed the air—"roast capon for supper. And there is the matter of those bones, Naomi. The baron has another think coming if he intends to starve me with a bunch of bones with all the meat gone."

"I promise I shall see that you are properly fed. You must remember, most dogs would be delighted with such a treat, and . . ." Naomi's voice petered out when she looked up to see the footman standing at the end of the stairs, staring at her with an odd expression.

At last he spoke. "Forgive me for leaving you standing about in the hallway, miss, but the upstairs maid, Abby, is under the weather and the butler and housekeeper are seeing to her."

Naomi came to where he stood. "Is she very ill?"

"Appears to have eaten somethin' what don't agree with her, is all."

Naomi knew a little spell that would have made the girl right as rain, but her aunts didn't wish her to practice her arts in town, so she offered a home remedy. "Perhaps I can help. Have Cook simmer a peach with half a cup of water and castor sugar. When the water thickens to a syrup, allow it to cool and have Abby eat only the syrup. It will make her feel better."

The footman nodded. "I'll tell Cook, miss." He gestured toward the stairs. "Miss Long and her ladyship are in the drawing room upstairs, miss."

Naomi hoped she had distracted him from what he had seen, but she could tell he didn't know what to make of her. She decided to play it off. "Come, Audric, Marion awaits."

The pair followed the footman to a drawing room upstairs where Marion and her grandmother, Lady Newlyn, awaited. Naomi had just a moment to whisper to Audric to be on his best behavior unless he wished to be residing in the cellars.

The dowager greeted her first, Marion shyly hanging back as if the years apart had somehow changed the relationship. "Why, my dear Miss Clayton, you are looking wonderful, is she not, Marion?"

"Q-quite," the girl replied, then her gaze dropped to the floor.

Naomi's heart sank. If it was possible, her old friend had grown even more bashful. She was fashionably dressed in a pale pink muslin afternoon gown, but her straight brown hair was resisting the elaborate curls, sticking out in several directions, which reminded one of a hedgehog. Not an image likely to make men fall at the young lady's feet.

"W-welcome to London, Naomi." Marion blushed, but managed a timorous smile.

If the girl were this way with an old friend, how would she be among a roomful of strangers? But that was something Naomi decided to worry about later. For the present, she would concentrate on regaining Marion's confidence. Then they would deal with improving her looks and manner before launching her into Society. After all, if worse came to worse, a little magic just might be called for despite her aunts' prohibition. Surely they would understand.

The door to the conservatory opened at six that same afternoon, and Peterson stepped into the room, carrying a tray with a wine decanter and a glass as well as several sandwiches and almond biscuits.

Lord Newlyn glanced up at the tinkle of rattling glass, then peered at the timepiece on his small desk. He sighed with frustration. His paper for the Linnean Society must be done by the end of the week, and he'd scarcely written two paragraphs all afternoon. For some reason, he'd had difficulty concentrating. His thoughts kept going to the young lady who'd disturbed his peace earlier. What had happened to the Miss Clayton he remembered from Yorkshire? She had been the perfect companion for a shy miss making her come-out. Marion would be completely missed in the swarm of swains who would come to pay tribute to the vicar's lovely daughter.

The butler arrived at the baron's side and slid the tray on the desk. "Her ladyship sent you tea since you failed to join them, sir."

"Send my apologies to my grandmother, and thank you, Peterson. How is Abby feeling?"

"Much better, my lord. Miss Clayton suggested a country remedy which seems to have done the trick."

Wyn was glad to hear that the young lady was still so practical, yet somehow he had a difficult time reconciling the beauty he'd met that afternoon with his memories of her in Yorkshire.

The white-haired servant poured out a full measure of wine, then bowed and left. The baron lay down his pen and took a sip of wine. He quickly ate the sandwiches, surprised at how hungry he was, and was about to finish his wine when movement caught his eye. He looked down to see Miss Clayton's hairy little dog seated at the foot of the desk, his dark eyes locked on the gentleman.

"How did you get in here?" Wyn rose and continued speaking to the dog as if he were a human. "I knew the moment I set eyes on you you were going to be nothing but trouble. I suppose you are wanting to go into the garden again."

The gentleman put down the glass and moved to the rear door, but the dog remained in the center of the room beside the desk. Opening the door, the baron whistled, but the animal's only response was to twitch one ear. The canine remained seated, his gaze fixed on the desk. Wyn suddenly wished he hadn't eaten all the sandwiches, for he could have used one to entice the animal to the door.

Before the baron could lure the dog outside, Peterson reappeared at the hallway door. "My lord, the gentleman from the potter's has arrived with the new pots you ordered. Where shall I have him put them?"

At once Lord Newlyn's attention was diverted to his first love, his plants. He left the door open for the pooch—after all, the garden was fenced—and Miss Clayton had assured him the animal wouldn't eat the plants, so he hurried toward the butler. "I should like to inspect them before they are unloaded."

His lordship went out to the potter's *fourgon,* pronounced his approval of the workmanship, and had the men carry the oversized pots into the conservatory. It wasn't until the workmen were gone and he was once again seated at his desk that he realized the little dog had disappeared. He went to the garden, but the animal was nowhere to be found. Perhaps he'd departed through the open door when the men were bringing in the pots. He went in search of Peterson, who he instructed to find the cursed animal and make certain he hadn't escaped.

At last Wyn sat down in the conservatory and reached for his glass of wine, only to discover it empty. Had he drunk it all so quickly? How odd. He would have sworn he took only a sip. He shrugged and went back to his paper.

A sharp knock sounded on the door and before the baron could respond, the portal opened. Without leave, Miss Ragsdale and her mother swept into the conservatory. The elder woman was a large female, much improved by her black widow's attire, but as for Miss Ragsdale, her white gown with black ribbons left her blond comeliness looking rather colorless—or was he merely comparing her looks with the healthy blush on Miss Clayton's cheeks? That would never do.

Wyn rose and grabbed his jacket, knowing how much Amaryllis disliked any lack of formality. "Ladies, did we have an appointment that slipped my mind?"

Mrs. Ragsdale tittered girlishly. "As if you would be so careless, my lord."

Amaryllis Ragsdale frowned at her mother, then asserted her role as the dominating one of the pair. "I assured Mother you wouldn't mind our presuming to stop by, since we are such old friends. 'Twas only that I remembered that Lady

Newlyn reminded us on our last visit that your friend, Miss Clayton, was to arrive today. I know how it is to be a stranger in town, so we decided to come and welcome her to London."

The announcement surprised Wyn, for Amaryllis had been quite adamant that she could fill the role that Miss Clayton was intended to play. Both she and her mother insisted there was no need to bring the lady from the country. Only after he assured her that his grandmother intended the visit as much for Miss Clayton to have a Season as Marion did the ladies end their protests. "How kind of you, Miss Ragsdale. I believe the ladies are still in the Green Salon."

He offered Mrs. Ragsdale his arm and led the ladies upstairs. He opened the door to the salon and froze in his tracks. To his and his companions' amazement, the tunes of a pianoforte could be heard as two young ladies twirled about the room doing the waltz.

On seeing the visitors, the dancers stopped and fell into giggles. Wyn had never seen Marion, her hair loose to her shoulders, cheeks flushed, looking quite so daring yet at the same time lovely. Beside her, eyes twinkling, Miss Clayton looked as if she were enjoying herself immensely.

With Marion quite speechless, Naomi said, "Oh, Lord Newlyn, I hope you don't mind, but we were practicing for our first ball."

Lady Newlyn, at the piano, ceased her playing and gazed at the visitors with a jaundiced eye, then looked at the clock. "Well, I certainly didn't expect callers so late in the day."

Miss Ragsdale was not the least dampened by her ladyship's comment. She eyed Miss Clayton with a superior air. "I do hope you are not encouraging Miss Marion to be waltzing before she has been approved by the patroness of Almack's. There would be nothing which could ruin her faster, I do assure you."

Marion and Lady Newlyn's faces grew stormy, but Miss Clayton merely smiled. "Why, you are quite mistaken, madam. Dear Marion was teaching *me* to waltz, for I have never seen the dance. It is quite delightful, is it not?"

Miss Ragsdale sniffed, "I would not know, for I have never danced in such a . . . reckless manner." It was clear by her pause that she intended to say *scandalous manner* but thought better of it.

Since the ladies were getting off on a wrong foot, the baron stepped in and said, "Miss Clayton, allow me to present Mrs. Lettice Ragsdale, widow of the noted botanist Amos Ragsdale, and their daughter, Miss Amaryllis."

The young lady smiled and said all that was polite, but Mrs. Ragsdale, being no fool, realized her daughter had allowed her tongue to get the better of her. "Lady Newlyn, we do not wish to intrude. We only wanted to stop a moment to make Miss Clayton's acquaintance."

Coolly, the dowager nodded. "Most kind of you, madam." Her ladyship made no offer to the ladies to sit down, since she considered the Ragsdales pushing creatures who would be encouraged by such polite treatment.

The widow slid her arm through her daughter's and began to tug her backward. "We will leave you to your rehearsing and hope that you might bring Miss Clayton to tea later in the week."

Lady Newlyn gave not an inch. "We shall have to see if we can find the time. Dear Naomi has only just arrived, and there is much to do to get her ready. As you know, the girls are making their bow to Society at Lady Huntford's ball."

Ignoring her ladyship, Amaryllis turned to Lord Newlyn. "Surely you will not waste *your* time with such foolishness. I believe you are to present a paper to the Linnean Society at this week's meeting."

Wyn stiffened at her censuring tone. He said coolly, "I know my responsibilities to the society, Miss Ragsdale."

It was evident to all that the young lady had overstepped her bounds with the baron. Not a fool, Amaryllis laid a hand upon his sleeve. "Oh, I did not mean to presume to tell you how to manage your affairs. Only I met Mr. Camden this week on Oxford Street, and he mentioned how much they are all looking forward to your paper."

Lady Newlyn made a snorting sound which caused Wyn to glare at her, but his grandmother innocently dabbed at her nose with a lace handkerchief as if she were taking a cold. He wasn't certain Miss Ragsdale had meant to sound so proprietary, and when he looked back her she smiled at him so sweetly he quite absolved her of such brazen conduct. She had only been concerned for his reputation, no doubt.

Yet something niggled at the back of his mind, telling him he really didn't know the lady that well for all the time she'd been in his presence. Still, he returned her smile. "While I might accompany my sister on random occasions as needed, I have no intention of attending Lady Huntford's affair."

To Wyn's surprise, Miss Clayton spoke to Amaryllis. "Do you have an interest in botany as well, Miss Ragsdale?"

Amaryllis's eyes narrowed as they rested on the vicar's daughter. "I am no bluestocking." She smiled up at the baron. " 'Tis my belief that I should leave such matters to gentlemen, who are better suited to such mental depths."

"Well said," Lady Newlyn pronounced from the piano. "A lady should know her own limitations, I always say."

The young lady's cheeks flamed red, but before she could respond, her mother tugged her from the room. "We must be on our way, dear Amy."

Wyn shot his grandmother a quelling look before he offered to escort the ladies out. As the door closed behind them, the dowager harrumphed. "Meddlesome jade."

Marion moved to the pianoforte. "Grandmama, you mustn't be discourteous to Miss Ragsdale. Wyn seems determined to have her."

"I won't have her mistake my feeling, child. I'm determine not to have such a cold, unfeeling woman be the mother of my great grandchildren."

Naomi's brows rose. "They are betrothed?"

"Not as yet, and not if I have anything to say about the matter." Lady Newlyn rose. "Come, no more about the annoying lady. You, dear Naomi, need to rest a bit before we dress for dinner. Marion and I shall make plans for tomorrow while you take a nap and write your aunts to assure them you have arrived safely."

Marion showed Naomi to her room. Before she departed, she squeezed her old friend's hand. "I am so glad you have come. I—I know Grandmama has plans for a great marriage, but I am not one of those who mingle well in Society."

Naomi kissed her cheek. "Don't you worry about that. Who knows but what you might end being the darling of Society?"

"Darling, indeed." The shy young woman laughed. "I shall be content to not be a laughingstock or struck utterly speechless at the wrong moment."

"That won't happen." Seeing doubt in the girl's eyes, Naomi added, "Besides, if you can think of nothing else, there is always that perennial favorite of the weather."

Marion laughed and nodded, informed her friend when supper would be served, then departed. Naomi closed the door and prayed she was right. In fact, even if she had to defy her aunts' ban on magic, she would make certain her friend didn't become a social disaster.

Suddenly a scratching sounded on the door. She opened it to find Audric there. "Where have you been?"

"Inspecting the lay of the land." The dog trotted into the room, then bounded up into a blue damask chair near the fireplace.

Naomi's eyes narrowed. "What does that mean?"

"You needn't look like I was chewing on the baron's slippers or such. I was down in the kitchens being all cute and cuddly, introducing myself to Cook and the maids. Not a pretty face in the lot, but they were very generous with the tidbits." He licked his chops, then grinned.

"And what if some handsome wizard had stopped by and you were nowhere to be found? I would have missed my chance, not realizing him a sorcerer." She put her hands on her hips while she chastised him.

"A wizard? Here with your stuffy botanist?" Audric guffawed. " 'Tis more like to snow in July, my dear. Besides, I saw the way you look at his lordship." With that he lay down his head and closed his eyes.

"Don't be ridiculous, Audric. His lordship is no wizard, and that is what I need. Besides, he is about to declare himself to Miss Ragsdale."

Without opening his eyes, the dog murmured, "That's as may be, my dear, but a wise man once told me the heart wants what the heart wants."

Naomi shook her head. She was beginning to wonder if bringing Audric had been the best decision. He seemed more likely to bring trouble than a suitable gentleman for her. She lay upon the bed to rest as Audric's assessment of Lord Newlyn swirled in her head. A stuffy botanist. A memory of the gentleman's smile came to her and she realized that stuffy didn't come to mind when she thought of him. She could certainly see what Miss Ragsdale saw in him. The question would be what he saw in her. She was passably pretty with her pale blond looks, but she seemed rather priggish and definitely humorless. But it was none of Naomi's affair. While he was an attractive man, he certainly wasn't what her aunts had had in mind when they sent her to London. She was here to help Marion, which she intended to do. If she found herself a wizard, all the better. No other choice made sense for a witch.

Over the course of the next few days, Naomi had little time to worry about the approaching ball or her attraction to the young baron. She met a grateful Abby, who arrived at nine sharp the following morning to inform her that her ladyship and Miss Marion desired her company in the breakfast parlor in thirty minutes.

The three women were soon on the go from morn till night. Lady Newlyn was determined that there would be nothing lacking in her granddaughter's first appearance in Society. In between shopping trips, the girls managed to slip away for a visit to the Egyptian exhibit at the British Museum, and to Hatchard's for the latest books. The highlight for Naomi was an afternoon spent with Lord Newlyn, who took the time from writing his paper to give them a tour of the conservatory and explain the new varieties of plants he was studying.

Naomi was surprised that he managed to explain his work without it being boring. Miss Ragsdale was a very lucky young woman. Naomi could only hope that she would be so lucky in finding her true love.

At last the evening of the Huntford ball arrived. Naomi, dressed in pale pink silk with a pink sarcenet overskirt shot with silver, hurried down to the drawing room, not wishing to be late. Audric trailed behind, averse to being locked upstairs for the night. She arrived to find the Green Salon empty. Surprised to realize that her nerves were jangling a bit even though it was Marion's evening, Naomi went to the piano and began to play a soft sonata which had always calmed her father. After circling the room once, her canine cousin jumped up on a nearby chair of green and white striped sateen.

"Get down, Audric. You leave black hair on everything."

He snorted, but complied. "Next you will be accusing me of stooping so low as to have fleas."

She heard the door opened and looked up to see Lord Newlyn standing in the doorway. She rose.

"Don't stop on my account, Miss Clayton. I was greatly enjoying the music."

He smiled that transforming smile and Naomi's stomach played tricks on her. "I was just passing the time until Lady Newlyn and Marion come down."

His gaze swept her and he said, "Then I shall keep you company until the ladies arrive." He went to the drinks table, offering her a glass of claret, which she declined before she sat down and continued playing. After pouring himself a portion, from which he took a sip before he set it on the table, he came and stood beside the piano. "May I say you are looking lovely this evening, Miss Clayton?"

Naomi blushed. "Thank you, sir. I quite feel like a fairy princess."

He arched one brow. "Don't tell me you are one of those who believe in fairies, elves, unicorns, and all that nonsense."

She had learned there was a great deal she didn't know about the world in the last year. "I believe there are many things which remain hidden from us. Even people often are not what they seem." A pang of guilt raced through her for her own deception of the Longs.

A frown appeared on the gentleman's face. "You sound like my grandmother. Has she convinced you as well of the inappropriateness of Miss Ragsdale as my future wife?"

"Miss Ragsdale?" Naomi asked, taken aback that he thought she was so presumptuous. "Why, no. I would never think to discourage a gentleman from marrying his true love."

"True love? Why, you are quite as fanciful as Marion. Marriage should be embarked upon on far sturdier ground than such a tenuous emotion, Miss Clayton."

A half smile played about her mouth as her gaze went to Audric. "I believe a wise man once said the heart wants what the heart wants, sir."

Before his lordship could retort, Lady Newlyn and Marion arrived. Naomi had convinced Marion to have her hair trimmed short, and a vinegar and water rinse had brought out golden highlights in her plain brown locks. Her maid had threaded a green ribbon through the curls and she looked quite different. A pale green silk gown embroidered with tiny yellow flowers on the sleeves and hem displayed her girlish figure to perfection.

Lord Newlyn hurried forward and took his sister's hands. "Why, Marion, you have blossomed into a beauty. You shall quite steal Miss Huntford's thunder at her own ball and become the belle of the night."

Marion shook her head and nibbled at her lip before she said, "B-but I still have two left feet when it comes to dancing and no witty conversation and I should be far happier here with a book than at this ball." It was evident to all that the young lady was terrified of her first ball.

Naomi came and stood beside her, slipping an arm through her friend's. "I am equally quaking, my dear, but my aunts always assured me that our nerves will quite disappear when we see that all the young ladies are nervous."

"Do you think that is true?" Marion clutched at her friend's hand.

"Of course it's true. Is it not so, Lady Newlyn?"

"You shall be fine, child. Now come along, or we shall be late."

Confident his sister would find her courage, the baron escorted the ladies out to the waiting carriage and he wished them a pleasant evening as he closed the door. He returned to finish his wine, only to find the glass empty. He looked down at the dog, then back at the glass, and shook his head, thinking it was impossible. He would be glad when he'd completed his paper, for he was overly distracted. On that thought he departed, but just before the door closed he would have sworn he heard that dog hiccup.

In the carriage, the ladies were full of high expectations for the ball. Unfortunately, as they stood in the receiving line at the head of the stairs, Marion's eyes grew wide with terror as she surveyed the crush below. Naomi did her best to calm her friend, but instead the girl grew progressively more withdrawn with each new gentleman presented to her. She stuttered or spoke not at all, she stumbled through her dances, and at last managed to slip away through the tall door that opened onto the terrace, where Naomi found her some minutes later.

"I—I cannot do this," she cried in her friend's arms. "I—I don't know a single p-person and e-everyone seems to be staring at me and I—I can think of nothing to say to the gentlemen. I—I want to go home."

Naomi tried to reassure her friend, but nothing would convince the girl that she was not making a spectacle of herself. At last they returned indoors, found her ladyship, and made their good-byes to the hostess and departed just after midnight.

In the carriage, Lady Newlyn sighed at the sight of her sadly distressed granddaughter. "I blame your father for your fears, child. You must realize that all gentleman are not such roaring beasts without patience. Did you not meet a single gentleman tonight who pleased you?"

Marion shook her head. "They were different from my friends back home. These gentlemen were all . . ." She seemed not to find the words she wanted.

Naomi offered, "They were all rather tiresome, in my opinion, with their talk of horses and fashion and gossip."

"Good heavens, girls. What else is there to speak of at a ball?"

Naomi looked out at the passing buildings. "I suppose Marion has been rather spoiled by Lord Newlyn's conversations. No doubt she expects more from a gentleman than a discussion of fisticuffs and fetlocks."

Her ladyship fell silent. But as the coach drew to a stop in front of the town house, she said, "I think we started too large, going to such a crush as Lady Huntford's. Perhaps a small musical evening would be more the thing for a shy young girl."

Naomi voiced her approval, but noted that Marion looked no happier than she had at the ball. It was clear that firing the girl off was going to be quite the task, but Naomi knew that eventually they would succeed, even if she had to resort to more interesting methods.

So two days later, they set out for Lady Willingham's musicale—but that proved an equal disaster. The hostess insisted that Marion, along with the other young ladies, each take their turn performing a song on the pianoforte. Thinking her friend might faint from fear, Naomi tried to beg off for the frightened girl, but Lady Willingham was determined. Marion managed to get through one verse of *The Prickety Bush* in a wavering voice before Naomi took pity on her and made a small vase at the rear of the room fly off the shelf to break on the floor. She knew her aunts wouldn't object to that little bit of magic—and, besides, every one had been looking at Marion.

Back at home that night as she lay in bed, Naomi realized she had to do something to help her friend. She knew her aunts had strictly forbidden her to do a love spell, but what if she were to give her friend a bit of courage? She sat up, blew on her candle, and a flame sprang to life. Then she pulled out her spell book and thumbed through the spells. At last she found what she wanted, but she didn't have the ingredients. Then she remembered that her aunts wanted her to go to an herbalist in the Seven Dials rookery to procure some of the rarer things they needed—eye of newt, goblin hair, and other oddities not sold at the local alchemist. She would go early before the ladies rose, perform the spell, and be at breakfast by ten. But where could she put the pot in which she intended to grow the seed of courage? Then she thought of the little maid who was so eager to thank her. Abby would know where she would be likely to be undisturbed while she performed the spell and where the seed could germinate without anyone interfering with the magic. With a plan set upon, Naomi blew out the candle and went to sleep.

Chapter Three

"Wake up, my lord." Peterson's urgent tone penetrated Wyndom's sleep-fogged brain. "It's urgent, sir."

The baron opened one eye. "What has she done that requires you disturb my slumber, man?" The gentleman was certain it had to be the lively Miss Clayton, for his servant had never before awakened him at this hour, knowing that he often worked late in his conservatory.

"She's set off for Seven Dials despite my direst warnings, my lord."

The gentleman bolted upright in bed. "Seven Dials! Great scot, man, what were you thinking to let an innocent girl go to one of the most dangerous rookeries in London?"

The old servant straightened, a wounded look on his lined face. "Truth be told, I'd already summoned a hackney cab before I fully understood what she intended. No matter my pleading, she was determined to go and swore that little dog was all the protection she needed."

Wyn tossed back the covers. "What time is it? Pray tell me you did not inform my grandmother of the girl's foolish trip. Where are my clothes? Have Thunder saddled and at the front door. I must go after the chit at once."

" 'Tis just after seven, my lord, and I came to you straight away." The butler handed the gentleman his shirt and breeches, then departed to summon his lordship's animal. Wyn knew he would have to apologize to Peterson after Miss Clayton was safely back in the town house.

While the baron was hurriedly dressing in Mayfair, across town Naomi peered out of the cab as the quality of the buildings and the pedestrians who moved about in front of them became progressively shabbier. Peterson had warned her, as had the hackney driver, but she had no choice, since her aunts needed the supplies.

"Audric, are you certain there was no other place I could have purchased what I need for this spell?"

"Grimmett's is where all magic folk come for their needs. Do you forget that you have great power to protect yourself, my dear? Nothing will go wrong, and we are likely to meet others who practice sorcery, which is what your aunts want."

The cab rumbled further into the depths of the London slums. At last it drew to a halt in front of an ancient shop whose windows were so grimy that one couldn't see inside. Flaking black letters on the door pronounced the shop to be for Herbs and Potions. Several sinister looking fellows stood near the corner and watched the cab with interest, but none made an attempt to approach Naomi as she climbed down along with her canine companion. She turned to the hackney driver. "Wait here. I shall be only a moment."

He looked about, but didn't say anything. Instead, he climbed back on his perch and watched the few fellows who were milling about on the street.

Naomi crossed the sidewalk and entered Grimmett's. A bell jingled above the door to announce her entry. "Good morning," she called to the empty store as her gaze roved over the jars and bottles that filled the shelves behind the counter. A heavy scent of cloves and dust filled the air, tickling her nose. One gloved finger under her nose helped her stifle a sneeze.

A wizened old man wearing a worn black suit stepped from behind one heavily stocked shelf. A fringe of white hair encircled his bald pate. "May I help you, miss?" He peered at her through thick glasses. His magnified eyes made him look like some exotic insect about to pounce on her.

"I have come for some items." Despite her nervousness, she handed him a list of what she and her aunts wanted.

He peered at the paper, then gave her a grin which exposed yellowed teeth. "Practicing the dark arts, are ye, miss?"

The one thing her aunts had stressed was to never admit to any kind of witchcraft to a single soul. "Do you have what I need, sir?"

"Aye, but it won't be cheap." He shuffled back behind the shelves, and she could hear the clink of crockery and the rustle of paper.

Suddenly the air around Naomi shimmered with energy, and a jolt of awareness warned her that she was no longer alone with the herbalist. She turned to see a young man of stout build with golden blond hair and eyes the tawny color of a lion's, dressed in the first stare of fashion. "Good morning, Grimmett, I need two dragon scales and . . ." His voice petered out when his gaze lit on Naomi. A smile lit his face. With gallantry, he drew his hat from his head. "Good morning, lovely lady."

Audric, who'd been sniffing at some crumbled leaves at the edge of the counter, looked up. "Why, Esmond, what are you doing in town?"

Without so much as a flicker of surprise, the young gentleman looked at the terrier, then arched one sandy brown brow. "Is that you, Audie? You were much larger and less furry when last we met in Rome. Haven't been able to convince Brassel to release you from doing penance for your dalliance with the lovely Tianna?"

The dog shook his head. "I'm not willing to stir his wrath any further by visiting him to beg his mercy. The punishment could have been for a thousand years instead of a mere century. Life isn't so bad—but, Esmond, enough of my fol-lies. Do allow me to present my cousin, Miss Naomi Clayton. Naomi, my old friend, Nathaniel Esmond."

Naomi had eyed the young man with interest as he'd non-chalantly chatted with her cousin. He had a pleasant face and a kind smile, but there was little about him that stirred her in the least. Was this the type of gentleman she was to spend the rest of her life with? Why didn't her stomach mis-behave the way it did with Lord Newlyn? She pushed disap-pointment aside as the gentleman extended his hand to greet her.

Before they could do more than exchange comments on how Esmond and Audric knew one another, Mr. Grimmett returned from behind the shelves and put a sack on the counter. "Here's yer order, miss. That'll be five guineas."

"Five guineas!" Mr. Esmond halted, drawing off his York gloves. "Good heavens, Grimmett, what are you selling the lady that could be so expensive?" The young wizard waved his hand, and the bag disappeared to reveal the contents. On the counter sat a bottle labeled wormwood oil, a pouch which stated mugwort paste, a ball of goblin hair, two tamarind seeds in a vial, and a small jar full of newt eyes. The young wizard picked up the bottle, pulled the stopper, and sniffed. "Just as I thought. Corn oil. And I would guess the seeds are mere flowers and the eyes from creatures caught in a mousetrap." He waved his hand, and in a puff of smoke Mr. Grimmett disappeared. Within seconds, a large rat ran out from behind the counter.

The little rodent reared on his hind legs and in a high squeaky voice cried, "My mistake, Mr. Esmond. I mistook the lady for a toad-witch."

"Toad-witch?" Naomi asked her new acquaintance as she struggled not to laugh, for the rat had on a tiny pair of spec-tacles.

"A witch who practices the arts but has no natural magi-cal talent, Miss Clayton. Most people avoid such witches be-cause they are always drawn to black magic." The young wizard waved his hand and Grimmett reappeared in his own form, his spectacles askew. He straightened the wire rims back on the bridge of his nose, then scooped Miss Clayton's order off the counter and hurried back behind the shelves to refill her list properly.

"Thank you for saving me from disaster, sir." Naomi shuddered at the thought of what would have happened had she used the wrong ingredients.

Audric cocked his furry black head, arching one fuzzy brow. "What brings you to London, Esmond? The last time we spoke, you were searching Rome for a talisman which would protect you from demons."

"Turns out it was mere myth, so I came home to England. Spyros is in town and has taken on two apprentices. I was lucky enough to be chosen as one of them." His eyes grew vague as he seemed to fall into a pensive daze. "Why, if I can learn even half of what such a powerful wizard knows, I would be happy." As Grimmett came out from behind the shelves, Esmond came out of his reverie. "Would you like me to speak to the master about your situation, Audie?"

The dog shook his head. "I know what price human form would be, and it's too high."

Naomi looked a question at Mr. Esmond. The wizard nodded his understanding and explained, "He would have to give up his magic."

"Here's ye order, miss." Grimmett stepped from behind the counter and eyed the young wizard warily before he added, "That'll be six farthings, please. I gave ye this nice sack for free." He handed her a small black bag which looked like a reticule."

She paid the herbalist, then turned to Mr. Esmond. "It was nice to meet you, sir. I hope you will come to visit us. We are staying at Newlyn House in Berkeley Square."

The gentleman bowed over her hand. "It would be my pleasure to call, Miss Clayton." Just then Grimmett threw a second bag upon the counter.

"Yer dragon scales, sir."

Esmond tossed several coins to the old man, settled his hat at a rakish angle, and disappeared with his purchase in a shimmering light. Then his voice echoed on the air. "Until tomorrow, my friends."

Naomi liked the young man very well, but she certainly had no desire to marry him, more's the pity. She slid the strings of the black sack on her arm with her reticule.

"Thank you, Mr. Grimmett." Naomi signaled for Audric to follow her. She stepped out of the shop. To her dismay, she was at once aware her hackney cab was nowhere in sight. A small crowd of dirty urchins had gathered as if waiting for her to come out.

"Wot ye reckon a fancy mort is doin' down 'ere lads?" a tall, gaunt lad of about fifteen called to the gathered crowd of riffraff. An unintelligible murmur ran through the group of boys, and their eyes glittered with avarice as they eyed her.

Naomi tugged her plain gray cape tighter as a chill of fear raced through her. She had the power to protect herself, if she must, but it could be used only as a last resort. At her feet Audric growled his best, then barked. Several of the young pickpockets fell back in fear. One of the lads reached out and tugged at her cape. "Wot ye goin' to give us to go away and leave ye be, miss?"

"A piece of my mind, if you don't stand back so I might pass." She sounded much braver than she felt. From the corner of her eye, she saw a lone rider approaching, and she prayed that the stranger would help her.

Several more lads reached out to grab at her cape. The ribbon holding it on her shoulders snapped, and the woolen cloak disappeared into the crowd. When the grimy hands began to tug at her green sprig muslin gown, Naomi swept her arm and shouted, "Away with you."

A sudden swirl of wind as powerful as a cyclone seemed to force the army of lads backward. Fright raced through the boys, who stared at the lady with fear. Just then the sounds of hoofbeats grew near and the lads scrambled away, leaving only the lady, whose knees trembled.

"Miss Clayton, are you unharmed?"

Naomi looked up and relief flooded through her. Seated on a dappled gray Arabian was his lordship, leaning down and extending his hand to her. Concern glimmered in the depths of his green eyes. She reached out her gloved hands and before she knew what was happening found herself lifted off her feet and settled on the pommel in front of the gentleman. His arms came round her as he took his reins and turned the horse back toward Mayfair. She sensed his anger, but at the moment she wanted only to feel the protection of those arms and to get away from the rookery. "Thank you for coming, sir." Then she called over her shoulder, "Come, Audric." The black dog raced behind the horse, his little legs churning to keep pace.

Through clenched teeth, the gentleman said, "Miss Clayton, what possessed you to come to one of the worst parts of London? Did Peterson not warn you it wasn't a proper place for a young lady? For that matter, it isn't a proper place for anyone, male or female, who wants to keep their life."

Naomi couldn't tell him that she had been in no real danger. It would have been only a matter of using more of her powers, but since she was grateful for his timely arrival, which had saved her from exposing herself as a witch, she merely said, "My aunts requested I go there, sir. I'm certain they had no idea Grimmett's was located in such a dangerous place."

There was a moment of silence as he drove the horse at a rapid pace back out of the dark slums. Only the sounds of the horse's shoes on the cobblestones broke the silence. Naomi peered over his shoulder and could see Audric was being left behind. "Could you slow down? My dog cannot keep pace."

The gentleman eyed the stores, which had grown more respectable, and slowed the horse to a brisk trot. After several moments, he said, "I would ask your promise that you won't go off again without consulting me or my grandmother."

Naomi could think of no reason why she should need to leave without an escort. "I promise," she meekly said, then added, "I was never so happy to see anyone in my life."

They rode the rest of the way to Berkeley Square in silence, but the entire time Naomi was patently aware of his strong chest pressed against her back. Soon she began to notice the strange looks they were receiving from the people walking abroad as they entered the square. All doubt was removed that it was most improper for her to be riding with the gentleman in such an intimate manner. When they approached Newlyn House, Naomi caught sight of two figures near the front door. In an instant she recognized Miss Ragsdale and her maid. It was clear by the expression on the woman's face that she was outraged to see Lord Newlyn riding with a young lady in his arms, and she grew even angrier when she realized the lady's identity.

Naomi felt his lordship's arms tense as he caught sight of the young woman. "Miss Ragsdale, what brings you to Newlyn House so early?"

Emotions openly warred on the young woman's features, but at last she managed to say in a civil tone, "Why, I came to consult you over several matters regarding my father's estate."

His lordship climbed down and lifted Naomi from the saddle. He smiled at Miss Ragsdale. "Pray forgive me for not being here, but there was an urgent matter I needed to attend to. I should be delighted to help you after I freshen up." He self-consciously ran a hand over his stubbled chin.

Amaryllis Ragsdale's gaze swept over the baron's unshaven face. "Newlyn, what can have possessed you to go out on the street in such condition?"

"I fear 'twas my fault, Miss Ragsdale." Naomi put on her warmest smile. She sensed they had shocked the young lady to the core. "I was so imprudent as to venture into a part of London that proved dangerous, and his lordship gallantly came to my rescue. Do join me in a cup of coffee while his lordship goes to change."

A muscle twitched in Amaryllis's jaw. Then she cooed, "I prefer tea, but, yes, I should like a moment to share my greater experiences in London with you, Miss Clayton. Perhaps your aunts never told you, but there are simply some things a proper lady must never do."

His lordship frowned, but without saying anything, he ushered the young ladies into the front hall where Peterson took Naomi's reticule and bonnet, not commenting on the missing cape. The baron excused himself and the ladies went to the upstairs salon to await refreshment. Miss Ragsdale's pleasant façade disappeared completely once the door closed.

"I am not fooled by you in the least, Miss Clayton. I know what a feather in your cap it would be to become Lady Newlyn. But I warn you, he is mine."

Naomi laughed. "You very much mistake the matter. I am looking for a different kind of gentleman altogether." But the truth was, he was exactly the type of man she would have liked, only her aunts had something else in mind.

Amaryllis's hand shot out and grabbed Naomi's arm. "You do not want me as your enemy, Miss Clayton. I have lived in London most of my life and have a great many friends. Gossip can be a very powerful tool when wielded by the proper person. One whispered tidbit from me could end your stay in London. With your ill-advised jaunt this morning, all I would need do is hint that you and his lordship are . . . paramours, and you would no longer be accepted anywhere."

Before Naomi could respond, Peterson arrived with a footman carrying a tray of tea and cakes. Despite her disgust for Miss Ragsdale, Naomi reined in her anger and took a seat, knowing that the conversation was not over. The butler quickly poured out the tea, which he handed to each young lady, then inquired if Miss Clayton needed anything else. With Naomi's assurances that they had what they needed, the old servant left.

Amaryllis took a sip from her cup and smiled smugly across the table at Naomi. "Have I made myself perfectly clear?"

Naomi put down her teacup. She had assumed that Lady Newlyn's dislike of the girl had been mere familial discontent with her grandson's choice, but she now realized it was because Miss Ragsdale was not a nice person. "My dear Amaryllis—I may call you that, may I not, since we are being so honest? In your vile ambition to capture Lord Newlyn's title and fortune, you have decided to declare war against me. Well, so be it." Naomi rose and smiled. "But be warned, you are inadequately armed for a battle, for I am not at all what I seem."

At that moment Amaryllis's teacup shattered in her hand, spilling tea all over the young lady's lavender morning gown. The lady gasped and jumped to her feet as a widening brown stain spread on the muslin fabric.

"My," Naomi said, "the tea must have been too hot for the fine china. You will forgive me, but I just remembered that I have things to do this morning." Naomi moved to the door, then paused and looked back, an intent expression on her lovely face. "Be warned, Miss Ragsdale. Any gossip about me would reflect badly on Marion, and I won't allow that to happen. Should one hint of scandal come to my ears, I would have to inform the family of your threats. Do you think her ladyship would doubt me? His lordship may not see you for what you are, but I think Lady Newlyn is not so unsuspecting." Naomi arched one dark brow. She politely bid the young woman good day and exited the room, well aware that her aunts would never have approved such a use of her powers—but she couldn't deny that it had given her supreme satisfaction to bring Miss Ragsdale down a peg.

Once upstairs, Naomi put the young woman out of her mind. She had a spell to do and she needed Abby to tell her where she might find some privacy.

* * *

When Wyndom came downstairs some fifteen minutes later, he discovered neither Miss Clayton nor Miss Ragsdale in the Green Salon. He went in search of Peterson, who informed him that one lady had gone to her room and the other had departed after spilling tea on her gown. He didn't mention the shattered cup, which he suspected Miss Ragsdale had broken in a fit of pique, for he couldn't think a delightful young woman like Miss Clayton would do such. Not only had she given Abby a recipe to soothe her stomach, but she also advised him to put rosemary in his tea after a hard day to relieve his aches and pains and had created a poultice for one of the grooms who'd rubbed a blister on his foot from borrowed boots. The entire staff liked Marion's new companion and woe be to Miss Ragsdale if she thought to drive her away.

The baron thanked his butler, then retired to his conservatory. It wasn't until he was settled at his desk that the thought came to him that he was relieved Amaryllis was gone. She would have been certain to ring a peal over him for having been out and about with Naomi that morning.

He bolted upright. Good heavens, when had he begun to think of Miss Clayton in such intimate terms? Was it the moment when he'd seen the joy on her face when she'd looked up to see him in her time of need? Or when she'd ridden back with him, nestled in his arms? Did it really matter when he'd begun to think of her so?

He plucked a sprig of rosemary and waved it under his nose. There was nothing wrong with his thinking of her as Naomi. After all, she was his sister's dearest friend. All he was certain of was that he had no more time to waste. He pulled his paperwork forward. The society was expecting his usual thorough work, and he would give them nothing less.

Audric sat perched on a straight-backed chair in the cluttered sewing room on the second floor at the end of the hall, his gaze riveted on Naomi as she performed the spell to give

Marion courage. With all the servants below stairs at their duties, and the noises from the street muffled by distance, the room was nearly silent. The novice witch consulted her spell book not once but thrice to make certain she had the proper ingredients and the words to the spell. She'd slipped away after nuncheon and borrowed a small clay pot from the potting shed at the rear of the garden, dug just enough dirt from one of the flower beds for her seed to germinate, then found the old sewing room which Abby swore no one ever used anymore except for storage.

Naomi patted the dirt in which she'd planted one of the seeds purchased that morning, then put three drops of worm-wood oil on top and half a cup of water. That done, she put a black ribbon round the pot as she chanted, "I bind Marion's fear." Then she placed the pot on a dust-coated windowsill to catch the morning sun and she sat on the floor, closed her eyes, and repeated the spell. "I conjure thee by night to come and bring to Marion a heart that's firm. As this seed's tendrils reach for the skies, so let Marion's courage arise."

The young witch opened her eyes and gave Audric a questioning glance. "Don't look at me, child. The only power I have now is to morph myself into different breeds. The rest all seems like gibberish." The canine gave a great sigh.

Naomi rose and brushed the dust from her hands as she looked about the neglected room. "I think my spell can be left here and won't be disturbed. Shall we go back to my room? I must change for supper, and I want to speak with Marion before we go down to dine."

With all taken care of, Naomi headed back to wait and watch for signs that her magic was taking effect. She knew the process would be slow, but that was good. The last thing she wanted was a sudden change in her friend to bring undue attention and questions.

That evening when Marion volunteered to join Lady Newlyn the following morning on her visit to Countess Littlebrook, a notoriously stern critic of young ladies new to Society, Naomi smiled a secret smile. She was certain the spell was the reason. When she looked up to see his lordship watching her, she politely arched one brow.

The gentleman crossed the room and took a seat beside her, which strangely heightened the pace of her heartbeat. "What pleases you so about the ladies' visit with the countess?"

Without so much as a blink of her eye, Naomi concocted, "Why, that I shall not have to go if Marion is so willing. As a penniless vicar's daughter, the lady will have no more interest in me than in a potted palm."

"But palms are quite interesting. There are over forty known varieties, which no doubt—" The gentleman ceased, then smiled, completely unaware of what that did to the young lady's heart. "Forgive me. I fear that my love of botany often makes me forget that others don't find plants so interesting."

"I fear that the Lady Littlebrooks of the world wouldn't be able to distinguish me from any variety of palm, but don't think that means that everyone is disinterested. Have you all forty varieties in your conservatory?"

"I have managed to collect only seven. They don't do well in our cold climes."

Miss Clayton and Lord Newlyn spent almost twenty minutes in conversation about palms and their possible value and use. Across the room, the dowager watched the pair with interest. It had never occurred to her to think in terms of the vicar's daughter as a possible wife for Wyndom, but the girl was certainly an improvement over the scornful Miss Ragsdale. If nothing else, Naomi might show the baron that a pleasant mein and kind heart made for a much nicer atmosphere in one's home. Amaryllis rarely opened her mouth save to criticize them. If only Wyndom didn't feel duty bound to marry the girl. What was needed was a suitor for Miss Ragsdale, but where one could find such a man, the dowager didn't have a clue. She would have to give the matter some thought.

The members of the household were much in harmony on retiring that evening. In the morning after breakfast, Lady Newlyn and Marion departed for their round of visits, his

lordship disappeared into his conservatory to work, and
Naomi went to the drawing room to write a letter to her
aunts. She had only just begun when Peterson arrived to inform her that a gentleman had come to call, a Mr. Esmond.

"Show him up, Peterson."

The old servant frowned, then cleared his throat. "Shall I
ask his lordship to join you, miss?"

It suddenly occurred to Naomi that Audric was not
enough companionship for her to be entertaining a gentleman alone in the drawing room. "Oh, there is no need to disturb Lord Newlyn. I shall come down to the hall."

Naomi entered the upper hall and halted at the top of the
stairs as Audric stood at her side. "Mr. Esmond, how delightful to see you again." With Peterson at their heels, Audric
barked a greeting, then raced down the stairs to where the
gentleman stood.

With a twinkle in his golden eyes, the young wizard
arched one brow. "Is this animal safe, Miss Clayton? I do believe terriers are known to be quite ferocious."

A smile played about Naomi's mouth as the butler moved
past her down the stairs. "You need not fear Audric, sir. He is
a lover, not a fighter."

"Ah, I do believe I heard that somewhere. Can't leave the
females alone. No doubt that will be his undoing." Mr.
Esmond and Naomi chuckled.

As the green baize door closed behind the departing butler, Audric mumbled, "Laugh it up you two, but remember,
eventually I shall get my powers back. Then you'd best be
wary. I fully intend to take my revenge."

Esmond winked at Naomi. "Never fear, Miss Clayton.
His bark has always been worse than his bite."

Audric rolled his eyes. "Good grief, no more of these
jests at my expense. I'm going to the kitchen to see if I can
coax some tidbits from Cook."

The dog trotted down the hall and pushed against the
door that led to the kitchens, then slid through the opening.

"Should I go after him and apologize?" Naomi worried

that they had been too free with the levity at her cousin's expense.

Mr. Esmond shook his head. "He is not in the least offended. My guess is that he acted thus as an excuse to leave us alone."

Naomi sent a questioning look at her new friend. She certainly hoped she hadn't given him the impression that she was casting out lures.

"Oh, did you not know? Whenever a single witch and an eligible wizard meet, the matchmaking begins. It is quite annoying, to own the truth." He took her hand, bending over it as he gallantly kissed it. "But in your case, I cannot complain, my dear."

At that moment, Lord Newlyn exited the conservatory on his way to request more ink from Peterson. He halted at the sight of a handsome young gentleman bending over Miss Clayton's hand. A strange emotion surged through him that he couldn't quite pinpoint, but of one thing he was certain: the sight left him feeling decidedly unhappy.

The young lady caught him watching, and her cheeks flamed pink. "My lord, do come and meet an old friend of my family."

She made the introduction and the two gentlemen eyed one another with, if not hostility, a wariness that did not bode well for future friendship. "You have known Miss Clayton for long, Mr. Esmond?"

The gentleman shook his head. "We are only recently acquainted, sir. But her aunts and her cousin have known me and my family for years."

A strained silence followed, and Naomi suddenly wanted Mr. Esmond gone, but before she could usher him to the door, Lady Newlyn and Marion arrived back from their visit. Introductions were made, and the dowager eyed the young man with interest. She insisted he stay for tea, and they all returned to the salon where, surprisingly, Lord Newlyn joined them. Naomi was nervous, uncertain how the young wizard would interact with the Longs, but she needn't have had any fears. He was charming and quite like any other young gentleman of the *ton,* flirting with the ladies, full of gossip, and well traveled. The dowager questioned him about his expectations and learned that he was heir to a tidy property in the north. Yet the more the baron seemed to hear, the less he seemed to like the young gentleman.

To Wyndom's dismay, his grandmother invited the gentleman to dine with them that evening. It wasn't until the young man had taken his leave, promising to be there again by eight, and the two young ladies had departed to their rooms that the baron took his grandmother to task over her invitation.

A smile lurked in the old woman's eyes. "What can you have to object to about such a nice young man?"

"I cannot like the way he lingers over Marion and Naomi's hands when he bows to them. Why, for all we know, he might be a rake."

"A rake?" A strange light settled in the dowager's eyes. "Yes, a rake just might do." Leaving her grandson puzzled, Lady Newlyn departed for her room without explaining. Wyn returned to his conservatory, but sat lost in worry that he might need to pay more attention to the young ladies' activities. His thoughts that Naomi would look out for Marion had been completely wrong. Beauty and a headstrong nature made her vulnerable, especially to someone she trusted like this old family friend. The baron decided he must make inquiries about the man.

Mr. Esmond arrived back promptly at eight, bringing two bottles of extremely fine French wine as a gift for his hostess. Despite the quality of the gift, Wyndom still couldn't find that he liked the young man, who again flirted with all the ladies. The baron drank deeply of the wine as the conversation flowed round him. When he ordered the second bottle opened, Lady Newlyn suggested they retire to the drawing room, convinced her grandson had had far too much to drink.

While Marion and the dowager showed Mr. Esmond the

family portraits, the baron pulled Naomi aside. "What can you tell me of your Mr. Esmond?"

A little in his cups, he had clutched her arms and pulled her close. Naomi was surprised that she didn't dislike the feel of his warm breath on her cheek. "Why, I know little other than that my cousin has vouched him a gentleman."

"Is he a rake? My grandmother was babbling something about a rake this afternoon."

"Are you worried about Marion? You needn't be, for she is not gullible in the least."

"I am worried about you both."

The gentleman stared into her eyes with such intensity it took her breath away for a moment. "I—I do not think you need be concerned for either of us, sir. He is friendly, but not in the least pushing."

Lord Newlyn's eyes seemed to linger on her mouth for a moment, and Naomi wondered if he meant to kiss her. Then a burst of laughter from the others seemed to awaken him from his trance. He released her arms and stepped back.

"Forgive me." He ran a hand over his face. "I don't normally behave in such a manner. I fear my protective instincts are heightened since my sister is on the Marriage Mart."

Naomi wondered what that had to do with his concern for her, but she didn't ask. "You needn't fear that Lady Newlyn and I won't watch out for Marion. She is as dear to us as to you. Trust us, sir."

Their eyes locked for a moment, and some undercurrent which had nothing to do with Marion seemed to flow between them. The moment ended when Lady Newlyn summoned them to come round the tea tray Peterson had delivered while they were in conversation. Naomi's thoughts were all jumbled as she accepted her teacup from her ladyship. Why did she continue to have such strange reactions when she was with the baron? He was practically engaged to Miss Ragsdale, and her aunts had strongly encouraged her to wed a wizard. She looked across at the young wizard, who would most please Bebe and Iona, only to find Mr. Esmond eying her and Lord Newlyn with a speculative gaze. Clearly he had observed the tête-à-tête between her and his lordship and wondered about them. Lady Newlyn drew his attention and the moment passed.

The rest of the evening passed uneventfully. Naomi saw nothing in Marion's behavior to think she was captivated by the wizard and so dismissed his lordship's fears. But every laugh or gesture from the ladies seemed to make Lord Newlyn's eyes narrow. It wasn't until the end of the evening that Naomi wondered if perhaps the baron was jealous. But that was too absurd, so she dismissed it from her mind.

Mr. Esmond departed just after ten, which was rather early during the Season. His excuse was an engagement at eight the following morning. Naomi knew he had lessons with Spyros that one mustn't miss. As he said his good-byes, Lady Newlyn engaged the young man to escort them to a ball on the following night. He promised to call for them at seven.

After his departure, the baron took his grandmother to the library for a private conversation. Naomi suspected he would read the lady the riot act about inviting Mr. Esmond to join them. Clearly he didn't like the man. The irony was he didn't even know the worst, or what he would think was the worst, if he were to know about the young man's powers. Not the least worried about Nathaniel Esmond's intentions toward Marion, Naomi suggested a game of chess to her friend, who pleaded fatigue. She requested they retire early instead. Naomi had no objection. Her life in London had been far busier than anything she had experienced in her sheltered life.

Summoning Audric from his spot beside the fire, the young ladies headed up to their rooms. When Marion wished her friend good night, the dog barked.

"I declare, one would almost think he understood our conversation." Marion smiled, then entered her room.

Naomi rolled her eyes at Audric and she warned, "Take care not to attract such attention."

"No one here will ever suspect I was once human. It is too far from reality in their minds."

With that, the pair entered Naomi's room and closed the door.

Just two doors further down the hall, the single bark by Audric had sent the occupants of the room into chaos. Two kitchen maids had taken the half-full bottle of French wine left on the dining table and slipped to the sewing room to enjoy a well-deserved drink, away from Peterson's disapproving stare. At the sounds of the dog and the ladies, one had rushed to the window to toss out the wine bottle before they were caught. Unfortunately for her, the window was stuck, so she poured the wine into the flowerpot on the sill. To her surprise, there was a strange sizzling and popping sound. She peered in the flowerpot and whispered, "What were in this?"

The second maid, her eyes riveted on the door, shrugged. "Just an old pot. Ye needn't worry."

Nell hid the wine bottle behind a trunk, then joined her friend. As the two maids trembled and waited, the hall grew quiet. After several minutes, they slipped upstairs to the servants' quarters unseen, each promising never to be so foolish again. As Nell reminded her friend, Lord Newlyn was the best of masters, but even he wouldn't tolerate such behavior from his servants.

Chapter Four

The following evening, a knock sounded on Naomi's door as she sat at her dressing table, putting the finishing touches on her hair for the ball. She had used artificial daisies through her dark curls to match her yellow silk gown. A fleeting thought of how his lordship would react when he saw her flashed through her mind. She shook her head in frustration at her continued fascination with the gentleman, then turned and called for the visitor to enter.

Marion stepped into the room, quite lovely in a pink silk gown with white lace at the bodice and sleeves. A small rouleau with tiny white roses was just above her hem. There was a twinkle of excitement in her eyes that Naomi had never before seen, and she suspected that her spell was beginning to take effect.

"Are you ready? We mustn't keep Mr. Esmond waiting." Marion stepped up behind her friend and peered at her reflection for a moment, then seemed satisfied. "Guess who is coming to the ball?"

Naomi knew who she hoped. "Your brother?"

"Wyn!" Marion laughed. "Not unless the hostess is displaying some exotic plants on the dance floor. He hates such affairs. 'Tis *Sir Charles Amberson*." She said the name with mock emphasis to show how unimpressed she was with the young man. "Grandmama had a letter from Lady Amberson this very day. I think she was hoping that grandmother would take him under her wing and open doors for him. Not that it matters, since Charlie isn't likely to be a nonpareil."

Naomi smiled at the memory of their old friend. After Sunday services when they were children, she, Marion, and Charlie had played freeze-tag behind the church while the adults stood about and talked. It was harmless fun, but the games had come to an abrupt end when Charlie knocked over a gravestone, which brought their illicit game to the notice of the adults. He had been quite clumsy, no doubt due to his girth.

"I thought he was still in the Peninsula with Wellington." Naomi grabbed her beaded reticule and rose, ready to go down to the drawing room. She had never been able to envision their lumbering friend a soldier, but then she hadn't seen him after he'd been sent to Harrow for his schooling.

"He sold out after his father died last year. Hurry, we don't want to be late. I have a feeling about tonight. I think I am going to meet someone special."

Naomi and Audric exchanged an amused glance before she called to him to be a good boy, then headed downstairs. They found Mr. Esmond and the dowager awaiting them. Naomi had secretly harbored the hope that his lordship would change his mind and accompany them, but to her disappointment, he was nowhere to be seen. They set out for the ball in Mr. Esmond's carriage, a splendid town coach which did much to raise the gentleman's stock in Lady Newlyn's eyes.

Like many of the early balls of the Season, the affair was a crush. Mr. Esmond escorted them through the receiving line and then found the ladies chairs against the wall until the dancing began. Lady Newlyn called Mr. Esmond to her side. Soon they were involved in a deep conversation, which puzzled Naomi, for Nathaniel was rather a lighthearted young man. But she was distracted from the pair when Marion eagerly pointed out the lovely decorations.

As the room filled with guests, several gentlemen they'd met at earlier balls came up and requested a dance with them. To Naomi's surprise, Marion was positively flirtatious. All doubt was removed that the spell was working.

When the strains of the first dance sounded, Marion rose to join Mr. Esmond and Naomi danced with a widower, Mr. Paulson, who'd come to town looking for a wife and mother for his four children. The dance seemed endless while she dodged questions about her housekeeping abilities, her background, and her interest in children's education. At last the gentleman returned her to Lady Newlyn's side, and Mr. Esmond was there to escort her out for the next dance as Marion went to the bottom of the set with Lord Fortesque, an old family friend. Before the music could start, Nathaniel leaned in and whispered, "What the devil did you tell Lady Newlyn about me?"

Naomi blinked in surprise. "Why, only that you are an old family friend."

"Then how did she come by the notion I am a rake?"

About to answer, Naomi paused when a gentleman entered the ballroom who struck a familiar chord with her. Yet she couldn't put a name to him. He was tall and slender, dressed in a well-cut blue coat. His hair was sun-bleached brown and he possessed a quiet reserve that she found appealing. She decided that he must remind her of someone.

Suddenly she wished Audric could be here to tell her if any of the guests were magical, for it did her no good to meet so many and not know. She looked up to see the wizard waiting for an answer to his question. "Pardon me, I fear I was woolgathering. What did you say?"

"Lady Newlyn thinks me a rake." His brows drew together as he glared at the old woman, who sat gossiping with her friends.

"I fear his lordship planted the idea in her mind. He suspects you of having designs on his sister and her fortune, but surely her ladyship didn't accuse you of such."

"More likely he fears I have designs on you." He arched one sandy brow in question.

"Me? We are but mere acquaintances, sir." Naomi's eyes widened.

"One does not look at a *mere* acquaintance with such intensity, my dear." At that moment, the orchestra began to play, and it was several moments before the movement of the steps brought them together to converse and he continued, "The dowager made no accusations. She only hinted that I should turn my charms on a Miss Ragsdale, as if I were some cursed fortune hunter. Who is she?"

Naomi thoughts were in turmoil at the wizard's assertion about Lord Newlyn. As she struggled to keep to the subject at hand, she looked across the room and gasped when Marion stepped from the line of dancers and threw her arms round the neck of the young man Naomi had admired earlier. Without the least reserve, Marion pressed her lips to his. A collective gasp could be heard from the guests. The music continued, but the dancers all craned their necks to stare at the young lady who'd practically ruined herself in front of the *ton*.

"Oh, good heavens, this is a disaster," Naomi uttered in despair, for she hadn't a single doubt her botched magic had induced Marion to behave with such abandon. "This is all my fault."

Nathaniel Esmond arched one brow at her. "Do I suspect a spell gone awry?" When she nodded, he pulled her from the line of dancers and began to stroll nonchalantly toward the refreshment room. "Oh, Anu, my old protector, save me from novice witches," he said, teasingly, then winked at her. "Come quickly. I think we can save your young companion from total social ruin."

He drew her into an alcove, then turned his back to the room. He folded his arms and stood in silence for a moment, then nodded his head before he called on the ancient gods to protect an innocent harmed by magic. Naomi was awed by the power that emanated from the experienced wizard. She wasn't certain if he truly glowed or if it was her own ability to see what ordinary mortals could not see. As the strains of the music died out, she heard a murmur race through the guests and she went to the archway to look out. A fashionable gentleman with impeccable grooming entered the ballroom and went straight to Marion and the young man, who seemed rather disconcerted by the girl's forward behavior. The newcomer greeted the pair, then stood in conversation with them for a moment. About to depart, he kissed Marion's hand and shook the young man's.

Nathaniel came up behind Naomi. She looked back at him. "Who is that?"

"Beau Brummell."

She had heard of the powerful arbiter of fashion. "What can he do for Marion?"

"His notice will do much to elevate her above the gossip. He shall now go about the room and inform all that Miss Long is an adorable innocent so overwhelmed with the safe return of her friend from the war that she quite forgot herself. Then he will declare her a true original and she will be made." The wizard smiled with satisfaction.

Naomi was amazed that Brummell could be so powerful. Then her mind locked on something Nathaniel said. "Her friend?"

"My spirit world guide tells me the gentleman is a Sir Charles Amberson, recently returned from the Peninsula."

"Charlie!" Naomi stared at the young man who, after Brummell moved to another group, had folded Marion's arm through his and taken her to her white-faced grandmother. There were only remnants of the boy from Yorkshire in the man beside her friend. As shocking as Marion's conduct had been, Naomi was greatly relieved that Marion hadn't kissed a complete stranger.

Beside her, Mr. Esmond put out his arm. "Shall we join the party?" He escorted her back to Lady Newlyn, where there was something of a reunion of the three old friends. Beside them the dowager sat speechless, staring at her granddaughter as if she were standing only in her shift.

Naomi only had moments to reminisce with Charlie before her next partner came to claim her for a country dance. The baronet escorted Marion onto the floor and later down to dinner. It wouldn't be until after the ball that the full impact would come of how close they had been to total disaster that evening, and all because she had been foolish enough to try casting a spell despite her aunts' warnings of no magic.

Thanks to Nathaniel, Naomi heard Marion being touted as one of Brummell's favorites of the Season and a certain success. With the wizard's help, they had averted social ruin. Naomi knew she owed him quite a debt.

At the end of the evening, Nathaniel duly delivered the ladies back to Berkeley Square. Last out of the carriage, Naomi whispered a heartfelt thanks and squeezed his hand. Nathaniel held on to her hand as the other ladies hurried into the town house. "If only I had met you first, perhaps . . ." He shrugged at fate's fickleness. "But love has its own kind of magic, and I think you and Lord Newlyn will have to find that out for yourself."

"But you are mistaken, we—"

The gentleman put a finger over her lips. "Don't give up true love for magic, my dear. With the right person, you can have both." He bowed over her hand before he climbed back into his coach, then lowered the window and added, "I believe there is a spell that you might want to put to an end—tonight." He gave her a knowing look as the coach pulled away.

Naomi, her thoughts so full of Lord Newlyn, had completely forgotten that the spell was still ongoing. She dashed across the sidewalk into the house, bid the footman good night, and followed the ladies upstairs.

When she reached the landing, Marion was waiting, her eyes shining. "Did you not think Sir Charles looked very well?"

Before Naomi could comment, Lady Newlyn came back down the hallway and said, "I should like to have a word with you, young lady, about that young man."

Marion's cheeks flamed red even as Naomi tried to intervene to protect the girl, but her ladyship ordered, "Go to bed, Naomi. I won't bite the child's head off, but I shall have my say." With that, her ladyship ushered her granddaughter into her room and closed the door.

Guilt raced through Naomi. It was her fault that Marion was getting such a trimming for her scandalous conduct, but her grandmother doted on her and would forgive her. Naomi went into her room to wait until Marion retired.

Audric sat up. "How was the ball?"

"A near disaster." She explained what had happened.

"The spell must be destroyed at once." Audric jumped down and came to stand beside her. They both stood and listened.

It was nearly fifteen minutes before Marion departed her grandmother's room to retire to her own chamber. There was no time to waste. Naomi took her candle and slipped into the sewing room, the small dog on her heels. She went to the window where the pot sat, appearing undisturbed. What had gone wrong with her spell? She picked up the pot and the strong odor wafted up.

"It smells like wine. How did wine get in the pot?"

"It doesn't matter. Destroy the spell."

Naomi hurriedly found a small carton full of yarn which she emptied before she dumped the dirt into the box. Sifting through the wet soil, she found the germinating seed. She held it in her hand and called, *"Terminar."*

The seed with its newly formed roots shimmered a moment, then disappeared like sparkling dust. A sigh of relief came from her lips and she brushed off her hands.

Audric trotted to the door and listened, then came back. "We need to get rid of everything so there won't be any questions."

Naomi stared at the soil and empty pot. "I will return everything to where I got it." She took the carton of dirt and pot, then hurried downstairs, Audric padding quietly behind her. The front hall stood empty and dark, except for her small circle of light. Without making the least noise, she opened the door to the conservatory. To her relief, no one was there, but the room was lit with warming lanterns to protect the plants against the night's chill. She followed Audric down the long rows of plants to the rear door, then stepped into the moonlit garden. The moon was full, bathing the area in silvery light, so she left her candle on a ledge near the door. Audric disappeared into the depths of the garden.

The chilled night air nipped at her as she hurried to the rear of the garden and dumped the box of soil. She leaned forward to push the carton under a small tree, promising herself to return in the morning and take the clay pot to the potting shed.

"Miss Clayton?" Lord Newlyn's voice sounded from behind her.

His unexpected presence startled her, and she almost tumbled headlong into the bushes. His lordship's strong hands grabbed her about the waist and pulled her back from the brink of an accident. As he pulled her upright, she lost her balance, and both his arms slid round her. She found her body pressed against his. A strange silence seemed to fall over the garden. For just a moment, he held her close in the moonlight's silvery glow. A tremble of something unexpected raced through Naomi as she turned her face up to his, wanting and longing for something that she shouldn't desire.

A magic as strong as any spell she'd ever done seemed to engulf them, and his warm mouth closed over hers. In that instant, as her body trembled from head to toe, she realized that, magic or no, she'd lost her heart to him.

Suddenly he released her and stepped back. Naomi felt abandoned.

"Miss Clayton, I apologize. I don't know what came over me." His voice was husky.

Clearly he was distressed by his actions, so Naomi, despite what she felt, made light of the kiss. "I suspect we were both bewitched by the moonlight, sir." She looked up at the glowing orb. "Is there anything more romantic than this silvery light?"

He stood silent for a moment, staring at her, then said, "No." Yet his tone was full of doubt. After a moment he asked, "What are you doing in the garden so late?"

Just then Audric trotted up beside Naomi. "Walking my dog."

"If he is finished, you should retire. You need your rest."

"Good night, sir." Naomi hurried from the garden, her thoughts in turmoil. She didn't say a word to Audric as they climbed the stairs. Once in her chamber, she bid him a terse good night and stepped behind the screen to don her nightrail and wrapper. But when she went to climb into bed, she saw her canine cousin eyeing her with a knowing glint. Had he seen what happened in the garden? "He is practically engaged, I tell you."

"Like I said, the heart wants what the heart wants." Audric settled his head on his front paws, never taking his eyes from Naomi.

She blew out the candle, but sleep did not come. How true were Audric's words. She was in love with a man who intended to ask another woman to marry him out of duty. As much as she might hope that he would change his mind, she still had the burden of her secret life—a life that few mortals understood. Why had she been such an utter fool as to fall in love with a man and not a wizard?

In the garden below, Wyndom was asking himself some hard questions as well. Why had he kissed Naomi with the eagerness of some schoolboy? Because she was beautiful and desirable as well as kind and intelligent, all characteristics any sensible man would want in a wife. But he had a duty to take care of Amaryllis. It was what her father wanted. He had criticized Naomi for wanting love, but he found himself contemplating such emotions for the first time in his life.

"Bah! Don't be a fool and mistake love and lust," he spoke in the empty garden. With clenched fists, he determined that he must do his duty and ask Amaryllis to marry him when her mourning was at end, but that thought didn't help push from his mind the memory of the soft feel of Naomi pressed against him. As storm clouds covered the moon, leaving the garden in darkness, he entered the house and tried to leave behind any thoughts of a future with Naomi.

Abbey woke Naomi just before noon the following day with the news that Miss Marion had awakened with a dreadful cough. They were hoping Naomi might have a home remedy. She rose and quickly dressed, then headed down to the conservatory, taking Audric with her. His lordship was nowhere to be seen, but she knew he would have no objection if she harvested a few leaves from his plants. Audric went outdoors while she scoured the conservatory until she found the horehound plant. It was no cure, but would relieve her friend's cough. She was in the process of plucking the leaves when she was interrupted.

"Miss Clayton, what are you doing to Newlyn's prized plants?"

Naomi didn't have to look up to know the querulous voice belonged to Miss Ragsdale. "I am going to make a remedy for Marion's cough."

"I shall have to inform him you have been damaging his plants." A smug look sparkled in the young lady's eyes.

"Do that if it makes you feel better. Come, Audric," she called toward the garden. "You must excuse me, but Marion is waiting." Naomi swept past the young lady and her maid without the least worry.

Amaryllis Ragsdale tapped her foot as she stared into the garden in thought. Nothing seemed to disconcert that conniving jade, and there was still a full month before she was officially out of mourning. Perhaps her mother was right. She should put herself in a compromising position with his lordship, and he would be forced to declare himself.

She turned to her maid. "Go wait in the hall."

"But, miss, ye mother said—"

"Go!" Amaryllis snapped, and the little maid disappeared.

The young lady's mind ran over the possibilities, and it suddenly occurred to her that pretending to faint would make him take her in his arms. All she need do was prolong the moment until Peterson or one of the footmen found them, and her task was done. A smile tipped her mouth as she hurried to the upstairs salon, where the butler had left her but she hadn't remained, for she was certain she might find Wyndom in his conservatory when he hadn't come.

Impatiently she waited until the butler brought the tea tray she had requested on arriving. She sipped the tea he poured and waited for him to depart. Then she rose and quickly removed her bonnet and tossed it on a nearby chair. She undid the ribbon that held the top of her bodice, exposing the mounds of her small breasts, which had been helped by her mother's tight lacing. After a glance in the looking glass, she pulled free several strands of curls. All was set when she looked down to see Miss Clayton's dog watching her.

"Go away, you stupid mutt—"

"I wouldn't be calling people names, for I can think of a few that would suit your present conduct—like strumpet or doxy." The dog grinned at her and waggled his thick brows.

Amaryllis's face blanched white, and for a moment it appeared she might truly faint. "W-what are you?"

Audric cocked his head and looked at her. It had occurred to him in the conservatory that as long as Miss Ragsdale was part of the scene, Naomi would never have her true love. So he had taken it upon himself to do what he could to reveal the woman's true nature. But how best to do that? Revealing himself would not be enough. He had to completely discredit her.

"I am Cupid, who has taken this form to promote true love." Audric watched her to see how she would take his lies. It was fortunate that she didn't know that Cupid was down in the tropics chasing some island beauty right now, for he detested the rain, cucumber sandwiches, and Prinny.

The lady eyed him warily, uncertainty on her face. It was not every day that one saw a talking dog, but she seemed to be interested in what this talking dog had to say. She questioned, "True love?"

Audric nodded. "True love between Miss Clayton and Lord Newlyn."

Amaryllis stamped her foot so hard the chandelier in the room below rattled, frightening the maid who was dusting there. "I forbid it. I have spent too much—"

In a puff of smoke, Audric changed his size and shape. When the smoke cleared, a huge brown mastiff, which was as menacing as he could be, stood there instead of the small terrier. "Don't take that tone with me. I could turn you, Miss Ragsdale, into a wharf rat."

The lady stepped back, her eyes like saucers. Then, as if she suddenly realized all that she had seen and heard, she began to shriek at the top of her lungs. The sounds of thundering footsteps could be heard in the hallway. Within moments, Lord Newlyn, without his jacket and with his cravat half tied, the dowager and Marion in their wrappers, Naomi, Peterson, and several housemaids with dust cloths entered the drawing room to find a rather disheveled Miss Ragsdale standing in the middle of the room in hysterics.

The baron went to her side as the others stood in the doorway and watched. "What is wrong, Amaryllis?"

"That—that dog is not a dog." She pointed to Audric, who was again a small black terrier. He was on the rug, chewing on the strings of the young lady's reticule with such gusto one would have thought it a beefsteak. While his lordship ushered Miss Ragsdale to a chair near the window, Naomi rushed to the dog and pulled the purse from him. In a whispered undertone, she asked, "What have you been up to?" Then in a louder voice she added, "Naughty dog."

The dowager arched one brow. "Just as I thought. All that fretting and fuming has weakened her mind."

Amaryllis sat forward. "I tell you that dog is—" She paused and seemed to think better of what she was about to say when she saw the looks on everyone's faces. She eyed the black dog thoughtfully. Then she said, "It must have been the tea. It was drugged."

A frown appeared on Lord Newlyn's face. "Drugged? By whom and why, Amaryllis?"

The malice was evident in the young lady's face as she stared across the room. "By her." She pointed at Naomi. "I found her plucking leaves from one of your plants, Newlyn. She is trying to discredit me in your eyes. She wants to steal your affection from me."

Everyone looked at Naomi, but she only saw his lordship's eyes, and his disapproving look frightened her. "I did take leaves from a horehound plant to make tea for Marion this morning. You can ask Peterson. He watched me brew it. It was to ease her cough."

When everyone looked to the butler, he shrugged. "In truth, I didn't pay much attention, for I was busy making tea for Miss Ragsdale. But it seems to have worked, for Miss Marion isn't coughing."

Marion nodded. "It worked wonderfully, but it tasted rather dreadful."

Amaryllis jumped to her feet. "She could have slipped something in my tea while he wasn't looking."

Marion, despite her sniffles, said, "How dare you, you vulgar creature? *I* might have been tempted to put something in your tea, but Naomi would never deliberately harm anyone."

"You are too spoiled to see what is in front of you," Amaryllis cried, then fell into his lordship's arms, weeping.

Lady Newlyn bristled. "Don't speak to my granddaughter in that manner."

"Ladies!" Wyndom's voice held such authority that they all fell silent. "We shall sort this out later. Amaryllis, I think your maid should escort you home and allow you to rest. You are overset. I shall visit with you this afternoon."

The young lady started to protest, but the baron directed Peterson to have her taken home in a carriage so there could be no further protest. After the butler escorted the young lady from the room, along with the maids, Wyndom urged his sister back to bed, and his grandmother to finish her toilette. When Naomi turned to depart as well, he requested that she stay and walked over to close the door.

At last he turned to look at her. "Have you malice toward Miss Ragsdale?"

"If you mean do I like her, no, I do not, but I did not drug her tea as she suggested." Naomi's ire rose that he would think her capable of such a heinous act. Was he so enamored with the lady that he took her side in the matter?

He folded his hands behind him. "I have known Amaryllis Ragsdale for most of her life, and while she can be a bit formal and"—he struggled a moment to describe the young lady—"authoritative, I cannot—"

"Sir, you are so involved with your plants, you are aware of little else. You have no idea what Miss Ragsdale's nature is, or you would not think to inflict her on your family." Naomi couldn't remember when she had been so angry. Her calmer self knew that there was no true reason for such anger, but it still simmered deep within her. Why could the man not see that Miss Ragsdale was a fraud?

The gentleman's eyes held a wounded look for a moment. Then he straightened. "I know that you are nothing like the young woman we remember from Yorkshire. I would never have put such a question to the vicar's daughter." He suddenly seemed to realize what he had just said and rubbed a hand over his face. "Naomi, how did we get to this pass? I could never think you capable of such an act, but how else to explain a woman of Amaryllis's intelligence having such a strange experience?"

The anger rushed from Naomi and only guilt remained. She loved this man and wanted to spend the rest of her life with him. It was clear he must know the truth. She straightened, fear racing through her at what she was about to do. She might be sending him straight into Miss Ragsdale's arms. Her mother had revealed the truth and it had destroyed her marriage. Better to know now than to have him end his plans to wed Amaryllis, only to find that he could not accept that Naomi was a witch.

"I am basically still that young woman whose father taught her virtues, but there is more to me, sir. Yet know this: I would never do harm to Miss Ragsdale or anyone else." She walked to the fireplace and pick up a crystal dove from the mantel, then turned.

The gentleman's brows rose. "What do you mean, more?"

She didn't explain. Instead she let her actions speak. She said the incantation needed, circled her hand once over the glass, and the porcelain bird sprang to life. It fluttered its wings, then sat in her hand cooing for a moment.

Disbelief etched the baron's face. "Was that some sleight of hand? Have you been keeping company with the tricksters from the fair? I should think your aunts would have kept a better watch on you." His gaze was locked on the bird, which Naomi took to the window and released.

She closed the sash and looked back at him, but it was clear he didn't understand. "It is no trick, I am—"

Audric rose and finished the sentence. "A white witch."

Lord Newlyn didn't say a word as his gaze darted from Naomi to the dog and back. All Naomi needed to know was written in the expression on his face. It was a combination of horror and mistrust. Suddenly nothing mattered when she realized the man she loved not only seemed to fear her, but suspected she would do evil because of that single word—witch.

He shook his head as he stared at her. "It's not possible. I am a man of science. I don't believe in witches or magic, black or white. I begin to think you have drugged us all."

His words were like a knife in Naomi's heart. Fighting back the urge to cry, she said, "Perhaps someday you will realize that there are some things science cannot explain. Good-bye, Lord Newlyn. Come, Audric." With that, she left the man who had no wish to possess her heart.

The door closed behind the girl, and Wyndom stood in the middle of the drawing room, his thoughts in utter chaos. He had kissed her last night and realized that he had feelings for her. Had she bewitched him? His thoughts ran through all their encounters, and he'd seen nothing to make him think she had manipulated him with spells, but did one know when one was under a witch's thrall? He couldn't grasp the concept of magic, except he'd seen her transform the statue with his own eyes and her dog had spoken.

He turned, running a hand through his hair, and caught sight of himself in a pier glass near the door. His cravat was only half tied and he still had to finish his toilette, for today was the day he was to present his paper to the society.

Despite what he'd just seen and heard, he had an obligation to fulfill his responsibility to the others in the botanical society. But the need to speak with Naomi further pressed in on him. Should he go and leave her here with his sister and grandmother? But in his heart he knew the girl was no danger to anyone under his roof. His paper must be presented in two hours. He would sort out his thoughts about Naomi when he returned. The baron hurried from the room.

"You are leaving us?" Marion sat up in bed, where her grandmother had insisted she return after the foolishness in the drawing room. "Don't let silly accusations by Amaryllis drive you away. Of course no one believed her."

Lady Newlyn, seated beside her granddaughter's bed,

added her voice of protest. "Wyn is too smart to believe that you would have drugged anyone, my dear. Of course you cannot leave. Marion still needs you."

After her encounter with Lord Newlyn, there was no doubt that Naomi would return to her aunts at once. In the safety of her room, she had debated whether or not she should confide in the ladies of Newlyn House. Audric had argued against it, but instinctively she knew she could trust them and had decided they deserved the truth.

She took a seat on the edge of her friend's bed and looked at the dog, who watched her with wary dark eyes.

"I think Marion has found what she is looking for in Charlie."

Marion blushed, then smiled. "Do you think he likes me?"

The dowager chuckled. "I think he never took his eyes off you when he wasn't dancing with you, child." A frown puckered the old woman's brow. " 'Tis quite fortunate he didn't take exception to your fast conduct." On seeing her granddaughter's blush, she raised her hand dismissively. "But there has been enough said on that matter."

Naomi sighed, seeing one more reason she must own up to her magic. "So you see there is no need for me to stay."

Marion leaned forward and grabbed Naomi's hand. "But I want you to have your chance to make a match—"

"That isn't likely to happen. I—I do not think I am suited for London. Besides, Lord Newlyn will want me gone."

The Longs exchanged a puzzled glance. Then the dowager asked, "Did you quarrel with my grandson after we left you, my dear?"

Naomi shook her head. "I revealed something to him I should have told you all when I first arrived." She took a deep breath, then said, "I am a witch."

Both Marion and the dowager stared at her with blank expressions, clearly not taking Naomi's meaning. Then Lady Newlyn laughed and waved a hand. "My dear, we have all been witches at one time or the other. My late husband used to say it's in the female nature to be witchy when—"

Naomi shook her head. "I'm not acting like a witch, I am a witch." She stood up, and with a wave of her hand she changed Marion's pink curtains and bed covers to a deep blue. Then she stepped to a nearby table and picked up a candelabra. Taking a deep breath she blew and all five candles flamed to life.

"Oh, my!" Lady Newlyn looked from the brightly colored fabric to Naomi, then to the flickering candles, which were once again on the tables. "If only I had been able to do that when I was a new bride at Newlyn Manor, it would have saved me a great deal of time and trouble with my mother-in-law. Well, my dear, you are certainly full of surprises."

Naomi was surprised at how calm her ladyship seemed on learning she had a witch under her roof. "You do not seem the least discomposed by my announcement."

The dowager sat back in her chair to eye the girl thoughtfully. "My dear child, the advantage to being my age is that you gain a bit of wisdom. Over time I have learned that no matter how much one knows, there is always something one doesn't know. Besides, you have been here for over a week and of one thing I'm certain. You haven't a mean bone in your body. A witch you may be, but not an evil one, I wager."

Audric sat up and smiled. "You are a great gun, my lady. I recognized it the first time we met."

Marion and the dowager stared at the animal with far more awe than they did at Naomi and her announcement. Lady Newlyn asked, "You speak?"

Naomi quickly explained who Audric was and the spell he must endure for one hundred years.

Lady Newlyn shook her head in amazement as she stared at the pair. "So a witch and a wizard all under our roof and us without the least idea."

Marion's eyes had grown round as she had listened to the exchange and gazed at the changes her friend had wrought. Then she smiled. "A witch, Naomi? What else can you do?"

"A great many things. But my aunts did not want me practicing magic in London. I am still a novice and things can often go wrong, like the spell I did to give Marion courage."

The Long ladies exchanged a look of dawning realization. "So that is why my granddaughter suddenly behaved like a little baggage. That is a great relief off my mind." Lady Newlyn looked at her granddaughter with renewed pride.

Marion sat up with her eyes narrowed. "And Brummell, was he part of your magic?"

Naomi shook her head. "That was thanks to Mr. Esmond. He is a powerful wizard and stepped in to help me. You won't tell anyone, will you?"

The dowager shook her head. "Of course not, child. Imagine, there are witches and wizards all mixing with the *ton.*" A wicked twinkle came into her eyes. "How I should like you to put a wart on Mrs. Drummond-Burrell's nose for all the times she has stuck it in the air to cut people over the years."

Naomi arched a brow at the lady.

"I was only teasing, my dear." Lady Newlyn grinned sheepishly.

Marion gasped, "Oh, Naomi, did you cast a spell for Charlie and me to fall in love?"

Naomi put her hands palms outward in a gesture of denial. "Love spells are forbidden. All I did was to bind your fear and release your true courage. Whatever you and Charlie feel is from your hearts."

A contented smile lit Marion's face. "He is wonderful, is he not?"

Lady Newlyn asked, "And what of your heart, Naomi? Am I wrong in thinking that my grandson—"

Naomi started up from the bed. "I am a witch, and, as my mother found out, not just every man would want such for a wife. I think it best I return home."

The dowager and her granddaughter did their best to convince Naomi to stay. But at last the ladies gave way when Naomi assured them she couldn't be happy at Newlyn House, especially with Miss Ragsdale soon to be his lordship's fiancée.

Her ladyship summoned Peterson and ordered the carriage be made ready for a journey back to Wiltshire that very afternoon. When her ladyship accompanied Naomi to finish her packing, Audric jumped from the floor to the chair to Marion's bed. The girl eyed him timidly.

"She loves him, you know."

Marion clutched at her covers. "Charlie?"

"No, your brother—and I'm certain he cares about her. Would you like to help them?"

"Me? How?"

"A little magic."

Marion frowned. "I should love to do that, but I am no witch."

Audric waggled his brows. "True, but even someone without power can do a spell if they truly believe in the power of magic."

A strange light began to glimmer in the young lady's eyes. She sat up. "What must I do?"

"I tore a spell from her magic book while she was distracted. It is tucked under the wardrobe in her room. Follow the directions exactly and Miss Ragsdale's dark heart will be revealed to Lord Newlyn."

Excitement made Marion's cheeks rosy. "So I, too, can do magic."

Audric jumped onto the girl, his paws pushing her shoulders back into her pillows. "Beware, Miss Marion. Do this one spell and only this spell."

"But why? Naomi is a witch. Why should I not—"

"Only a special few are born with true magical powers, child. It is a gift for doing good. If you do magic without the gift, you will be drawn into the dark forces. It is always so for witches. That is why the only ones you hear about are evil. Now, Miss Marion, promise me you will use the one spell, then tear it up and never again try to do sorcery."

Marion blinked, then nodded. "I promise."

Audric stared into her eyes and he believed her. "You must do the spell this very day or his lordship might be lost to Miss Ragsdale forever." The dog jumped down and hurried out of the room. Marion lay back, her mind reeling with what had just happened. Would she be able to do the spell? Of course she would. Anything to keep Wyn from marrying Amaryllis Ragsdale. She would sneak into Naomi's room later and find the paper. Perhaps it was best her grandmother hear what she intended to do later, just in case the magic went awry. Marion sneezed, then snuggled down into the covers to wait until the time for action was right.

By two o'clock Naomi climbed into the carriage to set off for home, with Audric to keep her company. The novice witch hoped her cousin would help her to explain what had gone wrong—that she, like her mother before her, had lost her heart to a mortal.

As the carriage pulled away from the curb, Marion slipped from her bed and ran to the window. The time was right, and she slipped into Naomi's room. The spell was where Audric had told her it would be. Without the least hesitation, she read what she needed and what she must do. She gave a nod of her head and set about finding what she would need. If she were lucky, her brother would be free from Miss Ragsdale by sundown.

Chapter Five

"Is everything as it should be, Wyn?" Ned Camden asked as he leaned back in the carriage and eyed his old friend thoughtfully. They had recently departed from the meeting of the Linnean Society.

"Why do you ask?" Wyn looked out at the street, his distraction making him snappish.

"You were a bit abrupt in there. Not your usual style after a presentation." Mr. Camden had known the baron since Eton and was well familiar with his friend's normal mein. Often he would stay for hours to answer questions on his presentations.

Wyn shrugged. "I have several things on my mind. Nothing you need concern yourself about. I shall come about soon." The frown on his face grew deeper.

"Perhaps a visit to White's might help? A drink and congenial conversation often helps me put my worries behind me." Ned couldn't imagine what had his congenial friend so out of sorts.

The baron shook his head. "I cannot. I promised to visit Miss Ragsdale this afternoon."

Ned sighed. "You know my thoughts on that young woman.

Just drop me on St. James's Street and I shall walk home from there." He had been quite vocal in his dislike of the lady. It was his opinion that Wyn was going beyond duty to be offering for Amos Ragsdale's daughter.

When the carriage reached St. James's, Wyn signaled the coachman to stop and the friends parted ways. In a matter of some fifteen minutes, the baron was outside Miss Ragsdale's door.

He was torn as to what he would say to Amaryllis about the incident that morning. There was no question that he would not betray Naomi's confidence. Amaryllis, no doubt, would want to burn the girl at the stake if she knew the truth. He lifted the knocker, but his hand froze when he heard a dreadful screeching inside the small house. What the devil?

Moments after he knocked, the door opened to reveal a maid looking as if she were afraid of her own shadow.

"Good morning, Sally. I have come to see how Miss Ragsdale fares."

The girl bobbed a curtsy. "My lord, I ain't certain she's receivin'." The maid looked back over her shoulder in doubt, even as a crash of glass sounded in the drawing room.

"I am expected." Wyn couldn't imagine what was happening.

With a shrug, the maid led the gentleman upstairs. She opened the door to a room in utter chaos. Flowers had been tossed about, magazines and books were strewn on the floor, and a teacup was upended on the table, the saucer shattered. Mrs. Ragsdale was standing in front of her daughter, holding onto her arm.

"Amy, dearest, you cannot behave in this—"

As Wyn stepped into the room, Amaryllis, unaware she had a visitor, drew back her hand and struck her mother full across the cheek.

"I don't have to do what you say. I shall send you away once I am married, and I won't ever have to listen to your simpering again."

The older woman grabbed her cheek and turned away.

She caught sight of his lordship standing in the doorway and gasped, "Lord Newlyn!"

The gentleman stiffly bowed. "I fear I intrude, madam." He addressed himself to the mother but his narrowed gaze was locked on the daughter.

Mrs. Ragsdale hurried to his side, fear in her eyes. "Sir, I do assure you that this is not what you think. She hasn't had one of these spells since her father died."

"Spells?" A deep sense of foreboding settled into Wyn. What didn't he know about Amaryllis? Had his loyalty to Amos blinded him to her faults, as everyone said? But he was certain he had never before seen her like this.

Mrs. Ragsdale wrung her hands. "Well, not exactly a spell. More like a little fit of pique over the merest trifle. You have a sister. Surely you understand. We do spoil our girls so."

With a hopeful look, she gazed up at him. Before he could deny that his sister had ever behaved in such a manner, Amaryllis put her hands on her hips ands glared at him. In every other way she looked normal, but her words were startling. "Well, so you have finally found time to pay a call. I could have been on my deathbed for all *you* cared. Can I assume you have at least sent that dreadful creature back home where she belongs? I tried to tell you and that obnoxious grandmother of yours that some country nobody didn't belong in London. No one heeds my advice."

"Amaryllis!" Mrs. Ragsdale cried. "What will his lordship think?"

The young lady raised her chin defiantly. "That I am tired of bowing and scraping to bring him up to scratch. I was bored to death with my father's incessant gabbling about plants, and I won't suffer a husband who is an equal bore. It is me or those cursed plants."

A stunned silence hung in the air for a moment. Without a word to the young lady, Wyn turned and bowed over Mrs. Ragsdale's hand. "Madam, I promised Amos that I should willingly look out for you and Miss Ragsdale. The lady has made it perfectly plain that she doesn't need or wish my assistance, but if *you* have need of any future advice, please feel free to consult with my man of business, Mr. Irwin, of Fleet Street." He leaned down and picked up a yellow tulip from the floor, the message to Amaryllis clear that he had made his choice.

Mrs. Ragsdale's face crumpled. "But—but I—"

"Good day, ladies."

It wasn't until Wyn was outside on the sidewalk that he realized a great weight had been lifted from his shoulders. He had tried to stand by his promise to Amos, but he wouldn't force the Ragsdale ladies to endure his company when all they needed was a good solicitor. He could check with his man of business from time to time to make certain the ladies were taken care of, but he no longer felt the bonds of obligation that had once shackled him. Amaryllis had set him free with her own words.

He climbed into his carriage. Then a sudden thought hit him right in the gut, making him sit down hard. He could hardly breathe. Had Naomi cast a spell on Amaryllis to make her behave in such a manner? The very thought made him ill. Would he have to go back and apologize, to once again face a marriage of convenience? He shouted for the coachman to take him home at once. He would know the truth.

The door to the drawing room banged open. Lady Newlyn looked up to see her angry grandson's face and frowned. "What is wrong?"

"Where is Naomi? I would speak with Naomi." He paced in front of the lady, his agitation so great he couldn't stand still.

"She left at two this afternoon, went back home." The lady went back to her fashion magazine. Then she calmly added, "And she didn't use a broomstick."

Wyn halted, distracted from his purpose. "She told you."

"Actually, dear Naomi showed us. You should be happy, dear boy. Marion's room has been redone in the finest blue silk and without the least expense to you. How I envy her gift!"

The baron stared at his grandmother in amazement. "That is all you can say? A guest in your home tells you she's a witch and you envy her? Well, let me tell you that I think your dear Naomi has cast a spell on Amaryllis, madam."

"A spell? While she was traveling in a carriage? I very much doubt that." A twinkle appeared in the old woman's eyes. "Did Amaryllis change into a viper? I think a viper would suit that girl very well, don't you think?"

At that moment Marion came into the drawing room, still dressed in her wrapper. "What is happening?"

"Newlyn is looking for Naomi." The dowager winked at her granddaughter.

"Well, she's not here. She knew you disapproved of her gift, so she went home."

"But . . . I never said I wanted her to go. I—" He broke off what he had been going to say and walked to the window to gaze sightlessly out at the traffic. In truth, he didn't know what he thought about her and her *gift*. He hadn't expected to find Naomi gone. They had sorted nothing out.

Marion appeared at his side. "What did Amaryllis do?"

Wyn turned to his sister. For a moment he struggled to get his thoughts away from Naomi. "Amaryllis? Why, she behaved like a complete fishwife. It was like seeing a different person. Did you know she hates botany? Demanded I give up my study of plants!"

Lady Newlyn snorted. "Unmasked at last."

Marion clapped her hands and ran back to her grandmother. "It worked. She revealed her true self."

The baron watched the two women celebrate. Puzzled, he asked, "What are you talking about?"

The dowager rose and slid her arm protectively around

Marion's shoulders. "Audric gave Marion directions on how to perform a truth spell to have your Miss Ragsdale be completely herself for the next twenty-four hours."

"Great heavens, you have involved yourself in this unholy business on the advice of a talking dog!" Wyn trembled, he was so angry that Naomi and her unnatural mongrel had drawn his sister into witchcraft.

To both the baron and dowager's amazement, Marion gamely stood her ground against her brother's wrath. "Unholy business! Did Naomi do anything but try to help those around her? You, a man of science, mustn't be mislead by old legends and superstition. We, none of us, had any notion that witches existed, but of one thing grandmother and I are certain. We would trust our lives to Naomi."

Lady Newlyn added her voice to Marion's. "You needn't look at your sister like that, my boy. It was a single spell which the dog ordered Marion never to repeat, and she gave her word. Besides, Naomi is gone from our lives, so there will be no more magic."

His grandmother's statement shook Wyn to the bone. Witch or not, Naomi was gone and not coming back. He ran his hands through his hair, aware there was now a hole in his heart. Yet perhaps it was for the best. He could not quite stomach the idea of a witch in his family.

He pointed at his sister to stress his meaning. "No more magic."

Without another word, he strode from the room and went straight to his conservatory. He stood at the head of the steps, overlooking his vast collection of plants, which often brought him such a spark of fascination and curiosity, but now there was no desire to work. Instead his gaze moved to the garden beyond the glass room and he remembered his moonlit encounter with Naomi, the feel of her in his arms, her lips beneath his. That night he'd tried to convince himself the kiss had meant nothing. He understood now his feelings of obligation to Amos had colored his thinking. With that burden lifted, he admitted to himself that Naomi had touched him in a way no other woman had. Could he allow her to walk away from him even knowing what he did about her?

He pondered her sorcery. His sister had called it a gift. Was she right? Were old legends and superstitions clouding his judgment, making him reluctant to fully embrace Naomi? She had been kind and caring with the servants, patient with his sister, and truly interested in his work—unlike Amaryllis, who'd only pretended interest just to marry him. In every way, Naomi was what a man could want, and he did want her. So what if she possessed a power he would never understand? He was certain she would never do anything wrong with her powers.

But she had left without a word to him. Did she possess any tender feeling for him after the accusations he'd made? She had seen through Amaryllis, as had that strange dog who'd encouraged Marion to perform a spell. A smile suddenly lit his face. Audric was responsible for the true Amaryllis being revealed. Did that mean he wanted Wyn to marry Naomi? One couldn't have a better ally.

The butler entered the conservatory at that moment. "My lord, her ladyship wants to know if you are joining her for tea."

"No, Peterson, have my curricle at the front door in fifteen minutes. I am going to Wiltshire and bring Miss Clayton back."

"All will be delighted to hear the news, sir."

The baron hurried upstairs and informed his grandmother of his mission and, as the butler had predicted, the lady was ecstatic. Within another ten minutes, he was on the road to profess his love to a witch.

Audric slicked the last of the brown gravy from the plate as if he hadn't eaten in days. At last he sat on his haunches and eyed the other treats on the table. "Did you want that last slice of beef?"

Iona shook her head as she glumly moved the food about on her plate. Behind her Bebe paced the floor, having given up on the pretense of dining.

Bebe tugged her cashmere shawl tighter as she drew near the open window. She peered out at Naomi, seated alone beside the pond. Then the old witch turned to glare at the dog. "How could you have allowed this to happen? Are you certain she loves this baron? This is dreadful."

The dog halted his eating for a moment. "Ladies, take it from me, from the moment those two met, I sensed . . ." Audric pondered the right word to use with two maiden aunts. "Attraction. By the time she met her first wizard, her heart was lost. Even Esmond took note."

"Nathaniel Esmond?" Iona asked, then sighed heavily. "He would have been perfect—magical and rich. Whatever shall we do, Bebe?"

"We must give her time for her broken heart to heal. She is young and needs time to master her magic. Perhaps in several years, she—"

"Ladies," Audric put his paws on the table, making him taller, and it helped to drive home his point. "Do not discount true love, even in a mortal."

Bebe snorted. "Kendra said much those same words—"

A knock sounded on the door. The terrier smiled and waggled his brows. "Like I always say, the heart wants what the heart wants."

Bebe opened the door to reveal a gentleman. Audric jumped down and hurried to greet him. "I knew you would come."

Wyn stared at the dog, bemused for a moment. "Forgive me. I'm still not quite used to conversing with a dog."

The aunts welcomed the baron into the cottage. After introductions, Bebe came straight to the point. "Why have you come, sir?"

"To ask Naomi to marry me."

Iona was all smiles, but Bebe was not so easily swayed. "And can you accept everything you now know about our girl? Don't think to marry her if you are going to try to take away her birthright."

The gentleman's eyes widened for a moment. Then he smiled. "Someone recently demanded I give up something that meant a great deal to me. I would never ask that of Naomi."

Bebe and Iona exchanged a pleased look. Iona rose from the table and came to take the gentleman's hand. "Then you have our blessing, if Naomi will have you."

He looked around, and Audric nodded with his head toward the rear door. "She's at the pond."

As the baron departed through the door, the dog looked at Bebe and asked, "Have you any more of those little macaroons that I had last time I visited?"

Naomi tossed a stone into the pond and watched as the ripples moved outward. She hoped that everything went well with Marion and Charlie, but when she thought about the Longs, her thoughts were drawn to the baron, and at the moment that was too painful.

Her aunts had been understanding about her sudden return, but she still felt guilty. They wanted a wizard, and she had fallen for a man who clearly was appalled by her magic. What was she to do now? Perhaps her heart wouldn't ache so much once she heard that Wyndom had married Miss Ragsdale. That would surely put an end to thoughts of the baron.

She lifted the magic book she'd pulled from the shelf and looked at the first spell on the page. Magic would help fill her time until the pain lessened. She read the words on the page. *"Susto flora."*

The bushes round the pond suddenly began to grow and bloom. White morning glories, blue foxglove, and pink wild roses unfolded to display a burst of color.

"It's beautiful," a voice spoke softly behind her.

Naomi started to her feet, the book tumbling to the ground.

She found herself facing the last person she would expect here in Wiltshire. "Lord Newlyn, why have you come?" Her heart was beating so loudly in her ears she was certain he could hear it.

He stepped up to her and took her hands. "To ask you to forgive a complete fool and to tell you I love you."

"What about Miss Ragsdale?"

He grinned, "She doesn't really like me or my plants, you know. Too much like her father, I believe."

Naomi frowned. "She told you that?"

"After Marion cast a truth spell on her."

Naomi's eyes widened and she shook her head. "But I swear I never told her—"

"I know. Audric gave it to her and made her promise never to do magic again."

"Audric." She said his name softly, then smiled. "One would never know, but he is quite the romantic. He knew I loved you even before I did."

"A dog, a romantic?" Doubt was etched on the gentleman's face.

"Actually, he's my cousin, under the spell of a powerful wizard." She watched the changing expression on Wyndom's face. Then the gentleman laughed.

"I hope that means he won't be living with us. It comes to me that he is rather too fond of my wine." He explained about the missing wine. As she laughed, he drew her to him and kissed her soundly. After several minutes, he drew back and asked, "But enough about him and magic. You haven't said. Will you marry me?"

For a moment, her doubts resurfaced. "I am a witch, and being your wife won't change that. Are you certain you fully understand? My parents' marriage proved to be an unhappy union because of my mother's magic. He never understood the nature of our power."

The baron placed his hands on either side of her face, tilting it upward. "Perhaps I am bewitched, and I should worry about your powers, but I cannot because I know that you are good and your magic will reflect that goodness. I love you and want you to be my wife."

A smile lit Naomi's face. "Oh, my wonderfully bewitched baron, I do love you, and I will marry you." With that she surrendered to the arms of the man she loved and who loved her, magic and all.

THE
BEWITCHMENT
OF LORD
DALFORD

Debbie Raleigh

Chapter One

The disaster was inevitable.

Lord Dalford had barely walked through the door of the drawing room when he managed to trip a passing servant, who promptly dropped an entire tray of champagne. In his haste to help the poor man back to his feet, Dalford reached down to offer his hand, only to knock into a small pier table and send the vase upon it crashing to the carpet.

Red-faced, Dalford stepped aside as a rush of servants dashed to clean up the mess. Predictably, he managed to step directly upon the toes of Mrs. Robinson, who promptly screeched in protest before slapping his cheek and hobbling toward her outraged husband.

Standing on the far side of the crowded room, Annie Winsome heaved a sigh.

She knew that there were a few things utterly inevitable in the world:

The sun would always rise in the morning.

It would always rain on the day of a picnic.

A carriage would always pass precisely when she was walking beside a puddle.

And at a large party, Lord Dalford would always manage to create an embarrassing scene.

She was never quite certain how her dear friend could possibly be so prone to catastrophe. He was, after all, an elegant, handsome nobleman with raven black hair, finely chiseled features, and the most astonishing blue eyes. He should have been the delight of every maiden in England.

But while he possessed the breeding, the position, and even the wealth to be the most eligible of gentlemen, his tendency to trip, stumble, or say precisely the wrong thing at the wrong time had made him rather a joke among the neighbors.

He was, indeed, cruelly referred to as "Lord Dolt-ford" by the other gentlemen, who took shameless delight in his clumsy habits.

Annie did her best to protect Dalford from the jests of others. Since he had purchased the estate next to her father's, she had treated him as an honored older brother. He was her confidant, her advisor, and her shoulder to cry upon. She would do whatever she could to ensure his comfort.

Unfortunately, he made it extremely difficult at times.

Swallowing yet another sigh, Annie moved forward, intending to join the embarrassed gentleman standing alone in the corner. She had taken only a few steps, however, when she was abruptly halted by a tall, overly handsome gentleman who deliberately blocked her path.

"Ah, Annie." Lord Stanwell offered a sardonic smile. "A lovely gathering."

"Thank you, my lord."

"A pity Doltford managed to create his usual elegant entrance. I cannot imagine what prompted you to issue him an invitation."

Annie instantly stiffened. She had never liked Stanwell, regardless of the fact that he was a favorite among most women in the neighborhood. To her mind, he was an arrogant braggart who took great delight in belittling others.

Just for a moment she considered how he would appear

with a large wart upon that aristocratic nose. Or perhaps a painful boil upon his . . .

Annie reluctantly thrust the temptation away.

Although a witch, she had made the difficult decision to live with her mortal father rather than with her mother, who had returned to the Witch's Conclave four years ago. Which meant that she was not allowed to use her powers or reveal her true nature to anyone.

It was not usually a difficult task. But at the moment she could not deny an overwhelming urge to teach the arrogant Stanwell a well-deserved lesson in humility.

Yes, definitely a boil, she thought grimly.

A big, raw, excruciating boil.

"Lord Dalford is always a welcome guest in my home, my lord."

The elegant, blond-haired gentleman cast a scathing gaze toward the distant corner. "I cannot imagine why. The man is a menace to society. Only last evening he managed to topple the poor vicar into a fountain and then proceeded to cause a scandal when he pointed out to Mrs. Monroe that her eye seemed to be twitching, when it was obvious she was shamelessly winking at Mr. Foster."

Annie determinedly hid her discomfort. She had already heard of poor Dalford's unfortunate incidents at the local assembly. And despite her best effort, she could not deny a tiny sense of relief she had not been present to witness the embarrassment.

And at the same moment, guilt at her relief.

A confusing combination of emotions that had been assaulting her all too frequently in connection to her dear friend.

"I would remind you that Lord Dalford is my friend," she said, perhaps more sharply than necessary.

Stanwell arched a golden brow. "A fact I find quite unfathomable. Tell me, Annie, what is it that attracts you to Dalford? Is it his ability to trip over his own feet? Or perhaps his manner of saying the most shockingly outrageous things?"

Annie regarded the handsome nobleman coldly. "I care

for Dalford because he is kind, thoughtful, and considerate of others' feelings. Quite unlike most gentlemen of my acquaintance."

The deliberate slight slid home and Stanwell's sensuous lips thinned with annoyance. "And of course the fact that he is considered one of the wealthiest gentlemen in England?" he sneered. "There is nothing like a fortune to make even a bumbling fool like Doltford appear attractive."

The gentleman had no notion of how close he came to being turned into a toadstool as Annie battled a flare of anger. "I would not care if he did not possess a farthing. As I said, Lord Dalford is all that a true gentleman should be. Unfortunately, his qualities are far too rare."

Stanwell offered a superior smile. "Brave words, my dear, but we shall see how you feel a few days from now."

Annie's eyes, which were a lovely shade of tender green with swirls of gold, narrowed in suspicion. "And what could you possibly mean by that?"

His smile was without humor. "You may not mind having Dalford cling to your skirts while in the depths of the country, but what will you do once you are in London for your Season? Do you not realize that you shall be the object of amusement for the entire *ton?* "

"You are being ridiculous," Annie retorted with a brave toss of her golden curls.

"You are incredibly naive, Annie," he mocked as he reached up to stroke her cheek. "Members of Society are always seeking some means to relieve their boredom. They will take great delight in shaming Dalford and any poor fool who is willing to stand at his side."

Despite her best intentions, Annie felt a chill race down her spine.

She had been anticipating her first London Season for years, perhaps for as long as she could remember. The mere thought of the lavish parties, the numerous sights of town, and the thrill of flirting with endless handsome gentlemen was enough to make her shiver with excitement. Now that she was only hours away from climbing into the carriage and being taken by her Aunt Doreen to town, she found herself rather uneasy.

She loved Dalford.

He was sweet and kind and utterly wonderful.

But not even she could deny that he was destined to create chaos in London. For goodness sakes, he could not even walk into the room without managing to trip a servant, knock over a table, and send Mrs. Robinson shrieking in pain.

And as Stanwell had so succinctly pointed out, even when he was not tripping or trodding upon others' toes, he always managed to say something outrageous.

Nor could she entirely dismiss the knowledge that she would be bearing at least a portion of his embarrassment.

What if she were excluded from the *ton's* invitations? Or made the object of jest?

Angry with herself for her renegade thoughts and the smooth, poison-tongued gentleman who was regarding her with a superior expression, Annie gave a loud sniff.

"I would think Society would have better things to gossip about than a mere debutante," she retorted.

"Ah, but gossip is the primary entertainment for most," he retorted. "And nothing is destined to titillate the jaded aristocrats more than a fumbling nitwit attempting to pass himself as a sophisticated gentleman. Can you just imagine the faces of the old tabbies when he drenches them in lemonade, or the enjoyment in the gentlemen's clubs when he utters some absurd comment?"

Annie sucked in a sharp breath.

She would not think of such things.

It only made her feel worse.

"You must excuse me, my lord," she said stiffly. "I would like to speak with Lord Dalford."

His lips twisted. "By all means. Perhaps you can convince him to remain in Kent rather than following you to London. I shudder to think of the spectacle you will present if he does make an appearance in town."

Sweeping past the arrogant nobleman, Annie headed directly toward the distant corner. *Blast and double blast,* she inwardly cursed.

She did not want to think of Dalford in London, not when it was inevitable that he would be the source of cruel amusement and treated with scorn. Perhaps even shunned.

It was utterly unfair.

Dalford was worth a dozen so-called dandies. A hundred.

Hoping that her unworthy thoughts could not be detected upon her countenance, Annie at last threaded her way through the vast crowd to stand before her friend.

As always, Lord Dalford was attired in a black coat that was rather too small and distinctly frayed about the edges. At least he had remembered to put on a fresh cravat, she thought with fond exasperation, and he had even styled his glossy raven curls to lie against his lean countenance.

A countenance that still bore the angry red mark of Mrs. Robinson's slap.

"Oh, Dalford," she said with a sympathetic smile. "Your poor cheek. Does it hurt very much?"

"My cheek? Oh." Shuffling his feet, Dalford gave an awkward shrug. "No, no. A trifling matter."

"Really, that Mrs. Robinson is the worse sort of harridan," she retorted with a flare of fury at the woman still moaning over her injured foot. "How dare she create such a fuss over a simple accident?"

He smiled with a rueful humor. "Well, I daresay that she feared her poor toes had been broken. Rather unfortunate, since I managed to pour a glass of champagne upon her gown only last week."

"Well, I wish you would spill a glass upon her tonight." Annie gave a dismissive sniff. "Why that woman continues to purchase that singularly ugly shade of puce is beyond all imagining."

"I suppose not all women can possess your own lovely sense of style."

Annie's eyes widened at the unexpected words.

"Why, Dalford, was that a compliment?"

"Oh, no . . . I mean . . . just a statement of fact," he hurriedly corrected, a blush staining his face.

She laughed at his hint of confusion, giving a shake of her head. "Still, the woman had no right to strike you."

He gave a faint grimace. "I fear that I have made a mull of your party."

"Nonsense. Mrs. Robinson was bound to have some complaint of the party," she said with a shrug. "After our last soiree, she assured everyone that the food was stale, the champagne was watered, and my gown fit for only a harlot."

The odd glint that flashed through his eyes might have been easily missed if she had not been staring directly into them.

"Did she?"

For a crazed, ridiculous moment she wondered if perhaps Dalford had deliberately punished Mrs. Robinson for her hateful comments. Then, just as swiftly, she was shaking her head. Dalford was barely aware of what was occurring beneath his own nose. He would never notice the woman's disparaging remarks about Annie's gown.

"So you see, you have done me a favor for giving her something to complain of beyond my dismal refreshments and shocking gown."

He smiled wryly. "You are far more forgiving than most maidens would be. This is, after all, your farewell party."

"Pooh." Annie gave a sudden smile. "You are my friend, Dalford. I could never be cross with you."

"Friend." His smile twisted in an odd fashion. "Yes, of course."

Wondering if he was more upset by the incident than he was allowing her to suspect, she frowned in confusion.

"Did I say something wrong?"

"Of course not." He gave a shrug. "If you will recall, saying something wrong is my sole province, my dear."

Her frown remained intact. "I wish you would not say such things."

"But why? We both know that I am always destined to say precisely the wrong thing or to tumble over my own feet. 'Poor Lord Dolt-ford' is a cry heard far too often to ignore."

"Only when you are in the company of others," she insisted sternly. "When it is just the two of us, you have no trouble whatsoever."

He regarded her a long moment before giving a vague shrug. "As you said, you are my friend."

She regarded the handsome features and blue eyes that always held a hint of tenderness. "Oh, Dalford, what am I to do with you?"

The raven brows arched at her sudden words. "What do you desire to do with me?"

"I . . ." She hesitated to put her rather unwelcome thoughts into words.

With a careful movement, he set aside his now empty glass and regarded her with a steady gaze. "Annie, what is it?"

"I wish to keep you here with those who know and love you," she explained cautiously.

"But I am here."

She hesitated again. Tomorrow she would leave for her first Season in London. A fortnight later Dalford intended to make his own way to town. It would be his first visit to London, and she very much feared that it would prove to be a painful experience.

How could it not be when he would soon be the source of amusement throughout every household in town?

"I mean, when I go to London," she said gently.

He stilled at her words, the blue eyes slowly narrowing. "You do not wish me to go to London?"

"Of course I wish you to go," she hurriedly corrected his low words. "I simply worry that you will be made to feel uncomfortable there."

The gaze never wavered. "Or perhaps you fear I shall make you uncomfortable there?"

"Do not be absurd," Annie retorted sharply, all too aware of her traitorous imaginings.

"Well, I suppose I cannot blame you," he said, something that might have been disappointment twisting his lips. "I do manage to appear rather the buffoon, not to mention being a constant hazard to those about me."

Realizing that she had hurt his feelings, Annie shifted her hand to grasp his fingers.

"Dalford, you could never make me uncomfortable," she insisted, with perhaps more emphasis than necessary. "But those among Society can be utterly cruel when they choose. I do not want you hurt."

He shrugged, his expression oddly unreadable. "I will survive. Besides, I cannot allow you to go off to London without offering my protection. The town is filled with charming rascals who would willingly turn a female's head."

Although not fully convinced he had believed her assurance that she was only thinking of him, Annie was eager to lighten the mood. Summoning a smile, she tilted her head to one side and flashed him a teasing glance. "I certainly hope so. It would be very dull without a few charming rascals."

"Well, they had better watch their step when I am about, or I shall soon have them set to rights," he warned in a mockingly gruff tone.

She gave his fingers a sharp squeeze. "Now see here, Dalford, I have told you I am going to London to thoroughly enjoy myself. I will not have you fussing over me like my father does."

"Someone had best keep you out of the bumble broth."

"Fah." She gave a laugh. "If I wished to be dull and stuffy, I would remain here in the country. This is my opportunity to spread my wings."

He gave a dramatic shudder at her light words. "That settles it. You are definitely not going to London with only an elderly aunt to chaperon you."

"You are being absurd, Dalford."

"I am being sensible. It is my duty to protect you."

The thought of this sweet, bumbling man actually protecting her nearly made her chuckle. Even if she were not a witch with enough powers to protect herself from any mortal dangers, she would not depend upon Dalford as her guardian. He would no doubt trip over his own feet and kill them both.

That thought reminded her once again of the danger awaiting him in London, and her smile dimmed. She could not bear to see him hurt.

"I still wish you would reconsider. It is bound to be . . . awkward for you to be surrounded by strangers."

He shrugged. "It does not trouble me."

"But . . ." She bit back her words, knowing that rather stubborn set to his jaw all too well. For such a kind, mild-mannered gentleman, he could be astonishingly determined when he set his mind to it.

He was going to London, and there was nothing she could do to stop him.

Even if it meant enduring one humiliation after another. Unless . . .

Annie was suddenly struck by a wicked, utterly tempting notion.

When she had decided to remain with her father, she had promised herself never to cast a spell on a mortal. It was considered extremely rude by other witches, not to mention it could bring unforeseen difficulties to her charade.

But she had never specifically made a vow not to use a potion, had she?

Specifically a potion that would merely assist Dalford in becoming a tad less prone to accidents.

After all, it would not alter him in any true manner, or induce him to act against his will. And it would last no more than a few months at most.

What could possibly be the harm?

"Annie, is something troubling you?" Dalford demanded as she regarded him with a narrowed gaze.

She unconsciously licked her dry lips, telling herself she was being ridiculous. Dalford was her dearest friend. She loved him as if he were her own brother. Could she truly contemplate deceiving him in such a fashion? Even if it was for his own good?

It was a moral dilemma that would need careful consideration, she told herself. And yet at the same moment she found herself conjuring a strained smile. "I should be getting back to the other guests, but . . ."

"Yes?"

"Will you come and see me tomorrow morning before I leave?"

He lifted his brows, almost as if he sensed that there was more to her invitation than she wished to reveal. "If you wish."

"I very much wish it."

With a last squeeze of his hand, Annie turned to make her way back through the crowd. She knew that she could not remain. Dalford knew her too well not to suspect that she had something upon her mind.

Besides which, she had never deliberately lied to him before, and the thought that she was even contemplating such a thing made her stomach clench in a disturbing manner.

Chapter Two

Lord Dalford was decidedly curious.

He knew full well that his future wife was up to something.

Something devious.

Not only had Annie refused to meet his gaze when she invited him to join her this morning, a sure sign she was not being entirely truthful, but there had been a hint of guilt in those beautiful green eyes that made him decidedly wary.

So the question was, had she decided to at last use the powers she had denied herself to force him to remain in Kent? Or did she have some other plot in mind?

A faint smile touched his lips as he left his horse in the care of the waiting groom.

After living for years in seclusion, Dalford had at last returned to the world of mortals with the intention of finding a wife. As a powerful warlock, he had naturally thought to find his mate among the witches, who had welcomed him with gratifying enthusiasm. But he had discovered himself remarkably indifferent to the various young maidens who had been paraded for his inspection. He desired a woman who possessed a heart that was true. One who would love him for himself, not his power as a warlock or the various material possessions he had accumulated over the centuries.

Then he had learned of Annie Winsome, the daughter of a renegade witch who had dared to wed a mortal and create a child.

It was said that Annie was different.

She did not use her gifts to enhance her own life or bend others to her will.

Instead, she had turned her back on her birthright and lived as a mere mortal with her father.

Intrigued, he had deliberately ensured that he was in a position to make the young woman's acquaintance. And just to be sure that she was all that was claimed, he had deliberately hidden his identity. She would not have her head turned by his powers as a warlock, or even by his wealth and position in the mortal world. If she were to come to care for him, it would be utterly for himself.

It had taken less than a few days to realize she was indeed the one.

She was just as lovely within as she was upon the surface, with an enticing spirit and lust for life that filled his heart with joy. Her kindness and staunch support of the bumbling "Dolt-ford" had proved she would make a wife he would want for all eternity.

Unfortunately, while he had decided that she was to be his wife, she had yet to realize that she loved him.

Oh, certainly she cared for him in a sisterly fashion, and she had showed time and time again she was his staunchest supporter, he acknowledged impatiently.

But she had yet to accept that they were destined to be together.

And now with her long anticipated London Season rapidly approaching, he was beginning to suspect she was not utterly enchanted with the notion of having him at her side and making her an object of amusement.

Well, she was not about to trap him in Kent while she went about flirting with every rake and rogue in London, he acknowledged grimly. Whether she knew it or not, she belonged to him. And until she accepted the truth in her heart, he was staying close to her side.

Climbing the steps to the small but graceful manor house, Dalford watched as the door was swept open to reveal the ancient butler. Everett was as much a part of the house as the seventeenth century stonework, and nearly as old.

"Good morning, my lord," the servant murmured with a bow.

"Everett." Handing over his hat and gloves, Dalford offered a small smile. "I believe I am expected."

"Yes, my lord, if you will follow me." At a stately pace, the butler led Dalford up the stairs into a lovely drawing room decorated with crimson wall coverings and elegant satinwood furnishings. "I shall inform Miss Winsome that you have arrived."

Strolling toward the lovely pieces of Wedgwood proudly displayed upon an oval table, Dalford glanced over his shoulder to realize that Everett was still in the doorway regarding him with a faint frown. "Is there anything the matter, Everett?"

"I . . . perhaps you would care to have a seat?"

Realizing that the elderly butler feared for the safety of the china, Dalford hid a smile. "Thank you, I am quite comfortable."

Heaving a resigned sigh, the servant gave a nod of his head. "Very good, sir."

Dalford allowed himself a chuckle as the butler disappeared. He had managed to destroy a goodly number of vases as well as a few chairs over the past three years. He had always been careful, however, to ensure none of them held any true sentimental value. He had, in fact, done Annie a favor by ridding her home of the singularly ugly pottery her father was prone to buy whenever he visited the village.

Still standing beside the table, Dalford felt that peculiar tingle that raced over his skin whenever Annie was near. With a slow movement, he turned to regard the woman he had chosen to be his wife.

In the early morning sunlight, she appeared as fresh as spring. The vision was only enhanced by the buttercup muslin gown and tumble of golden curls held back by a simple ribbon.

Dalford's heart missed a beat as he met her golden-green eyes. He had waited centuries for this woman.

"Good morning, Annie," he said in low tones.

"Dalford, how good of you to come," she said with a smile that did not quite reach her eyes.

Dalford once again experienced that rush of unease. "You did not believe that I would allow you to leave without a proper good-bye?"

She hesitantly moved forward, her usually buoyant spirit subdued. "No, of course not."

Dalford tilted his head to one side as he regarded her with a narrowed gaze.

"You appear rather ill at ease, my dear. Is anything the matter?"

"No, nothing," she assured him even as a faint blush rose to her cheeks.

"You are certain?"

She shrugged, no doubt realizing she could not entirely hide her unusual tension. "I suppose that I am a bit nervous at the thought of traveling such a great distance."

"You, nervous?" he demanded in disbelief. He did not doubt Annie would face the dragons of old without a blink of alarm. "That is most unlike my daring, incurably optimistic friend. You have been anxious to enjoy your first Season for a goodly time."

"Yes, but now that it is here I discover the thought of being so far from home and Papa rather disheartening."

He smiled at her absurd words. "Do not fear. Once you are gadding about London, you will soon discover your spirits reviving."

"No doubt." There was an oddly awkward silence. Then the round form of the cook entered the room carrying a large tea tray. "Oh, Mrs. Brown, thank you."

Setting the tray upon a low table, Mrs. Brown straightened and placed her hands on her hips.

"I put them cakes upon the tray just as you asked, although why a proper scone would not do is beyond me."

Annie's blush deepened at the chiding words, making Dalford more curious than ever.

"That will be all, Mrs. Brown," she managed to mutter in low tones.

With a decided sniff, the servant turned to leave the room and, strolling forward, Dalford regarded the flustered maiden with a searching gaze. "Mrs. Brown appears to have her nose rather out of joint."

Annie gave a vague wave of her hands. "I decided to make you my special plum cakes, and Mrs. Brown unfortunately regarded my presence in her kitchen as a direct insult to her skills."

Dalford lifted his brows in surprise. "You baked me cakes?"

"Yes." Annie's gaze shifted away from his own, assuring him that she had something to hide. "I thought you might wish to try an old family recipe."

An old family recipe?

Dalford was beginning to comprehend precisely why Annie had demanded that he visit this morning. "Just for the matter of record, was this recipe handed down from your mother's branch of the family?" he demanded smoothly.

She gave a startled flinch as her gaze snapped back to his carefully bland countenance. "Yes, why do you ask?"

He shrugged. He did not doubt that any recipe handed down from Annie's mother contained a specific potion, one he suspected was to give him a sudden ability to move without tripping over his own feet. He could not deny a faint pang of disappointment. "Mere curiosity."

Swallowing heavily, Annie moved to collect the small plate of plum cakes. With a jerky motion, she held it toward him. "Will you not try one?"

Dalford eyed them with open suspicion. "I am uncertain."

She blinked in surprise. "What?"

"I have never tasted your cooking before. Indeed, I did not realize you had ever before entered the kitchen. How can I be certain I shall not be made ill?"

"Dalford," she exclaimed in shock.

"Well, it is a possibility."

"It most certainly is not," she retorted with a hint of temper. "Really, I would think that you would be more appreciative of my efforts."

"Oh, I am quite appreciative," he drawled. "But perhaps I shall wait until after you have tasted one first."

Annie barely resisted the urge to stomp her foot at his unusual perversity. "You are being quite provoking, Dalford."

Dalford allowed a wry smile to touch his lips. He supposed that he should be a bit more forgiving of Annie's youth. Even in mortal years, she was quite young. It was perhaps understandable that she would be less than enthusiastic to face the scorn and embarrassment of the *ton*, even in defense of a friend.

But a part of him could not resist the notion of revealing just how shallow such concerns were.

No matter how young, Annie must discover that she could not go about altering others to suit her own needs.

It was not only poor etiquette for a witch, but it could also be dangerous.

Appearing the picture of innocence, he sent Annie a puzzled frown. "Are you angry, my dear?"

Her lashes fluttered downward, no doubt to disguise the guilt in her eyes. "No, I merely wish you to enjoy the treat I have prepared for you."

"Is it that important to you?" he demanded in somber tones.

There was a long, breathless pause before she gave a reluctant nod of her head.

"Yes."

He heaved a resigned sigh. "I see."

She held the plate toward him. "Will you?"

"To please you, Annie, I will do whatever is necessary,"

he assured her softly, reaching for one of the cakes and taking a large bite.

Covertly watching him from beneath her lashes, Annie waited until he had polished off the small cake and wiped his fingers upon the napkin she had handed to him.

"Well?" she demanded.

He lifted his brows. "What?"

With obvious impatience she set aside the plate. "Is it any good?"

"Oh yes, it is quite delicious."

She licked her lips in a nervous manner. "And I wager you do not feel ill?"

Realizing that had he been mortal he most certainly would have felt some reaction to the powerful potion, Dalford forced himself to give a small frown. "Not precisely."

She instinctively moved forward, her expression concerned. "What is it?"

"Nothing. I am fine."

"Are you certain?"

He lifted a hand to press it to his temple. "Just a moment of dizziness."

With swift motions, she was pouring a cup of the hot tea and pressing it into his hands. "Here, perhaps some strong tea will help it pass."

He eyed the steaming liquid with a wary gaze. "You did not brew this yourself, did you?"

She gave a reluctant chuckle at his teasing. "No, I assure you I would not dare to tamper with Mrs. Brown's tea."

He took a tentative sip. "Ah, delicious."

Clearly torn between delight at having achieved her goal and a certain amount of remorse for having deceived him, Annie regarded him with a searching gaze. "Are you feeling better?"

"Yes, quite." Setting aside the cup, Dalford decided that he needed time to consider what was to be done next. Certainly he would plan his arrival in London with great care. "Still, perhaps it is best if I return home."

"You will be in London within the fortnight?" she demanded anxiously.

"Do not fear, I shall not abandon you to the cruelty of London Society," he assured her in wry tones.

She bit her bottom lip, as if already regretting her impulsive potion. "I daresay we shall have great fun."

A decided twinkle entered his blue eyes. "Oh yes, I intend the Season to be most enjoyable."

Unaware of his inner amusement, she offered him a small smile. "Good." Without warning, she stepped forward to place a light kiss upon his cheek. A bolt of sizzling pleasure shot through his body, making him long to wrap her in his arms and put an end to their games. All he desired was to make this woman his wife and have her at his side for all eternity. Unfortunately, she was already pulling away before he could move. "Take care until I see you again."

"And you, Annie." He reached out to softly stroke her cheek. The time had not yet arrived. But soon, he assured the painful longing in his heart. Very soon. "I shall see you in London."

Chapter Three

"Oh, he is glancing in our direction," Elizabeth Ward whispered, her fan fluttering so fast that the dark curls that framed her heart-shaped countenance danced in the candlelight. "No, Annie, do not look."

Ignoring her friend's appalled plea, Annie turned to openly regard the handsome dandy who was the current darling of Society.

"Why ever not?" she demanded as she flashed the golden-haired Adonis a flirtatious smile. "He is looking."

Far more prone to accept the unwavering stricture that a maiden must appear modestly shy at all times, Elizabeth gave a sharp tug upon the sleeve of Annie's pale green gown.

"He will believe you to be fast."

"Pooh." Not nearly so concerned with the dragons who hovered in the distant corner prepared to shred the reputation of any young woman who dared to oppose their rigid strictures, Annie gave a shrug. "I must look somewhere, and since the room is crowded to the rafters, it is inevitable that I be looking at someone. Far better it be a handsome young gentleman than a sour old tartar."

"Oh, Annie, you are incorrigible." Elizabeth gave a nervous chuckle. Of the same age and both enjoying their first Season, it was rather inevitable that the two maidens would have been drawn to each other, although Annie often felt years older than the more timid Elizabeth. "But do not allow your aunt to discover you making eyes at a mere baron. She is quite determined that you will capture no less than an earl."

Annie grimaced at the mention of her Aunt Doreen. Since their arrival in London two weeks ago, the older woman had done everything short of kidnapping an eligible gentleman to see her engaged. Gads, she had half expected to awake one morning to discover a poor victim tied to her bed. It had become something of an embarrassment to realize that the entire *ton* believed her to be desperate for husband, especially when nothing could be further from the truth. "She can plot all she desires. I have no intention of wedding an earl or any other gentleman."

Elizabeth looked momentarily dumbfounded. Then she gave an uncertain laugh. Clearly it was unthinkable to the young maiden that any woman would not desire to be wed as swiftly as possible. "Oh, you are merely teasing me."

"Not at all."

The dark eyes framed by thick lashes widened in confusion. "You cannot mean to say you will never wed?"

Annie gave an indifferent shrug. "It is highly doubtful."

"But . . . why?"

Annie's lips twisted with rueful humor. She could hardly confess that she was a witch and that the handful of warlocks she had encountered had been so filled with arrogance and pompous conceit that she would rather live alone than be tied to them the rest of her very long life.

"I suppose I am far too particular in my taste," she forced herself to say in light tones, unfolding her own fan to combat the thickening heat that filled the room. The one thing she had discovered since arriving in London was that each social occasion was more crowded than the last. "I do not believe I could ever discover a gentleman who truly could bring me complete happiness."

"Not even the delicious baron?" Elizabeth demanded coyly.

Annie gave a shake of her head as she turned her gaze from the preening gentleman.

"Especially the delicious baron. He might be all that is handsome, but I would wager my last grout that he would devote more attention to the cut of his coat than to his wife."

"No doubt," Elizabeth agreed with a tinkling laugh, her own gaze moving over the baron before abruptly narrowing. "Oh, my."

"What is it?"

"He is here," Elizabeth breathed in soft tones.

Puzzled, Annie followed her gaze, unable to see over the pressing crowd. "Who? Who is here?"

"The gentleman I told you was riding in the park yesterday."

Annie felt a stab of disappointment. She had harbored hopes of at last encountering the prince, or at the very least Brummel. Instead it was no more than another puffed-up popinjay who seemed to capture the interest of fickle Society with tedious regularity.

"Ah, the raven-haired demon that you claimed was stealing hearts faster than Byron," she said dryly.

Clearly in raptures over the dandy, Elizabeth breathed a deep sigh. "Yes, he is . . . magnificent."

Craning her neck, Annie attempted to peer over the heads of the milling guests.

"Blast, I wish I were not so short," she complained. "I can see nothing."

Elizabeth abruptly grasped her arm in a fierce grip. "He is walking this way," she hissed, only to give a sudden grunt of disapproval. "Oh."

Not for the first time cursing her diminutive stature,

Annie could only depend upon her friend for the progress of the mysterious stranger. "What is it?"

"Mrs. Wilkins has accosted him with that horrid daughter of hers. You should see the shameless way that hussy is attempting to flirt with him."

Annie gave a startled blink. "You must be jesting."

"Not at all. Miss Wilkins is all but tossing herself at his feet."

Annie was impressed in spite of herself. "He must be magnificent indeed to have stirred Julia to put herself forward. She far prefers to force her devoted admirers to scrape and plead for her attention."

Elizabeth gave a snort of disapproval, her usually sweet expression hardened with jealousy. "I assure you that she is being quite shameless. Why, she even has laid her hand upon his arm. And now Mrs. Smith has joined him. I swear, one deep breath and the widow will burst out of that indecent bodice."

"Good heavens, this gentleman must be a wonder," Annie retorted, becoming increasingly intrigued. It was said that the lovely Mrs. Smith shared her favors with only the most exclusive gentlemen among the *ton*. "Let us see if we can get a better view."

"No, no." Elizabeth kept her death grip upon Annie's arm, preventing her from so much as taking a step. "He is once again moving this way." The young maiden abruptly turned to stab Annie with an apprehensive gaze. "Do I appear flushed? Is my hair still tidy? Perhaps I should . . ."

"You look as beautiful as always, Elizabeth." Annie broke into the breathless chatter with a wry smile. Really, her friend was not usually so prone to act like a perfect simpleton over a mere man. "Although you are in a definite twitter."

Elizabeth pressed a dramatic hand to her heart. "I have never before encountered a gentleman who could make me tingle all over."

Annie experienced a startling flare of envy. Of all the numerous gentlemen she had managed to meet in London, not one of them had managed to so much as make her heart miss a beat. "Is he as handsome as the baron?" she inquired with a faint frown.

"Yes, but it is not that." The maiden gave an impatient shrug. "It is simply something about him . . . dear heavens, he is almost here."

Anxious to catch a glimpse of her friend's dashing rogue, Annie cast etiquette aside and childishly went up on the tips of her toes. "Where?"

"There. Beside Lord Lundfield."

At first Annie could see nothing beyond the high turban of a passing matron. Then, spotting the elderly Lord Lundfield, she eagerly scanned for sight of the masculine paragon.

It took a long moment to at last spot the dark-haired gentleman, who was attired in a black coat fitted to near indecent perfection and knee breeches that revealed very fine legs. For long moments, she simply allowed herself to appreciate the hard, lean lines of pure muscles. Far too many gentleman of the *ton* were forced to pad their coats or squeeze their waists to achieve even a poor imitation of a decent silhouette. This gentleman, however, was . . . perfect. A delicious, rather wicked warmth spread through her body as her gaze paused upon the wide chest. What would it feel like to be held against such a masculine frame?

With embarrassing reluctance, her gaze slowly lifted to the finely chiseled profile—a profile that was oddly familiar.

Familiar?

Suddenly, abruptly, shockingly her heart lurched to a full halt.

No.

It wasn't possible.

This elegant, captivating gentleman could not be shy, awkward Dalford.

"Good heavens," she breathed in disbelief.

"Is he not utterly delightful?" her friend retorted, her eyes glowing with a disturbing warmth.

"But . . . that is Dalford," Annie said in blank shock.

Elizabeth widened her gaze in amazement. "You know him?"

Turning back to where Dalford was easily chatting with the nobleman, Annie suddenly wondered if she did know him.

She hadn't heard the crash of furniture or the cry of an injured maiden. There had not even been the usual rush of servants who were sent to clean up whatever catastrophe had occurred when Dalford entered the room.

Even in appearance he was different.

Gone was the bashful gentleman who hid in the nearest corner and who rarely recalled to have his cravat starched, let alone tied in an intricate knot. In his place appeared to be a confident, decidedly sophisticated gentleman with an innate air of elegance who was attracting more than a little attention from the numerous women about the room.

Gads. She had hoped that her potion would help prevent Dalford from making a total fool of himself, perhaps even give him a bit of self-assurance that he had never before possessed.

She had never dreamed he would suddenly appear in Town and create such a flutter.

And in truth, she was not at all certain she liked this unexpected turn of events.

"Annie."

With great reluctance Annie turned her gaze from the handsome gentleman to meet her friend's impatient frown. "What?"

"I asked if you knew him."

"Of course I do," she retorted with a frown of her own. "He is my neighbor, as well as a dear friend."

"But how wonderful," Elizabeth breathed in awe. "You can introduce me."

Not at all enamored of the notion of introducing the lovely, clearly infatuated maiden to Dalford, Annie shook off her friend's clinging fingers.

"Perhaps. Now you must excuse me," she muttered, firmly beginning the task of pressing her way through the large crowd.

"Oh no, I am not leaving your side until I have an opportunity to meet this Mr. Dalford," Elizabeth retorted with uncharacteristic determination, following closely on Annie's heels.

"Lord Dalford," Annie corrected, wishing her friend would simply disappear. She needed to speak with Dalford in private.

"He is titled?" Elizabeth heaved a charmed sigh. "Oh, it is too good to be true."

"It most certainly is," Annie agreed in dark tones, at last pushing her way past the circle of admirers that had surrounded Dalford to stand at his side. "Good evening, my lord."

Half expecting Dalford to drop his glass of champagne or stumble over his feet in shock at her sudden appearance, Annie was amazed when he smoothly turned and offered her an elegant bow.

"Annie," he murmured, his dark blue eyes shimmering with an odd glow as he allowed his gaze to skim over her elegant gown and her artfully arranged curls. "May I tell you that London agrees with you? You appear even more lovely than I thought possible."

"Thank you." An unwitting frown tugged at her brows as she regarded the worldly gentleman who abruptly seemed more a stranger than dear friend. "Why did you not let me know that you had arrived in Town?"

He gave a lift of his shoulder, the gesture abruptly making her aware of the ripple of lean muscles beneath the fitted coat. Muscles that she had been undeniably ogling only moments before.

Indeed, she seemed aware of many things she had never noted before. The rich gloss of his raven hair, the hint of power that was etched onto the striking features, and the rather disturbing scent of clean male skin that suddenly filled her senses.

"After hearing you had taken Town by storm I did not know if you would wish to be burdened with such a dull old friend."

"That is absurd," she said sharply, realizing that she was more than a little hurt that he had deliberately been avoiding her.

His brows lifted at her obvious annoyance. "You did say you wished to spread your wings, Annie."

"Yes, but . . ." Her words came to an abrupt halt as Elizabeth's insistent tugs upon her gown threatened to rip the expensive silk. With a rising annoyance, she turned to glare at her friend. "Elizabeth, you need not pull my gown off," she muttered, reluctantly giving in to the inevitable. "Dalford, may I introduce my new friend, Miss Ward? Elizabeth, this is Lord Dalford, a neighbor to my father."

Simpering like a schoolgirl, Elizabeth swept a deep curtsy, coyly glancing beneath her lashes as Dalford offered a bow.

"My lord."

"Miss Ward." Dalford smiled with a lethal charm that made Annie blink in shock. "Had I realized that Annie had befriended the most beautiful maiden in London, I should have rushed to town much sooner."

"Oh," Elizabeth breathed, her eyes wide with dazzled pleasure.

Annie gave a loud snort.

Really, her friend was behaving like a twit.

And Dalford . . .

Well, she was not at all certain she had done him any favor, she decided with a sour feeling in the pit of her stomach.

Oh, certainly he was more sophisticated and there was an air of confidence that seemed to attract the attention of the entire room. But the sweet tenderness that she had always admired within him appeared to be buried beneath the artificial gloss.

Suddenly he was no longer her Dalford but a handsome, utterly eligible gentleman who would be the target of every maiden, lustful widow, and courtesan in England.

The sourness turned to an odd pain that might very well have been jealousy if it had not been so ludicrous.

"Now that you are here, Dalford, I trust that you will call upon me?" Annie interrupted the light flirtation with sharp tones.

Dalford returned his attention to her with a hint of surprise. "Certainly, although I have a rather busy schedule over the next week."

Her lips thinned with annoyance. "Too busy for an old friend?"

"Never." His head tilted to one side. "But you did request that I not interfere."

Annie felt a pang of guilt. Had she unintentionally hurt his feelings by her insistence that she be allowed to enjoy her Season without being overly sheltered?

Ignoring the avid interest of the crowd, Annie reached out to lightly touch his arm. "I have missed your company, Dalford."

His expression softened as he gazed into her concerned eyes. "And I yours, Annie."

"So you will come?" she demanded.

He smiled wryly. "Of course."

Just for a moment Annie found it impossible to glance away from his blue eyes. The party and guests seemed to fade into the distant background as she unconsciously moved closer to the gentleman she had missed more than she had ever realized. She wished they were alone so that they could share the teasing banter that always lifted her spirits. Or perhaps walking through the woods so that they could simply enjoy one another without fear of interruption.

But with a tenacious boldness, a lovely matron with dark curls and sultry beauty abruptly shoved herself between

Annie and Dalford, grasping his arm with a possessiveness that set Annie's teeth on edge.

"My lord, how lovely of you to grace my little ball," the woman purred as she pressed herself indecently close to the smiling gentleman. "I will even forgive you for being so unconscionably late. Now there are dozens of eager maidens just dying to meet you."

Annoyingly Dalford did not seem at all put out by the woman's brassy manner. Indeed, he smiled in a manner that seemed to invite all sorts of intimate liberties. "Of course." Turning to the fuming Annie, Dalford offered a half bow. "If you will excuse me, ladies?"

Not giving Annie an opportunity to protest, Dalford was being ruthlessly pulled away.

Not that he seemed unwilling, Annie thought with a jaundiced frown. He was clearly enjoying his newfound popularity among the ladies of Society, a realization that did not make her nearly as delighted as it should have.

"Oh, I think that I have just met the gentleman of my dreams," Elizabeth breathed, clearly unaware of Annie's suddenly dark mood.

Watching the cluster of maidens that surrounded the gentleman she had perhaps unwittingly considered as her own, Annie gave a low growl. "And I think I have just created a monster."

Chapter Four

There were less than a handful of people strolling through the British Museum located on Great Russell Street.

Standing in the shadows, Dalford patiently awaited the arrival of Annie.

A hint of amusement touched his lips.

There could be no doubt that she had been startled by his sudden arrival in town. And perhaps a bit put out by his obvious success, especially among the fairer sex.

She clearly had not considered the consequence of her potent potion, beyond, of course, the hope that he would not prove to be an embarrassment.

Perhaps rather spitefully, he was taking full delight in her reluctant jealousy.

After waiting nearly three years for her to accept that she loved him as more than a friend, he surely deserved a bit of retribution.

Running a hand over the mulberry coat that had been expertly tailored to mold to his lean muscles, Dalford waited patiently for his reluctant bride to arrive.

He had received a note before breakfast had even been

served demanding he meet Annie at the museum—a note that held more than a hint of pique at his determined refusal to call upon her.

She would not be late.

In fact, she was ten minutes early.

Entering the museum with a harried maid in her wake, Annie glanced anxiously about the large room. She appeared beautiful, as always, attired in a rose muslin gown with a pretty bonnet upon her golden curls.

Dalford felt a familiar tingle of pleasure as she noticed his large frame beside a marble statue and hurried forward, waving her persistent maid aside before she reached his side in a flurry of muslin and sweet violet perfume. "Dalford."

He performed an elegant bow, careful to keep his gaze from hungrily devouring her delicate features. "Good day, Annie."

"Thank you for agreeing to meet me."

His lifted his dark brow at her hesitant tone. "It is always my pleasure, although I must say I was surprised to receive your note to meet you here rather than at your aunt's home. Does she refuse to allow you to indulge your love for art and history for fear you might appear a bluestocking?"

"Oh no. Aunt Doreen has been very indulgent. Indeed, she has allowed me several afternoons to view the sights of town and even to purchase a number of books for Father's library."

Dalford could not deny a flare of surprise. Mrs. Doreen Levet was very much a lady of Society, who believed a maiden's only accomplishment should be landing a husband of suitable birth and rank. Certainly she had never approved of Annie's insatiable desire to learn. "Indulgent, indeed."

Annie abruptly wrinkled her nose with rueful humor. "Well, I am under strict instruction that I am not allowed to discuss such tedious subjects with others."

"Ah." He paused for a moment, carefully observing how

she toyed with the ribbons holding her reticule. Most unlike his bold, carefree Annie. "I still do not know why I was requested to meet you here."

She glanced over her shoulder—to where her maid eyed them with obvious disapproval—before turning about to meet his questioning gaze squarely. "Because I wished to speak with you in private."

"Of course. Aunt Doreen would no doubt be hovering near whenever a gentleman comes to call." His lips twisted. "Even an old, dull friend like myself."

Surprisingly, her features hardened at his teasing words. "Actually I was thinking more of the hordes of acquaintances that have suddenly begun to fill our drawing room upon a regular basis."

Dalford squashed his very mortal flare of jealousy. He did not wish to think of the handsome, charming gentlemen filling her drawing room.

"I had heard you were quite popular." He forced a smile. "My congratulations."

"They are not there to visit me," she retorted tartly.

"No?"

"No. Once it was discovered that I was the neighbor of the Dashing Dalford, every maiden in town has been making calls in the hope you might make an appearance."

The tartness of her tone swiftly returned his good humor. She was the one who was jealous.

Now, this was much more to his liking.

"Dashing Dalford?" he retorted mildly. "Surely you jest."

"Not at all." Her lips thinned. "You have created quite a stir since your arrival in town."

He grimaced. "I always create a stir. Unfortunately, as a rule, my presence makes maidens flee in terror."

She allowed her gaze to openly move over his large form, now elegantly attired in the latest fashion.

"Not any longer. They have badgered me for an introduction to you for this past week. I cannot turn about without some marriage-mad female assaulting me."

Dalford could not keep his lips from twitching in amusement. He feared she might rip the ribbons right off her reticule. "Why, Annie, you sound rather miffed," he said in deliberately innocent tones. "Shall I spill some punch upon the hopeful maidens or trip over their feet to make them halt pestering you?"

"No, of course not," she swiftly denied, a faint hint of color touching her ivory cheeks. "I am very pleased you are having such success."

He lifted his brows at the patent lie. "You do not appear pleased."

She hesitated for a moment before regarding him with a rather rueful gaze. "If the truth be told, I fear I am not accustomed to having to share you with others."

His heart gave a leap at her reluctant confession. For a crazed moment he longed to gather her in his arms and prove that she would never have to share him with anyone, no matter how many centuries they were together.

Instead, he regarded her with an expression of surprise. "Annie, are you jealous?"

She stiffened at the soft accusation. "Jealous? No, of course not. I merely wish to spend time in your company without having to battle with your adoring crowd."

He glanced pointedly around the nearly empty museum. "I believe you must be exaggerating, my dear. As you can see, there is no adoring crowd within sight. Indeed, I believe you must be thinking of some other gentleman. I have never had an adoring crowd. I have always been 'Dolt-ford' to the ladies."

His rather self-mocking words brought an instant expression of contrition to Annie's delicate features. "Forgive me, Dalford, I am being horridly selfish," she said softly, her amazing eyes soft with regret. "I am truly happy you are enjoying your stay in London. And I assure you that the ladies find you quite, quite irresistible."

His studied her upturned countenance. "And what of you, Annie? Are you enjoying your stay?"

Her expression cleared as an enchanting smile curved her lips. "Yes, indeed. It has been wonderful."

"No doubt you are a favorite among the gentlemen?"

She gave an indifferent shrug. "Hardly a favorite, but I am not entirely a wallflower."

Dalford could not imagine any gentleman not tumbling at this woman's tiny feet. She was adorable, delightful, and utterly irresistible. "Any gentleman who does not consider you the loveliest maiden in London must be a fool."

She laughed, although there was a rueful glint in her eyes. "I have discovered that a maiden's loveliness is in direct proportion to her dowry, which makes me barely passable."

"As I said, fools."

"Thank you, but it does not trouble me a whit. I am here to enjoy the sights and parties, not to push myself in the Marriage Mart."

Dalford smiled wryly. Perhaps he should be relieved that she wasn't anxious to toss herself into marriage with the first gentleman to turn her head. But in truth, her determined resistance to the mere thought of taking a husband was wearing upon him like a sore tooth.

What the devil was so horrid about a husband and family, he questioned in silent annoyance?

"One never knows when love might strike," he said in low tones.

Her eyes widened at his unexpected words. "Why, Dalford, you sound like a poet."

He refused to be distracted by her teasing words. "You do not believe in love at first sight?"

Opening her mouth to give a flippant retort, Annie abruptly halted as his steady gaze probed deep into her eyes.

Slowly she gave a shake of her head.

"Not true love," she at last admitted. "Surely such a deep emotion is based upon more than a physical attraction. I would hope that friendship, mutual interests and a commitment to each other's happiness were equally important."

He blinked in surprise as he realized that Annie had actually given love and all it entailed a great deal of thought. Surely he could take heart from the knowledge? No maiden utterly opposed to marriage could have devoted such time to thoughts of romance.

Of course there was one very important aspect of love and marriage she seemed to have forgotten.

His entire body tingled as he stepped close enough to smell the sweet violet scent that clung to her warm skin. "Very well said, my dear," he said softly. "But I believe that you have left out an important ingredient of love."

She stilled as if she suddenly sensed the shift of atmosphere. "What is that?" she asked in hesitant tones.

"Desire."

A wild flush rose to her cheeks. "Dalford."

"What?" Covertly his hand moved to trail slowly up the length of her arm. His heart gave a sudden shudder as he felt a tremor race through her body. He had waited a long time for this moment. Far, far too long. "Surely you wish to experience passion in the arms of your husband?"

Her gaze searched his countenance, as if truly seeing him for the first time. "I . . . I suppose."

"Suppose?" Without warning, his hand shifted to grasp her upper arm. Tugging sharply, he managed to force her to stumble toward the small alcove he had already discovered. Another tug, and he had her safely hidden in the small storage room that was filled with shrouded works of art.

"Dalford, what are you doing?" Annie protested, her eyes growing wide as he pulled her into his arms and hauled her close to his aching form.

"Hush," he commanded softly.

"But . . ."

Whatever her protests, he gave her no opportunity to voice them as he determinedly lowered his head and claimed her mouth in a soft, searching kiss.

For a moment Annie stiffened in shock. Dalford had not

so much as held her fingers for a moment longer than convention allowed. Certainly he had never before hauled her into a closet and attempted to seduce her.

But even as he feared that he had pressed his luck too far, Annie slowly relaxed against his taut form, her hands fluttering to land upon his chest.

Her sweet surrender sent a flare of heated pleasure racing through Dalford, and he lifted his hand to cup the back of her head. Nibbling, stroking, and tasting, he explored the satin softness of her mouth.

He had, of course, imagined this moment on a hundred occasions over the past years. But not even the seductive dreams that had plagued his nights could compare with the exquisite reality of her soft curves next to his own.

His breath halted as her satin lips tentatively parted in invitation. He pressed her closer, shivering at the heady sensations racing through him.

The urge to toss caution to the wind and teach Annie just how delightful passion could be raced through him.

He wanted to press her against the wall and explore those perfect curves. He wanted to stroke his lips over the silky skin and . . .

With a deep, heartfelt groan, he slowly pulled back to regard her dazed eyes with a barely restrained need. He felt rather dazed himself. He had always known that he loved Annie, but he had not fully realized just how desperately he desired her. "Annie," he said softly.

She drew in an unsteady breath. "Oh."

He gave a low chuckle as he gently pushed back a stray curl. "You see, my sweet, passion should never be underestimated."

Appearing as bemused as he felt, Annie lifted her fingers to press against her faintly swollen lips. "Why did you kiss me?"

"Because I wished to do so." He tilted his head to one side, his hungry need suddenly pierced with a flare of amusement. She looked as if she had just been tossed off the edge of a cliff. "Do you wish an apology?"

"I . . ." She paused before giving a slow shake of her head. "No."

Warm satisfaction filled his heart at her simple words. "Good, because I do not feel any particular remorse. I quite enjoy kissing you."

"Do you?"

"Yes." He gave a rueful grimace. "Unfortunately this location is not particularly proper for such pleasurable pastimes. I would not desire to embroil you in unnecessary gossip."

As if suddenly hearing the distant sound of voices, she gave a wary glance toward the still open door. "No."

Taking her hand, he tenderly laid it upon his arm and urged her out of the secluded room.

He had achieved what he desired, he told his protesting body. Annie was now forced to consider him as more than a clumsy friend who caused her constant embarrassment.

When she thought of him now, she would have to recall the blazing passion that had momentarily exploded between them.

Frustrated, but content with the progress he had made, Dalford steered Annie toward her outraged maid. Feeling her sudden squeeze upon his arm, he glanced down to meet her darkened gaze.

"Dalford?"

"Yes, my sweet?"

She unwittingly licked her lips, making Dalford's entire body tighten with a lingering excitement. "When will I see you again?"

He wanted to assure her that he would be at her house within the hour. Sweet heaven, he would willingly camp upon her doorstep if it meant a chance to catch a glimpse of her.

But he had already learned that being at this woman's

beck and call had done nothing more than encourage her to take him for granted.

A new strategy was clearly in order.

"I fear I cannot say, my dear," he said with a faint shrug. "But do enjoy your entertainments."

With an elegant bow, he removed her clinging fingers from his arm and turned to leave the museum.

He could feel her outraged gaze following his retreating form and a smile curved his lips.

Yes, matters were progressing quite nicely.

Quite nicely, indeed.

Chapter Five

As rescues went, this one was spectacular.

One moment Miss Jane Huntwell was tooling her handsome curricle through the park. The next, her horse had taken fright and began bolting toward the Serpentine.

The elegant onlookers watched in horror as the carriage jolted over the wide expanse of grass, the screams of the terrified maiden echoing through the spring air.

Only one brave gentleman managed to do more than gawk in scandalous disbelief.

With the daring of a knight of old, Lord Dalford charged across the park. Coming alongside the terrified horses, he leaned sideways and grasped the reins that had been lost by the poor maiden.

Then, with near impossible strength, he had pulled the charging pair to a slow halt.

Not surprisingly, Lord Dalford was swiftly hailed as a hero throughout London.

Miss Huntwell's father had offered Dalford his daughter's hand in marriage, along with a vast estate and an unseemly dowry.

The prince had commanded a dinner in his honor.

The hostesses became frantic to secure his presence at their gatherings.

And Annie Winsome stewed with a growing sense of frustration.

It was absurd, of course.

After her fears of Dalford's being ridiculed by the *ton,* and in consequence herself as well, she should be delighted by his success.

Not only was he not an embarrassment, but he had captured the jaded *ton*'s interest and become the current darling of Society. The very fact that she was acquainted with Dalford ensured that she achieved a far higher status in town than she ever dreamed possible.

She could not have dared to hope for such results when she had given Dalford that potion.

Oh yes, she should be all that was delighted.

So why was she standing in a shadowed corner of Almack's when she could be laughing and dancing with the vast crowd that filled the hallowed dance floor?

She did not have to look far for the answer to her question.

She could see no more than the top of Dalford's raven head through the crush that surrounded him. But it was far more than she had seen of him in the past fortnight.

Since the afternoon when he had grudgingly agreed to meet her at the museum, he had been increasingly elusive. He never called, never sent notes or flowers, and even when they encountered one another at the endless Society functions, he barely offered her more than a nod of greeting.

It was exasperating.

After that kiss she had expected . . . what?

That he would be as startled and amazed as herself by the shock of desire that raced between them? That he would suddenly look upon her as something more than just an old friend? That he would discover his heart racing and his palms sweating at the mere thought of her?

She unconsciously scowled at the growing crowd that surrounded Dalford.

She wished that she had never given him that blasted potion. She wished . . .

"Good heavens, Annie, you look as if you just swallowed a lemon. Are you not enjoying your first visit to Almack's?"

With a great deal of reluctance Annie wrenched her gaze from the top of Dalford's head to regard her friend Elizabeth, who had come to a halt at her side.

She had looked forward to this evening for months, perhaps years. To actually be within the rarified walls was a dream of every debutante. Now she could only wish that the evening were through.

"It is very stuffy and not at all as elegant as I had expected," she complained, waving her ivory-handled fan until her curls bounced in the breeze. She wasn't about to admit that her disappointment with Almack's had far more to do with a certain Lord Dalford than with the plain furnishings and ghastly lemonade.

"No, it is rather dismal," Elizabeth agreed with a faintly disappointed sigh. "I suppose it is only the fact that it is so terribly difficult to receive vouchers that makes it seem so imperative that one attend." Her expression suddenly brightened. "Still, I am glad that I came, since Lord Dalford chose to make an appearance."

Annie turned her jaundiced gaze back toward the clutch of toadeaters nearly crushing Dalford in their desire to be next to him. "I do not believe he had much option. Lady Jersey threatened to have him tied, gagged, and hauled here this evening if he did not come of his own free will."

"Well, you cannot blame her. His name is on the tongue of everyone in London. Had Lord Dalford chosen to attend some other gathering, there would not have been a soul here this evening, including me."

Annie gave a sniff, not wishing to dwell upon whether she would have attended or not. "There is little point in attending a gathering that includes Lord Dalford. Not unless one enjoys gazing at him from afar."

"True enough." Elizabeth heaved another sigh. "Ever

since his heroic deed in the park, it has become nearly impossible to catch his eye. And I suppose it would do no good even if I could capture his interest. Not now."

A frisson of unease shivered down her spine as Annie slowly turned back toward her friend. "What do you mean?"

Elizabeth widened her eyes at Annie's seeming stupidity. "Surely you have heard that he is only waiting until the end of the season to claim Miss Huntwell as his bride?"

If the ceiling had fallen upon her head, Annie could not have been more shocked.

Dalford to wed Miss Huntwell?

Impossible.

Utterly, completely, absolutely impossible.

"Absurd," she retorted in sharp tones, not at all amused at the ridiculous gossip. "He is barely acquainted with Miss Huntwell."

"It is said that he has called upon her every day since the accident to ensure she is well."

Every day?

Why, the toad!

No wonder he had not had the opportunity to spare a moment for her.

"Dalford has always been a kind and thoughtful gentleman," she forced herself to say, not certain who she was attempting to convince. "That does not mean he intends to wed the chit."

Elizabeth shrugged. "It is also rumored that Miss Huntwell's father has offered fifty thousand pounds and an unentailed property in Surrey if Lord Dalford agrees to the match. What gentleman wouldn't leap at such a generous offer?"

Annie's fan came to an abrupt halt as her brows furrowed in growing unease. "I cannot believe that Dalford would wed for a fortune. He has ample wealth of his own."

"When has a gentleman ever had ample wealth?" her friend demanded in dry tones. "Besides, Miss Huntwell is very lovely. She would no doubt be an Incomparable even without her indecent dowry."

"Yes." Annie grudgingly conceded, wishing she could think of something not perfect about the delicate, sweetly tempered maiden. "Still, Dalford has never spoken of marriage. Why should he suddenly desire a wife?"

"Good heavens, Annie," Elizabeth breathed, as if pressed beyond all patience. "Gentlemen never think of marriage. Not until they are too dazzled by a woman's beauty, or more often, her dowry."

"Not Dalford," Annie retorted stubbornly.

A speculative expression descended upon her friend's countenance. "Perhaps you do not know Lord Dalford as well as you think you do."

Annie slowly turned to watch as Dalford led out a simpering Miss Huntwell to the dance floor.

Her heart contracted with a sudden pain.

Could it be true? Was it possible that Dalford was actually considering marriage to another woman?

No. It was simply unthinkable.

"You must excuse me, Elizabeth," she muttered as she headed determinedly in the direction of her aunt.

Something had to be done. And done quickly, she decided with a grim determination.

Now she only had to figure out what that something was.

Dalford was pleasantly weary by the time he reached his town house in Mayfair.

All in all, he thought the evening had progressed nicely.

Although he had only been able to catch glimpses of Annie throughout the night, he had seen enough to realize that she was far from delighted at his sudden fame, and even less delighted with his dance with the lovely Miss Huntwell. He had not missed the manner in which she had stormed from the room when he had led the maiden out on the floor.

Giving the butler his hat and gloves, Dalford made his way down the hall to his study. He always indulged in a glass of brandy before retiring for the night.

Pushing open the door, he entered, expecting to find the usual books, heavy walnut desk, and lovely Dresden figurines he had collected over the years. What he had not expected to discover was a golden haired witch standing beside the fireplace, a defiant expression upon her beautiful features.

"Good God," he muttered in shock.

"Is there a problem, my lord?" the butler called from down the hall.

"Not at all," he forced himself to retort in what he could only hope were normal tones. "You may go to bed. I shall see to the fire."

"Very good, my lord."

Waiting for the butler to disappear toward the back of the house, Dalford firmly shut and locked the door before stepping toward the unruly minx. "Annie, what the devil are you doing here?"

She gave a tilt of her chin at his chastising tone, but Dalford did not miss the manner in which her fingers were twisting together.

"I had to speak with you."

"Tonight?"

"Yes."

He gave a shake of his head as he moved toward her, not certain whether he should drag her into his arms and kiss her insensible or turn her over to her aunt for a good tongue lashing. "You do realize that if anyone happened to see you enter, your reputation will be in shreds?"

A wry smile tugged at her lips. "No one saw me."

Dalford suddenly realized that she must have used her magic to whisk herself to his study, and he reached for the nearby brandy to pour a healthy measure.

He feared he might need it before this encounter was finished. He took a deep drink while she watched in tense silence.

"Forgive me, but you have rather shaken my nerves," he retorted in all honesty. Whatever he had expected, it had not been for Annie to appear in his study in the middle of the night.

"The heroic, dashing Dalford unhinged by a mere female?" she retorted with an edge in her voice.

He lifted his brows in surprise. "Surely you did not risk your Season and reputation simply to mock me for the absurd gossip that is flying about town?"

She had the grace to blush. "No, I am not here to mock you, Dalford. You know I have never done so."

"True enough." He polished off the brandy and set the glass aside. "You have always been the one friend I could depend upon."

"Then as your friend, I must know . . ." She paused to take in a steadying breath. "Are you to wed Miss Huntwell?"

Ah. Dalford hid a sudden smile of satisfaction. So that was what this was about. "I see you have been listening to the rumor mills," he said mildly.

Her lips thinned. "I would have to be deaf not to. Everyone is speaking of the generous dowry you have been offered."

"And you believe me to be on the hunt for a fortune?"

She paused, clearly knowing that he would never stoop so low. "No, but she is very lovely."

"Yes, she is." He allowed a reminiscent smile to curve his lips.

Annie swiftly stiffened in annoyance. "Blast it, Dalford. Are you or are you not going to wed Miss Huntwell?"

He slowly crossed his arms over his chest, quite enjoying the display of jealousy she could not hide. And why should he not? He had waited long enough.

"That is rather a private matter, my sweet," he softly chided. "I have not put you through the Inquisition for every gentleman you have encountered since arriving in town."

"You have done more than merely encounter Miss Huntwell," she accused, the gold in her eyes shimmering with a fascinating glow in the firelight. "It is said you have called upon her every day."

He gave a faint shrug. "I was naturally concerned for her welfare. She had endured quite a frightening experience."

"Hardly that frightening," she retorted in scornful tones.

"It was not as if she was thrown from the carriage or overturned."

Dalford deliberately lifted his brows. "Why, Annie, that is not very kind."

Without warning she abruptly turned away to peer down at the smoldering logs in the fire. Clearly she did not wish him to read her revealing expression. "Are you going to marry her?"

Knowing that he was testing the limits of his control, Dalford slowly moved to stand directly behind the woman who haunted his dreams. He had waited far too long to have her in his arms to waste such a perfect opportunity. "What does it matter to you, Annie?" he demanded softly.

"I . . . am concerned for your happiness."

Dalford's lips twitched at the blatant lie. "You do not believe Miss Huntwell will make me happy?"

"Do you?"

Not in a million years, Dalford silently answered. Only one woman could fulfill his desire.

"I do not know her well enough to say," he vaguely retorted. He watched as her entire body stiffened with the jealousy that burned within her.

"Have you kissed her?"

Dalford shivered as the ready heat flared through him. Gads, did she have any notion what she was doing to him?

Obviously not, he wryly conceded.

She would be deeply shocked to realize the vivid images racing through his mind.

Unable to halt himself, Dalford lowered his head, allowing his lips to trail softly along the line of her exposed neck. "Like this, do you mean?" he questioned in husky tones, gently nipping at the lobe of her ear.

She gave a startled gasp at his sudden caress, but much to his delight made no effort to pull away.

"Dalford," she whispered.

Placing his hand on her shoulders, he turned her about so he could taste the lips he had ached for over the past weeks.

He gathered her close as he drank hungrily of her sweetness, coaxing her lips apart as he cupped her face in firm hands.

A groan rose in his throat as honey heat thickened his blood and stirred his body with a dangerous desire.

He had tried to be patient, to await this woman to discover the truth for herself. But he was not made of stone. He wanted her with a desperation that was growing increasingly difficult to hide.

Scattering kisses over her upturned face, Dalford felt Annie's arms tentatively lift to encircle his neck. She was pressed close enough for him to feel the soft thrust of her breasts and slender length of her legs. A sharp, fiercely painful need surged through him, and with a moan of reluctance he abruptly pulled away.

Suddenly bereft of his touch, Annie regarded him with a shimmering frustration. "Dalford, what is it?" she demanded in strained tones.

He shoved his hands through his hair, his entire body revolting at his attempt at sanity. "It is time you were home in your bed, Annie," he said roughly.

"But . . ."

"I cannot have this discussion with you now, Annie." He interrupted her pleading words, not about to give in to temptation now. He would not have her accusing him of seducing her into marriage. When she came to him, it would be with her heart, mind, and soul. "I am a man like any other, and the desire to do more than taste of your lips is very powerful."

Expecting her to be horrified by his confession, Dalford was nearly undone by the bewitching warmth that burned in her eyes.

"I do not wish to leave you."

"Annie . . ." With a groan, Dalford leaned forward to place one last branding kiss upon her lips before firmly putting her away. Soon he would have her in his home, in his arms, and in his bed. Soon. "Go home. We will finish this conversation tomorrow."

Chapter Six

The note came before Annie had even finished breakfast the next morning.

Annie,
> *The prince has commanded my presence during his excursion to Brighton. I shall call upon you when I return.*

> *Yours,*
> *Dalford*

Annie crumpled the note and tossed it upon the table. *Blast the prince,* she silently seethed.

She had paced the floor the entire night waiting for Dalford to arrive this morning.

Over and over she had gone through the words to tell her dear friend that she had been a perfect idiot.

She would tell him she had foolishly taken him so much for granted that she had never realized how important he was in her life.

So important that the mere thought of his marrying another was enough to make her feel physically ill.

What did it matter that she had sworn never to tie herself to either a mortal or a warlock? Or that by caring for Dalford she had made herself utterly vulnerable in a manner she barely comprehended?

She needed to tell him how she felt before it was too late.

And now she would have to wait for his return, all the while wondering if he was flirting with another woman, or even considering his engagement to Miss Huntwell.

It was truly more than any witch should have to bear.

On the point of leaving the breakfast room, Annie was halted by the sudden appearance of the butler.

"Pardon me, Miss Winsome."

"Yes, Wallace?"

"Mrs. Winsome is awaiting you in the front parlor."

Annie gawked at the servant in disbelieving shock. She would have as soon expected the mad king to arrive upon her doorstep as her mother. "Good heavens," she muttered. "Mother is in London?"

"I believe she has just arrived."

Attempting to collect her wits, Annie gave the butler a stiff smile.

"Thank you, Wallace. I shall join her in a moment."

"Very good." With practiced ease, Wallace faded from the room, leaving behind a decidedly disturbed Annie.

What the devil could her mother be doing here? It had been nearly a year since she had last seen the woman who had given birth to her, although they kept in close contact through magical means. It was utterly unlike Minerva Winsome to simply appear without warning.

Giving a shake of her head, Annie forced her reluctant feet to lead her out of the breakfast room and up the stairs to the front parlor. Upon entering, Annie barely noted the Palladian beauty of the marble fireplace and gilded mirrors. Instead her attention was directed upon the slender, golden-haired woman seated upon a rosewood sofa.

At her entrance, Minerva rose to her feet, appearing as young as Annie in her soft peach gown.

"Darling," she murmured as she crossed to gently kiss Annie's cheek.

"Mother . . . this is a surprise."

The older woman gave a small chuckle as she firmly led Annie back to the sofa and settled them both on the brocade cushions. "A pleasant surprise, I hope?"

"Of course."

Minerva waved a hand toward the large tray that was situated upon a nearby table. "I ordered tea. I hope you do not mind?"

Annie frowned, wondering what her mother was up to. It was entirely unlike her to be hedging about in this manner. "Of course not."

"It was such an exhausting journey." Minerva gave a charming grimace. "I had forgotten how dismal traveling by carriage could be. Unfortunately, I did not believe you would desire me simply popping in and frightening the staff."

Annie shuddered at the mere thought. Her mother's unexpected appearance was bad enough without having her materializing from thin air. "What are you doing here?"

There was a pause before her mother slowly leaned back and regarded her with an all too knowing gaze. "I thought you might have need of my advice."

Annie furrowed her brows in puzzlement. "Your advice?"

Minerva shrugged. "Well, I may not be the most traditional of mothers, but I do understand the temptations of falling in love with a mortal gentleman."

"I . . ." Annie lifted a hand to her heart, which had skidded to a complete halt at the unexpected words. "What on earth makes you believe I have fallen in love with anyone?"

"I did not use my powers, if that is what you are worried about," her mother assured her in dry tones, clearly reading Annie's wary expression. "It does not take a witch to realize that when a daughter fills her conversations with a certain gentleman's name, her heart is involved."

Too late Annie realized that she had indeed spoken of little other than Dalford over the past few weeks. Not surprising, she grudgingly accepted, considering that she had thought of nothing beyond him for longer than she cared to admit.

Still, she belatedly wished she had been a bit more circumspect.

Her emotions were still too new to be easily discussed with anyone.

Especially her all too shrewd mother.

"I suppose you came to warn me of the dangers of loving a mortal?" she retorted in unconsciously defensive tones.

A rueful smile curved her mother's lips. "I am not so foolish. No one, not even a witch, can control the dictates of her heart. I do, however, think that you should consider the consequences of such a relationship."

Annie unconsciously plucked at a ribbon upon her pale lemon gown. Good grief, she had barely acknowledged to herself that her feelings for Dalford were more than friendship. She did not want to dwell upon on the reasons it was impossible. She attempted to divert the inevitable lecture. "I am well aware of the consequences."

"Are you?"

"Yes."

Minerva gave a sad shake of her head, easily sensing her daughter's reluctance to discuss her feelings. "Before I begin, I wish to assure you that I am here only because I love you and want only the best for you, Annie. I do not interfere lightly."

A portion of Annie's tension eased at her mother's pleading words. She had never doubted this woman's love, nor the fact that she would do whatever necessary to ensure her happiness. Reaching out, she lightly patted her mother's hand. "I know that, Mother."

There was a short pause before Minerva at last met Annie's gaze squarely. "When I first met your father, I intended no more than a light flirtation. My own mother had already chosen a suitable warlock to be my husband, and I wished for a bit of excitement before I was forced to settle down."

Annie could not halt a startled chuckle. Although she dearly loved her father, she would never have thought of him as the sort to choose for a brief, exciting flirtation. He was a quiet, gentle man who preferred books to people upon most occasions.

"And you decided upon Father for this flirtation?" she demanded in disbelief.

A reminiscent smile tugged at Minerva's lips. "Oh, he was very handsome and quite dashing in his regimentals. More than anything, he was extraordinarily tender."

Now that Annie did comprehend. After all, it was what had attracted her to Dalford in the first place. His tenderness, his gentle humor, and his utter lack of arrogance. "Yes."

Her mother heaved a sigh. "Before I knew what was happening, I had tumbled desperately in love—so much in love that I ignored all the warnings and accepted his offer of marriage."

Annie shifted uneasily upon the cushion, already aware of where her mother was leading her. It was a lecture she did not want to hear. Not now. "I am well aware that you regret marrying Father," she retorted in low tones.

"Of course I don't regret marrying Fredrick," her mother astounded her by denying in shocked tones. "Without your father I never would have had you."

Annie frowned in puzzlement. "But you left him."

"I had no choice."

Recalling the pain that lingered in her father's eyes even four years after his wife's abrupt departure, Annie gave a sharp shake of her head. "Of course you had a choice."

Minerva suddenly reached out to grasp Annie's hand in her own. "My dear, have you truly considered the sacrifice you must make to live as a mortal?"

Annie shrugged. "I have no desire to use my powers."

"It is more than just your powers," her mother insisted, her elegant features hardening as she attempted to make Annie understand her fears. "It is denying who you are deep inside. It is living a lie for year after year."

"It has never bothered me before," she retorted stoutly.

"Because you are very young. There will come a time when you long to be among those who truly understand you."

Annie was not swayed. The thought of being separated from Dalford was far more painful than any vague desire to be with her mother and other witches. Besides, she could always visit the Conclave if she felt the need to be with those of her kind.

"None of us can predict the future, Mother," she said. "Just because you felt the need to be with other witches, it does not necessarily follow that I will feel the same."

Minerva heaved a sigh at her daughter's adamant refusal to heed her warnings. "That is not the most important reason I left, Annie."

"Then why?" Annie demanded warily.

It was her mother's turn to shift in discomfort, clearly not eager to reveal her most inner emotions. "When I met your father, he was young, virile, and in the prime of his life. Twenty years later, he was rapidly aging to become an old man."

Annie was shocked in spite of herself. She had never believed her mother to be a shallow woman. "He could hardly help growing old," she loyally defended her dear father.

"Of course not." Minerva smiled with a haunting sadness. "But I was not. Twenty years later I was precisely the same as the day we wed. It was inevitable that your father would begin to resent the fact that most people assumed I was his daughter rather than his wife. Or even for him to begin brooding upon the ridiculous notion that I would soon be seeking a younger, more attractive gentleman."

Annie caught her breath.

It was true.

As a witch she would live for centuries, while any mortal husband she might choose would grow old before her very eyes. Would Dalford come to resent her? Perhaps even worry that her love would not remain true?

She licked her suddenly dry lips. "I realize that could be difficult."

Minerva gave a slow shake of her head. "No, I do not believe that you do, Annie. It is not just a matter of your husband aging while you remain as youthful as ever. It is watching him become more frail with every passing year. Watching him without being able to do a thing to halt the inevitable. I was not strong enough, Annie. I could not remain knowing what the near future held. Could you?"

Annie abruptly rose to her feet, at long last understanding why her mother had left.

The realization made her heart freeze.

Gads, she did not want to think of Dalford as growing old and dying. It was unbearable.

But on the other hand, could she walk away from her feelings just because of that fear? Mortals wed every day without knowing if the one they loved might be there tomorrow. Would she be any happier to turn her back on the only man she would ever love just to avoid future heartache?

"Annie?" her mother prompted softly.

"I do not know, Mother," she said in low tones.

Minerva rose to her feet to lay a comforting hand upon her shoulder. "At least think upon what I have said."

"I will."

"And, Annie?"

Annie turned her head to meet her mother's steady gaze. "What?"

"If nothing else, you must tell him the truth of yourself. No relationship based upon lies can possibly last."

"The truth?" Annie regarded her mother as if she had just requested that she turn herself into a fish. "Dalford will never understand."

"It is essential," her mother said in relentless tones. "If you truly love this gentleman, there should be no secrets between you. Secrets will destroy you both."

Annie pressed a hand to her quivering stomach.

Her mother was right.

Of all the barriers that stood between them, the lie she had been living was the greatest.

Dalford deserved better.

He deserved a wife who could be as honest and candid as himself. A wife who offered the same lack of guile and precious sincerity.

She could only hope he would not be too horrified to see that beneath her powers she was simply a woman who was desperately in love with a man.

Chapter Seven

Dalford deliberately awaited the arrival of Annie in the same location in the museum as he had before.

He had been surprised when he had been handed her note requesting his presence this morning. He had every intention of calling upon her as soon as he could decently do so.

In truth, he had struggled to find some means of luring her to a private location. After being apart from her for the past week, he was desperate to have her in his arms.

More importantly, he was desperate to end this game once and for all. He wanted Annie as his wife. And he would do whatever necessary to make his desire a reality.

But without causing a scandal, the best he could do was hover close to the storage chamber and hope to sneak her into the dark privacy without too much damage to their reputations.

He could at least steal a kiss, if nothing else.

Barely preventing himself from pacing like a caged animal, Dalford was deeply relieved when he caught sight of Annie hurrying toward him, attired in a pale green gown.

His entire body filled with joy at the sight of her beautiful features. He longed to sweep her in his arms and take her far away from the milling crowd, someplace where it could be just the two of them with no distractions.

Instead he was forced to perform a small bow as she halted before him.

"Dalford."

His gaze greedily searched her expression for some clue to her inner thought. The fact that she had demanded to meet with him seemed to bode well. He had hopes that she had at last come to her senses. Her tense expression, however, sent a quiver of alarm through him. "Good day, Annie. You are looking particularly lovely."

"Thank you for meeting me."

He smiled wryly, knowing she only had to lift her finger to send him running to her side. "Did you think that I would not?"

Her lashes fluttered at his soft words. "How was your journey?"

With an effort, Dalford bit back his impatience. Annie was clearly not yet prepared to discuss their future. He would have to follow her lead for the moment.

If worse came to worse, he would simply haul her to the nearby storage room.

"It was tedious, at best," he retorted with a grimace. "Remind me to become violently ill on the next occasion the prince demands my presence."

He was rewarded with a sudden smile. "I have heard that his entertainments can be quite lavish."

Dalford shuddered in horror at the memory of the endless entertainments he had been forced to endure. "They are interminable. I felt like a Christmas goose being stuffed and roasted in the Pavilion. The only surprise was that no one came along to baste me."

Annie softly laughed. "It could not have been that bad."

"No." He gazed deep into her wide eyes, his heart refusing to stay out of his throat. "I simply did not wish to be away from London."

Her smile slowly faded as she regarded him with a hint of uncertainty. "Because of Miss Huntwell?"

Dalford gave an impatient click of his tongue. "You know Miss Huntwell has nothing to do with my desire to return to London."

She remained unconvinced. "No?"

Quite willing to prove just how wrong she was, Dalford abruptly reached out to grasp her arm and smoothly tugged her into the shadows of the storage room. Once alone, he encircled her in his arms.

"Dalford," she gasped in shock.

"Gads, but I missed you," he muttered, before swooping downward to claim a wholly possessive kiss. For a moment she stiffened. Then, with a faint sigh, she surrendered willingly to his demand.

Time stood still as Dalford explored her satin mouth, his hands running a restless path down the curve of her spine. This was surely paradise, he dizzily acknowledged, even with the dust, cobwebs, and shrouded statues that surrounded them. What did it matter where they were as long as Annie was returning his kisses with a passion that stirred his very soul?

At last he reluctantly pulled back to study the green eyes that glowed with a shimmering gold.

An utterly tempting smile curved her mouth. "I missed you as well."

"Did you?" he demanded in husky tones.

"Very much."

He scattered restless kisses over the satin skin of her face. "Annie, my sweet Annie. Can it be you have discovered that I can be more than a dull, plodding friend?"

Her hands lifted to lie upon his chest, her expression suddenly somber. "I have considered you as more than a friend for quite some time."

His breath caught at her low words. "Because I no longer stumble over my own feet?"

Her hand lifted to gently stroke his cheek. "Because you kissed me."

Dalford groaned as he stole yet another delicious kiss. "Good heavens, when I think of all that time I have wasted when I only had to do what I had longed to do since I first caught sight of you."

She frowned at his soft words. "All that time?"

He gave a low growl at her puzzlement. "You impossible, stubborn woman. I have been in love with you forever."

Her breath caught as a dazzling glow entered her eyes. "You have?"

"Yes."

"But . . ." She gave a shake of her head. "You never said a word."

"Because you considered me only a friend," he pointed out in dry tones. "How could I lay my heart bare when you were destined to reject me? I could not risk our friendship in such a manner."

Her expression darkened, almost as if she were regretting the months she had put him through purgatory. Or perhaps it was merely wishful thinking on his part, he acknowledged wryly.

"I was a blind fool," she admitted with a grimace. "I have always considered you my own. When I heard you were to wed Miss Huntwell, I thought I would perish."

His lips twitched as he recalled her bold manner of appearing in his study. "I will admit your seeming jealousy did give me a measure of hope."

"Beast," she said with a small laugh.

Dalford shook his head. "No, just desperate."

Her expression became somber as she regarded him with a searching gaze. "No more desperate than I have been over the past few weeks."

His blood heated as he allowed his hands to softly trace down her back. "Ah, I like the thought of you desperate."

"You are shameless," she complained, although she could not hide the shiver of pleasure that raced through her. A pleasure that echoed deep within Dalford.

His hands came to rest on the gentle curve of her hips, his fingers flexing as he battled the ready tide of need that washed through him. "I would like nothing more than to be shameless," he growled in frustrated tones, his eyes dark with the effort to maintain control. "Unfortunately, I believe we shall have to wait until I can procure a special license." He was abruptly struck by a distinctly unpleasant thought. "Unless, of course, you prefer to wait and have a more traditional wedding?" Having thought of nothing more than marrying this woman for the past three years, Dalford had somehow simply expected her to be delighted with the notion of a wedding now that she had recognized her love for him.

Instead, with a suddenly stricken expression, she pulled from his embrace. "Dalford."

A sharp stab of unease pierced his heart as he regarded her darkened eyes. Blast it all. He had waited three years for this moment. Surely she was not about to prove reluctant?

"What is it?" he demanded cautiously.

"We must talk."

His gaze narrowed. "Not until you agree to marry me."

She bit her bottom lip, making his unease deepen to an alarming level. "No, I cannot. Not until I have told you the truth of myself."

Dalford stiffened as he suddenly realized what truth she was about to reveal.

The truth that she was a witch.

No.

He was not yet prepared to confess his own sins. Not until she was his.

Moving forward, he clasped his hands upon her shoulder and gazed deep into her eyes. "Just tell me one truth, Annie."

"What?"

"Do you love me?"

She drew in a shaky breath. "More than I ever dreamed possible."

"Do you wish to spend your life with me?"

"Yes, but . . ."

He halted her unwelcome words with a brief, burning kiss. He was too close, he told the treacherous voice that warned the truth would soon come out. Too close to risk losing her now. "That is all either of us needs to know."

"But it is not, Dalford," she persistently argued, although in far less certain tones. "There is something that you must know about me."

"We have much to learn of each other, my sweet." He softly stroked the satin of her cheek. "We have the rest of our lives to make such discoveries."

"It might alter your feelings for me."

Realizing that her guilt would not be easily salved, Dalford determined it was time to bring a strategic end to their encounter.

He would send her home. Then this afternoon, he would procure a special license. He would have her wed before she knew what had happened to her.

Perhaps not the best means of handling the delicate situation.

But a desperate man was willing to go to any lengths.

And he was very, very desperate.

"Nothing could alter my feelings for you, Annie," he assured her in rough tones. "Nothing whatsoever. Now we must leave here before we are discovered together in such a scandalous position. I will not have your reputation tarnished."

Without further ado, he firmly grasped her arm and led her from the storage closet.

No doubt he would suffer for his lack of honesty at some point.

It did not matter as long as that point came after Annie was safely his wife.

After that he could deal with anything.

Chapter Eight

Knowing that she was being a coward, Annie meekly allowed herself to be led from the storage closet.

In truth, she could not deny a flare of relief that Dalford had refused to listen to her confession.

She did not want this wonderful dream to come to an end.

She wanted to be Lady Dalford. She wanted it so badly that the mere thought of losing him was enough to make her heart freeze in dread.

There would still be time, she attempted to quiet the voice that warned her she was making a terrible mistake. It would surely take days to acquire a special license. What could it matter if she told him today or two days from now?

At least in the meantime she could enjoy basking in the warmth of Dalford's love.

Unfortunately, that niggling voice refused to be dismissed.

Even when she told herself she was being a nodcock for not simply enjoying this wondrous moment.

Even when she attempted to convince herself that she was only waiting for the proper place.

Coming to a slow halt, she turned to regard her fiancé with troubled eyes.

"Dalford, about our wedding . . ."

"Do not fear, my sweet," he interrupted with a smile. "I will take care of all the necessary details. A pity there will not be time to call upon your father and formally request your hand in marriage. I do not doubt he will be shocked."

Annie wryly thought of her father's amazement at the announcement. She had firmly denied any intention of ever taking a husband for so long that he was bound to wonder if she had lost her wits. "I think that is a safe assumption," she said dryly.

"But I do trust to win his favor." His astonishing blue eyes twinkled with sudden humor. "I am nothing if not persistent."

She bit her lip, willing herself to be courageous. "Yes, but I still . . ."

"Annie, do not fear," he once again interrupted, his tone urgent. "All will be well as long as we are together."

"I wish I could be so certain," she whispered softly.

"Trust in me."

She met his pleading gaze, knowing that she would trust this man with her life. "I do."

He smiled. "Thank you."

An odd tenderness swept through Annie as she realized that Dalford felt just as vulnerable as she. Goodness, how could it ever have taken so long for her to realize just how much she loved this man?

For a perfect, breathless moment they stood gazing into each other's eyes, like two moonstruck simpletons, until the sound of a familiar voice had Annie spinning about to watch her mother hurrying in her direction.

"Annie, there you are," Minerva exclaimed in impatient tones.

Annie briefly closed her eyes, deeply regretting that moment out of time was over.

Now reality was closing in upon her, attired in a plum satin gown and determined expression.

So intent on her sense of disappointment, Annie failed to notice as Dalford discreetly turned away.

"Mother, what are you doing here?" Annie demanded as Minerva came to a halt before her.

The older woman heaved a martyred sigh. "I could not bear the endless chatter of Doreen another moment. I thought we might visit the shops."

"I . . ." Annie wished to refuse her mother's request. She did not desire to traipse through endless shops when she had so much on her mind. She wanted to do nothing but think of Dalford and how she would tell him the truth. Still, she knew that brooding upon the inevitable would do no good. Her courage was lacking, not the proper means of telling him. "If you wish."

Peering over Annie's shoulder, Minerva lifted her brows at the silent gentleman hovering so near. "Are you not going to introduce me to your companion?" she demanded in arch tones.

Annie grimaced, suddenly realizing it was not Doreen's chatter that had driven her mother to seek her out. It was pure motherly curiosity.

"Of course." Turning, she was startled to discover that Dalford had shifted until his back was toward her. "Dalford, I would like for you to meet my mother, Mrs. Winsome."

Just for a moment she thought he might actually ignore her words. Then, with obvious reluctance, he slowly turned to meet the inquisitive gaze of Minerva.

As he turned, her mother gave a sharp gasp. "Raphael?" she demanded in shock.

He bowed, his expression unreadable. "Hello, Minerva."

"What on earth are you doing here? And with my daughter?"

Dazed by the unexpected exchange, Annie glanced from Dalford toward her mother. "You know Lord Dalford?"

"Dalford?" Minerva gave a tinkling laugh as she reached

out to teasingly bat the gentleman with her ivory fan. "Do not tell me that you have dug out that ancient title?"

Dalford gave a lift of his shoulder, his body coiled with a near visible tension. "It is as good as any other."

"What?" Annie gave a slow shake of her head. "How do you know Dalford, Mother?"

Her mother regarded her as if she must be a bit dense. "I suppose I should know one of the most powerful of all warlocks. We have been acquainted for centuries."

Pure shock cascaded through Annie as she turned to meet his wary blue gaze. "Warlock?" she whispered in disbelief, not able to accept that she had been so mistaken in this gentleman. "You?"

With an impatient glance about the growing crowd, Dalford moved forward to grasp her upper arm. "Annie, let us go somewhere we can talk in private," he said in urgent tones.

She attempted to shake off his arm, but she might as well have attempted to shift the angle of the moon. Instead she was forced to content herself with a furious glare.

This man was a warlock.

An arrogant, bloody warlock.

All this time he had deliberately lied to her. Made a fool of her.

"So now you want to talk?" she hissed in anger. "Well, it is too late. You can find some other naive sapskull to play your games with. I am leaving."

Minerva regarded her with startled eyes. "Annie, what on earth are you making such a fuss about?"

Annie's gaze never strayed from Dalford's hard countenance. "I do not enjoy being deceived and manipulated. Good day, my lord."

"Oh, no, you don't," he muttered, abruptly tugging her back toward the storage closet.

Indifferent to the scene they were no doubt creating, Annie attempted to dig in her heels. Unfortunately her slippers could find no hold on the slick floor and she discovered herself being ruthlessly pulled back into the shadowed darkness.

"Blast it, Dalford . . ." she began to mutter. Then, without warning, the darkness disappeared, and she was suddenly whisked to a barren stone room where the sound of the distant ocean could be heard out the barred window. She realized that Dalford had used his powers to take her to some isolated castle where she was now his prisoner. She was not frightened. She did not believe for a moment that Dalford would harm her or use his powers to hold her captive. She was just bloody furious. "Take me back," she gritted.

"No," he said calmly, although his eyes glittered with a hectic light. "Not until we have talked."

Annie angrily thought of her own pathetic attempts to talk to this man. She had wanted to be truthful, which was more than could be said of Dalford. He clearly intended to keep his charade intact indefinitely.

"We have nothing to say to each other."

His lips thinned at her stubborn expression. "Actually we have a great deal to say to one another. Beginning with the fact that neither of us has been completely honest with the other."

The fact that he was right did nothing to ease her temper. "I never deliberately set out to deceive you," she retorted, tugging her arm free as she glared at him in frustration. "I simply preferred living as a mortal."

"While I wished to discover a witch who could love me for myself and not for my powers or for the position I have acquired over the centuries."

Annie crossed her arms over her quivering stomach. "You behaved like a dolt to win my sympathy."

His expression abruptly softened to reveal that unnerving tenderness. "No, I desired to discover if your heart was as kind and generous as I hoped it to be. And it was." He reached out to lightly touch her cheek, an odd yearning in his eyes. "When all others made me an object of jest, you were there defending me with all the fierce loyalty I could ever dream of."

Although she could not halt the small twinge of longing

in her heart, Annie attempted to remain immune to his undoubted charm. He had made a fool of her. "Then it was a test?" she demanded.

He gave a rueful grimace. "I suppose in a sense it was."

"That is despicable."

His brows lifted at her fierce words. "No more despicable than you giving me a potion so I would not be an embarrassment to you in London."

Annie suddenly blushed a vivid red. Blast, she had almost forgotten that ridiculous potion—and she had not considered the notion that he must have known what she was doing from the very beginning.

"I . . . I did that for you," she lamely attempted to counter. "I feared you would be made miserable by the mockery of the *ton*."

He gave a disbelieving shake of his head. "Annie, you feared I would ruin your Season. And I will admit I was rather hurt that you were ashamed of me, and I was willing to have you suffer a bit."

"By making me jealous?" she gritted.

"Yes." He allowed a smile to curve his lips. "I also hoped it would make you realize that I was more to you than a mere friend."

She abruptly spun away, her emotions in turmoil. Despite her lingering anger, she could not wholly deny a desire to toss herself in his arms and remain there for all eternity. "You must have found it all very amusing," she said, revealing the heart of her anger. The mere thought that he had been toying with her for three years made her teeth clench.

She felt his hands lightly settle on her shoulders, his breath stirring the curls at the nape of her neck. "No," he denied in low tones. "There is nothing amusing about being so desperately in love with a maiden that you will go to any length to win her regard. And I do love you, Annie."

She shivered, his words touching her deep in her heart. "I never wished to wed a warlock." She desperately attempted to fight her own desire. "They are unbearably arrogant."

With gentle but determined pressure, Dalford turned her until she was forced to meet his burning gaze. "Not this warlock. I have never felt so vulnerable and uncertain in my life." He reached down to grasp her hand and pressed it to his wildly beating heart. "Feel what you do to me, Annie."

Her breath caught in her throat. "Dalford."

"I asked you earlier if you trusted me. Do you?"

Annie bit her lip, unable to lie beneath that searching gaze. "Yes."

"And do you love me?"

"I . . . yes."

He abruptly tugged her close, folding her in strong arms that promised paradise. "Oh, my sweet Annie, we have nothing to worry about."

Annie could not halt snuggling closer to the warm strength of his body. She felt so right here in his arms. As if she were suddenly made whole.

A rueful smile curved her lips.

They had both made mistakes.

She had been just as deceptive and manipulative as Dalford.

Obviously they were made for one another.

A small smile curved her lips as his hands compulsively ran down the curve of her back. "I suppose if you become too arrogant I can always brew another potion," she murmured.

He gave a soft laugh as he bent his head to tenderly nuzzle her neck. "Oh, no, my sweet, no more potions. I am quite bewitched as it is."

THE LOVE
POTION

Jeanne Savery

Lady Samantha Forsythe backed away from her lifelong friend, shaking her head.

"You must! Sammy," wheedled Mary Pringle, "you *do* want me to be happy, do you not?"

"Yes, but not this way." Samantha's mouth firmed. "It won't work."

"Of course it will. You gave my first governess one, and she caught her vicar, did she not?"

"They don't *always* work," amended Samantha. "You *know* that. Besides—" Samantha frowned ever so slightly. "—I was never certain she didn't pour it out into that potted palm. If you will recall, she looked distinctly guilty when she turned back and discovered us watching." Samantha shook off old memories and drew in a deep breath. "Mary Pringle—" She pointed a long slender finger at her friend. "—you are as stubborn as our gardener's pet pig!"

"It is *you* who is stubborn, Samantha Forsythe." Mary folded her arms and turned away. "You don't *care*. You don't *want* me to be happy."

Lady Samantha sighed. "Mary, think. Who is the witch here?"

"You are. The seventh daughter of a seventh daughter. No question, is there? That is why I come to you for help."

"Then should you not listen to my advice?"

Mary pouted. *"I need that potion."*

Samantha eyed her friend. "Do you really want a man who must be tricked into wedding you?"

"Oh, yes." Mary fell into a pose denoting rapture. "So manly. So handsome. So *rich* . . . and a proper earl, too! He is *perfect* in every way." Mary's eyes glowed, and she nodded her head several times in a row. "Have you *seen* him, Sam? I mean *recently?"*

"I don't want to see him," grumbled Samantha. "The only two times I've seen him were disastrous." Why she felt a teensy-weensy niggling irritation that that was so, she could not—or would not—explain.

Mary giggled. "If you weren't so like that funny man in that Spanish story . . ."

"Don Quixote." Lady Samantha's lips compressed once again. "If men didn't have this idiotic urge to destroy anything that moves, it would be unnecessary for me to interfere."

"You know as well as I that foxes must be destroyed."

"Some, perhaps," Samantha agreed, but only with reluctance. "And even if it is true, that particular fox was a friend of mine." More strongly, she added, "And to hunt with *hounds!* Abominable! Barbaric! Besides," she added as a clincher, "if men didn't also destroy birds, then the foxes would eat the birds and the chickens would be safe."

"What a clanker."

"A what? Mary! What a word."

"Clanker?" Mary grinned, a wide smile that involved her whole face and drew one in, teasing one to forgive Mary very nearly anything—even her wearing-down persistence of water dripping on stone when she wanted something. "It means a lie, Sam. I learned it from my brother."

Samantha debated arguing about whether she had lied. She had not, but she would never convince Mary, who was the daughter of an avid fox-hunting rider to hounds. Instead of arguing, she changed the subject. "Is your brother home from Oxford, then?" she asked. *Anything* was better than talking about their neighbor. Rath Burnside, Lord Dalreath, was *not* a subject with which she felt at all comfortable. "I thought James was not due for another week."

"Shall I tell my brother you wish him to call?" teased Mary.

"No!"

Mary giggled.

Samantha grimaced. "Mary, you will tease me once too often and I will cast you off."

Mary hid her giggles behind her hands, her eyes twinkling.

"James," continued Samantha, "is a very nice man, or he will be when he has matured—" Samantha ignored the fact that James was nearly three years older than she. "—but you know I've no wish to encourage that ridiculous infatuation he feels for me. The whole of his last holiday, I felt like a cornered rabbit. Do not laugh, Mary, I beg you. It was not at all comfortable."

Mary grinned again. "You need not concern yourself. I caught him writing odes to the earlobes of some young miss in Oxford. I told him I believe her to be a barmaid, but he *insists* she is the daughter of his tutor."

"Perhaps one day soon you will have a new sister," suggested Samantha.

"I don't want a new sister." Mary's expression changed to one of determination. "I want a husband. You must—"

Samantha rolled her eyes. Mary would not cease demanding a vial containing a love potion, however many diversions were offered.

"—do it for me, Sammy."

Ten years previously, having earned the sobriquet *Lady Sam* by riding astride in a pair of Mary's brother's old trousers, she did not demure at the disliked nickname. But she did lift her eyes to Heaven and then squeeze them closed before she asked, "Will it satisfy you if I pack the necessary herbs so that, if we find it *truly* necessary, I can make up a potion after we are in London?"

Mary nodded, satisfied. The offered compromise was more than she had expected given Lady Samantha's stubborn insistence she did not *want* to be a witch, because it was not at all comfortable being a witch for the simple reason that, more often than not, a particular potion did not work as it was *supposed* to do, but behaved instead in a mischievous or disastrous way that all too often caused pain rather than doing good.

"Oh, Sam," Mary added, able to put behind her the need to cajole her friend into doing something against her inclination, "are you not excited? In only three more days we are off to London."

Samantha was not at all excited. In fact, her feelings were very near the reverse. Very like her father, a countryman to the bone, she didn't *want* to go. She still did not understand—despite any number of sometimes contradictory explanations—why her mother insisted it was necessary.

So, less than a week later, Lord Forsythe, Lady Sam's father, reluctantly entered his London club. He nodded to the porter who, though Forsythe was rarely to be seen in the rooms, recognized him and welcomed him instead of instantly moving to eject him. Continuing on to the paneled reading room, his lordship sent a searching glance around it, hoping—or, perhaps more accurately, *not* hoping—for a glimpse of the man for whom he searched. A man to whom he had promised to speak. Not that he *wanted* to talk to Rath Burnside. The current Earl of Dalreath was not a man after his own heart, not a farmer, his estates his greatest interest, his duty to them done with alacrity and enthusiasm.

On the other hand, the man was a neighbor—not that he was often in residence. Just at the moment, it was far more important that he was a noted member of the *ton*. At least Lady Forsythe insisted his lordship's knowledge of tonnish

things was what was needed. She also insisted that his tonnish lordship could, for once, put himself out a trifle and do
his duty by a neighbor, making up for his dilatory behavior
toward his estate and local problems. Lady Forsythe had
talked and talked and talked until Lord Forsythe had, with a
distinct lack of enthusiasm, promised to find Lord Dalreath
and put the question to him.

"*Ha,*" muttered Lord Forsythe, catching sight of his
quarry. Eyeing the younger man, his lordship took a moment
to gird himself for a confrontation he dreaded.

Lord Dalreath stood near the fireplace, his arm along the
mantel. He smiled with sleepy looking eyes at his shorter,
very slightly overweight cousin, James Morrison, who was
saying something to him in soft urgent tones. As Lord Forsythe
made his way across the room, he saw Dalreath grin at whatever was said.

Morrison, whose eyes were never still, saw Lord Forsythe's
determined approach. He quickly finished his story and added,
"Looks like someone's after your hide, Rath. You been chasing some unfledged chit and I not know it?"

Lord Dalreath glanced toward the round-shouldered little
man stalking across the room, zigging and zagging around
the furniture—overpadded chairs occupied by overfed and
dozing elderly gentlemen and the tiny tables beside them
that were traps for unwary feet. Dalreath felt his brows rise
up his forehead. Quickly he brought his features back to the
relaxed, not quite bored expression he'd adopted years previously and never found reason to change.

"Lord Forsythe," he said and bowed as the baron, reaching
a position a few feet away, stopped and glowered. Dalreath
repressed a chuckle when the man grew red in the face, then
white, then opened his mouth, and then shut it. "Have you
met my cousin James?" his lordship asked politely, gestur-
ing at Morrison.

Sidetracked—and not unwillingly—Lord Forsythe enthusiastically greeted the other young man, shaking his hand

so thoroughly that Morrison inspected it carefully once it was returned to him to assure himself it had not been damaged.

The introduction finished and time for business arriving, Lord Forsythe tugged at his suddenly overtight cravat. A silence fell. His lordship shifted from one foot to the other.

Finally Dalreath took pity on the older man. "Can I help you in some way, my lord?" he asked.

"You can do your duty," blurted Forsythe.

This time Dalreath's brows arched and stayed arched. "My duty?"

"Don't give a rap for your land or your tenants," muttered Forsythe. "Don't do a thing for the county poorhouse or the village church. Not that it's entirely your fault," grumbled his lordship, determined to be fair. "Inherited too young, didn't you? Very likely no one ever taught you the way to go on, but, by God, you *can* put forth an effort where you *do* know the ropes!"

Dalreath heard a rustle from a newspaper hiding a peer with whom he was not on the best of terms. Not much farther away a book slowly lowered an inch or two, and deepset eyes under grizzled brows peered over the top, staring at him.

"My lord," said Dalreath, gritting his teeth in order to retain a smiling expression, "perhaps we should discuss this—whatever it is—elsewhere." He took Forsythe's arm and drew him back across the room and out the door. "A glass of wine, perhaps. James, would you be so kind as to . . . oh, no, you don't!" he said. He caught James's elbow—

James had been doing his plump best to sneak away toward the front door.

—and turned him the way he wished him to go. "You are coming with us and you can use *your* expertise to choose the wine."

At that particular moment, no one occupied the small room where writing desks, paper, pens, ink, and wax wafers awaited any member's sudden urge to send off a note. It was not something that happened all that often so, once the door was shut, the three of them were unlikely to be interrupted. Dalreath, with charming grace, soon had them, all three, settled there.

The wine chosen by James was, as Dalreath had known it would be, excellent. When Forsythe had drunk off a glassful and held another filled with the ruby red liquid, the younger peer cleared his throat. "Now, Lord Forsythe, perhaps you would be so kind as to explain that extraordinary and exceedingly embarrassing statement you made in the reading room?"

"Embarrassing?" Lord Forsythe blinked. "Embarrassing?" he repeated, having no notion at all what was meant.

"You implied, my lord, that I've a duty to perform, and since you are a man considerably older than myself and are known to have brought a daughter of marriageable age to London for the Season, then it is likely there will be a great deal of gossip about Lady Samantha and myself. Actually—"

James was taking a sip of wine and, with a great deal of difficulty, refrained from spewing it all over.

"—gossip linking the two of us will quite definitely be all over London before the day is out."

Forsythe, who had just swallowed, turned bright red. "Gossip about my Samantha? Can't have that!"

"I would prefer it were otherwise myself," said Dalreath politely.

"But," asked a bewildered Forsythe, "what sort of gossip? What could anyone say? From where would such nonsense come?"

"From you yourself," said Dalreath, answering the last question. Lord Forsythe looked such a combination of confusion and outrage that Lord Dalreath turned and reached for the bottle in order to hide the smile that teased his countenance, an expression that would, if noticed, be unacceptable to Lord Forsythe. He poured them all more wine as he explained, *"You* suggested it, my lord. You said I'd a duty to fulfill. It will be suggested that duty is toward your daughter, and having a duty toward a young woman implies one thing and one thing only. It will be said I ruined her and must make amends."

"But . . ."

"Exactly."

"But . . ."

"We must see the gossips are confounded, my lord," said Lord Dalreath gently.

After a moment's thought, Forsythe sighed gustily. "I detest London. I did not want to come to London. I wanted to keep to home as we always do, where I would enjoy the spring weather and newly growing things and riding over my acres and . . ." His voice trailed off.

"And?" asked Dalreath politely.

"Never mind. *You've* no understanding of the joys to be found on our land." Lord Forsythe sighed lugubriously and held out his glass for still another refill when, sympathetic, James offered to pour it for him. "I cannot understand why we had to come to town when each of our other daughters had no difficulty at all finding a husband. All six of them shot off from the village church and quite happy with it! Still, my wife insisted that *this* time it *was* different." This time Forsythe sighed gustily. "Have to take Samantha to London, she said. No way out of it, she said. And Mary," he added as an afterthought. "Brought her, too, since we were coming."

"Mary?" asked Dalreath frowning. "I thought you'd only the one child remaining under your roof, my lord."

"Hmm? Mary? Pringle's chit. My Sammy and his Mary have been friends since the cradle. The wife thought Mary's nicer ways might rub off on our Samantha, you see."

This time Dalreath was caught with a mouthful of wine. He, too, barely managed to swallow and not embarrass himself.

"My Sammy is a delightful chit, you know," said Forsythe earnestly, "but there is no getting around it. She's got an odd kick to her gallop and she *will* go her own way. She always

thinks she knows best, you see, and will not allow that older
and wiser heads have a thing to tell her."

"Hmm," said Dalreath noncommittally. He remembered
when he'd first discovered just how stubbornly intolerant
Lady Samantha could be when certain she had the right of
something. She'd been no more than an engaging child on
that occasion, perhaps as much as ten years of age, but the
second time they'd come to verbal blows, she'd begun to
enter adulthood . . . and Dalreath had never been able to forget her. Had not particularly wished to forget her. "I do seem
to recall she's rather opinionated," he said carefully. "At least
about some things."

"Yes. That's the problem, you see. Lady Forsythe says she
will be thought an oddity and either scorned or taken up for
her very differences. My wife says she needs someone here
in London to give her the nod. To make her eccentricities a
good thing, rather than a thing about which others will laugh.
So—" Lord Forsythe straightened in his chair and pointed a
long, rather bony finger at Dalreath. "—you, my boy, will do
your duty by your neighbor. You will bear-lead her about,
give her your approval, and introduce her to proper young
men. *Your* approval will make her just the thing, even if you
are only *half* as up to snuff as I'm told you are. Oh," he finished irritably, and waved his glass so that the wine sloshed
perilously near the rim, *"you* know the thing."

Dalreath frowned.

"And no nonsense," blustered Forsythe, seeing the creased
forehead and remembering his wife's arguments. "You haven't
paid the least attention to your duties back home. You can
just take care of one here in London. As compensation."

Dalreath's mouth compressed. He would not reveal it to a
soul, but, at some point in the last year or three, his rather
heedless life in and around London had become a dead bore.
He had wondered, more than once, if it were not time to return to the home from which he'd escaped at an early age,
and accept that the house and lands were not responsible for
his feelings of antipathy toward them. His guardian—who

had finally stuck his spoon in the wall eighteen months earlier—was responsible. Jealous, convinced he himself should be the earl, Dalreath's uncle had made life a misery for the growing boy and ignored him as he grew older. But his uncle was gone now. The place was free of his influence.

Still . . .

Dalreath drew his attention back to Lord Forsythe and discovered his lordship was raking him over the coals for his neglect of his property and didn't care for it. Not at all. It was one thing to tell oneself one needed to reform one's ways—but it was no business of this country peer, a man who was obviously very out of place in London.

"Well?" blustered Forsythe, his color rising again.

Dalreath realized the older man was more embarrassed than angry and relaxed slightly. "I have been thinking, my lord. Since you have managed to tar your daughter and me with a brush of nasty gossip, something must be done to right the wrong to the girl. To myself as well, of course."

Forsythe rose abruptly to his feet. "If you are suggesting a duel . . ."

"No such thing!" exclaimed Dalreath, rising automatically to his own feet. "My lord, *think!* That would only make everything ever so much worse."

Forsythe sank back into his chair. "Sorry. Don't know if I'm coming or going. Don't know what to do. Thought maybe you would," he added, looking under grizzled brows at Dalreath. "At least," he added with more honesty, "my wife thought it."

"Well, I, too, think I do, my lord," said Dalreath quietly. "To begin, you and I must appear to be the best of good friends. And your suggestion that I squire your daughter about town, showing her the sights perhaps, and that I introduce her to friends . . . I am forced to agree that is a good suggestion, my lord."

"Forced?" Forsythe bristled.

"Surely," said Dalreath silkily, "you do not think it is something I will do from the goodness of my heart?"

Forsythe's bristles took on a look of an angry hedgehog. "Don't like it."

"Don't like what, my lord?"

"Don't like you implying you are forced to come to Sammy's aid. Seems like you should *want* to help a neighbor feel comfortable in this ridiculously uncomfortable town!"

Dalreath chuckled. "My lord, you knew very well it was an odd request, or you'd not have come blustering at me before we'd ever said hello."

"Well—" Forsythe seemed to grow smaller, to collapse in on himself. He nodded. "—if you must have it, I *did* know it."

"When one's wife insists . . ." suggested Dalreath with sympathy, but allowing the thought to remain unfinished.

Forsythe muttered something incomprehensible about his wife.

"It is nothing particularly out of the way, my lord. One sees that sort of thing all the time, actually. A mother brings a daughter up to London for the Season," continued Dalreath in soothing tones, "and wishes to do her best by the chit. Frankly, more often than not, she becomes quite unreasonable in the process, so you need not feel badly, my lord, that you have been drawn into Lady Forsythe's plotting. When a matchmaking mother takes the bit between her teeth, determined to marry off a daughter, it is best if we men step back out of the way and do our best not to ruffle their feathers. Shall we have one more glass of wine and toast our plan?"

"Plan?" asked Forsythe, holding out his glass with alacrity.

"Our plan to place Lady Samantha's steps on the right social path?"

Forsythe drank. "Better warn you," he said when he'd set his glass aside.

"Warn me?"

"Hmm. Have to take Miss Pringle, too. Not that she'll be any problem," he added hurriedly. "Nice little thing, Miss Mary."

"But you think Lady Samantha *will* be?" asked Dalreath

in that overly polite manner that usually set Lord Forsythe's teeth on edge.

This time, however, his lordship didn't appear to notice. Instead, his features revealed a morose look that very nearly had the two younger men laughing. "Bound to. Just the way she is, you see?" He rose to his feet. "Well, if that is all, my lord . . ."

"But it isn't!" said Dalreath, also rising. "We must lay our heads together and come up with specific notions. For instance, the weather is surprisingly delightful for this early in the year. And, too, the more quickly we begin the better, so do you think the young ladies would care for a ride in the park this very afternoon? At the hour of the promenade?" Dalreath nodded, answering his own question. "Yes, just the thing with which to begin. James and I," he continued—and hid a grin at his cousin's scowl, "—will stop by to pick the young ladies up at . . . about five, I think." He frowned down at James, who was shaking his head in horror and making negative gestures with his hands. "Tomorrow," he continued, firmly overriding anything his cousin might wish to say, "we will squire them to the Tower, a suitable monument with which to begin our seeing of the sights, and, while driving there and back, we may discuss with them what other particular edifices and things of interest they wish to see while residing in London. Ah! Another thing. We must be informed which parties you have been invited to attend, and if James and I have not received a bid to them, then we will join your party, and, of course, we will ask you to the theater and supper after. Let me think . . ."

"Almack's," muttered James in faintly strangled tones. Quite obviously he wished to have no part in the whole, but could not bring himself to remain silent on such an important point.

Rath snapped his fingers. "Yes. *Most* important. Has your wife the entrée there? Or should I put a word into the ears of one or two of the patronesses? Perhaps," he added, seeing how bewildered poor Lord Forsythe had become, "that is something I should discuss with your lady wife?"

"Yes. With Lady Forsythe," said his lordship, as if Dalreath might not know his wife's name. He mopped his brow with an overlarge handkerchief, this talk of London social activities depressing him all over again.

Dalreath hid a grin. "I'll do that very thing," he said politely. "And now, one more thing, my lord."

"Eh?" Forsythe looked dismayed. "There is more?"

"I said earlier that you and I must be seen to be on the best of terms. I think," said Dalreath, eyeing his lordship thoughtfully, "that, if you do not object, I will put it about that you have agreed to teach me what I need to know to better manage my estates, which, as you pointed out, are in sad condition. Since I am in need of your good advice, what better way to show our mutual esteem?"

His lordship's eyes goggled.

Rath frowned. *"Do* you object?" he asked.

"Er, do you mean it," asked Forsythe cautiously, "or is it merely a ruse?"

"That I want your advice?" asked Dalreath.

"Yes."

Dalreath stared across the room for a long moment. "Hmm. I wonder . . . yes," he said slowly, his brows very slightly arched. "Yes, now I think about it, I *do* want it." He smiled.

Lord Forsythe blinked.

"Well?"

"Well? Of course it is well. Just been saying you need to have more to do with your lands, have I not?" blustered his lordship.

"We are in *London!*"

"Bah," retorted Lady Samantha.

"How can you not be the least little bit excited?" asked

Mary, her face glowing as she tried to look in all directions and still, without stumbling, keep up with Lady Forsythe and Lady Samantha.

"I would much rather be at home. Mary, it is spring. How can you think to enjoy it here with all the dirt—"Samantha wrinkled her nose at the smells. "—and noise and crowds and . . . and no trees showing that lovely first bit of green against the sky and no early flowers to brighten our walk and no new nests with tiny perfect eggs and . . . ?"

"And," interrupted her mother sternly, "all those other childish things you must now put behind you. You are a young lady, Samantha. It is time you thought of marriage and your nursery and all that goes with it."

Mary turned bright red. Lady Forsythe's words reminded her of the lecture her mother had given her just before they left for London about *all* that was a part of marriage, but Samantha, who had long had more knowledge of all *that*— she had been reared in the country, after all—than her mother might have though quite proper, merely scowled.

"Bah!" said Lady Samantha again—but said it softly, not wishing to endure still another of her mother's lectures.

At Lady Forsythe's mantuamaker's establishment, it was more of the same. Lady Forsythe and Miss Pringle enthused over the styles and fabrics, and then over buttons, laces, fringes, spangles, and other decorative bits while Lady Samantha sat, her arms crossed, scowling at the toe of her shoe.

She finally roused herself when her mother raised the topic of a new riding habit. When it came to riding habits, Lady Samantha had Views. When she had Views, she was not the least shy about making herself and her needs understood and did so now, succinctly and clearly.

"But, Samantha"—Lady Forsythe didn't exactly wail her daughter's name, but one could tell she wished to do so and was only prevented by the fact that she was very much on her dignity—"you cannot have thought! What you suggest is so starkly plain!"

"If I had my way," growled Samantha, *"all* my gowns would be *equally* plain."

The modiste, who, off and on, had cast a sapient eye over her newest client, straightened in her chair. She peered at Lady Samantha, who glared back. Suddenly, the woman rose and pulled a resisting Samantha to her feet. Samantha stood there, growing more and more angry, while the mantuamaker prowled around her and then around her once again. She turned her head to one side and then to the other as she attempted to see what the seamstress was doing.

"No. It would not do. One could not go so far as no decoration whatsoever . . ." muttered the woman, her voice trailing off. Then she nodded—one firm nod. "Lady Forsythe, your daughter has the right of it. That tall, wonderful form is very nearly sufficient decoration all on its own. She doesn't need a frill to make the bosom look more than it is or draping and flounces to detract from a bottom that is, perhaps, a little too wide. She is perfect just as she is."

Samantha, who never blushed, turned bright red. Mary, who was cute and pert, and perhaps a little too wide at the bottom, but nevertheless the belle of their home region, pouted.

"I," continued the woman, "will use all her good points in designing her gowns. I saw, in my mind, just the sort of wardrobe she requires when she finished describing the riding habit. Perfect. She will set a new style. Others will attempt to imitate her and will, of course, fail. You, my dear—" She turned a knowing eye on an increasingly irritated Mary. "—are far too *intelligent* not to *know* that *slavishly* following fashion will not do. Each form has its own requirements. Now, you've a *very* pretty face with a perfect pink and white complexion and that *lovely* golden-blonde hair, which is the fashion this year. Are you not a lucky girl? But we must call attention to it. Your hats will be particularly important. And you are so very graceful. You will want fabrics which flow about you as you move, short trains on your evening gowns, perhaps, which swing about, and a habit which . . ." Her discreetly blackened brows arched. "No habit?"

"I do not ride." The tactful modiste had overcome Mary's peevish response to the enthusiasm for Lady Samantha's form and returned her to her usual spirited state. "Lady Sam is a goddess in the saddle, but I—" Mary spoke with great earnestness. "—am no more than a lump of clay. I will not sit a horse while we are in London where one's every appearance must show one at one's best. I will not require a habit."

"Very well spoken," approved the dressmaker.

Mary beamed with pleasure at the compliment. Admitting her fault had been the right thing to do, however painful it had been to denigrate herself and add to Samantha's consequence.

Samantha, despite herself, discovered a growing interest in the gowns suggested for her. Now that she knew she would not look like a fleecy cloud or an ambulating flower garden when she strolled among the *ton,* she was willing to take a part in the discussion, insisting on certain colors and fabrics and eschewing others. Well over an hour was then spent standing still and being stuck, over and over, by carelessly inserted pins as several gowns were designed right upon her chemise-clad figure.

Sam hated it.

She had always detested being still. Movement. Lightning and wind and fast-moving water. That was Samantha. She became tense and unhappy, a stagnant pool, when required to be still, as was necessary for fittings. Finally, even though she knew that for the first time in her life she'd have gowns that suited her, she could bear no more.

"Mother, did you not say we were expected at Lady Hemplewhite's at three?" she asked when she could not, for another moment, stand still as a stone while yet another length of fabric was pinned around her.

Her ladyship looked at the tiny watch pinned to her bodice. "Oh, dear, I'd no notion it was so late. Perhaps we should make another appointment?"

The mantuamaker looked at the fabric yet to be draped and sighed. "We have enough to be going on with, but you must return in the morning, my lady," she said sternly, holding Samantha's gaze. "If these were the usual styles, I could simply take your measurements as I did with Miss Pringle and be certain I would supply exactly what is needed, but in your case, where the material itself is the most important thing and not the decoration, we must try each design as we go. Do you understand?"

Lady Samantha shrugged. "Surely at some point you will have made a sufficient number to have the trick of it."

The woman smiled. "Oh yes. Eventually. *But not yet.*"

Samantha sighed. "I *knew* I did not wish to come to London," she muttered.

The modiste laughed. "You wait until you begin to receive well-deserved compliments. You will feel quite differently."

Samantha looked thoughtful. "Will I?" she mused. She shook her head. "I doubt it."

Mary sighed. "I will never understand you, Sam. Do you not wish to dance the night away? Do you not wish to find the man of your dreams? To wed him and . . . and . . ."

Mary didn't wish to think about what followed that *and,* but she had every intention of suffering through it. With Lord Dalreath, of course! Surely such a perfect gentleman would not embarrass her too dreadfully. She sighed again, but it was a far more blissful sigh as she went back to daydreaming about her one true love—or, rather, the man she *hoped* would be her one true love—and, fully occupied, she didn't bother to listen as Lady Forsythe made the arrangements for their next fitting.

"Rath," said James once Lord Forsythe had had a final glass of the truly excellent wine and, with a handshake and other expressions of goodwill—all done where several of the club's greatest gossips would see—departed from the club.

"Hmm?"

"That Lady Samantha . . . isn't she . . ."

"Dub your mummer, you fool," said Rath looking around quickly. Luckily, no one was near, not even the doorman.

James still wished an answer, but he spoke more softly. *"Is* she?"

"The one who stole that fox? The one who made my birds wild as bedamned?"

"Yes, that's what I'm asking."

"Yes, she is."

James blinked. "Then she's the one you mean to . . ."

"I wish I hadn't had quite so much to drink that night," interrupted Rath, an edge to his voice.

"But you did, and you said . . ."

"One more word, James, and you and I will have a falling out, is that clear?"

"Just as soon as you admit she's . . ."

Once again Rath glanced all around. "Yes," he said softly. "She's the one I mean to wed. I admit I hadn't thought to do so just yet, but if her mother means to marry her off, then I'll just have to see that she marries the chit off to me."

"Ah! But . . ."

"What now?" asked Rath.

"You don't even know her."

Rath grinned, his eyes twinkling. "I know what I need to know. That girl is a storm, a tempest, a wild thing . . . and—" He spoke with satisfaction. "—I will tame her."

James, alarmed by such a thought, wished to remonstrate, but before he could form his words to tactfully say what he wished to say, Rath continued.

"But not *too* much," mused Rath. "I would hate to harm that wonderfully free spirit in any way."

Ah. That is all right then. James relaxed.

Lady Samantha followed Mary from the carriage in which Lord Dalreath and James Morrison had taken them to the park. She grimaced at the sight of her friend, red of face, her chin ducked down, and her tongue tied in knots. Lord Dalreath smoothed over Mary's gauche behavior, telling them both what a delightful excursion it had been in the company of two such beautiful ladies.

"Delightful, my lord?" asked Samantha, drawing his attention from her blushing friend. "What a . . . a clanker," she added, recalling Mary's word for a lie.

He chuckled. "What a . . . a word," he mimicked, teasing her.

Samantha felt heat in her ears and, silently, chided herself. Why would she care what this man thought of her? Besides, he was the man her friend had an interest in, so it would be outside of enough if she were to even pretend to set her cap at him. And as to that, from where had the notion of setting her cap at *any* man come? Samantha's chin rose. "Would you deny that you lie?"

His expression sobered and his eyes narrowed. "Lady Samantha, I never lie. I may indulge in the occasional social exaggeration, but I do not lie."

She felt reprimanded and didn't understand why. He had, whatever he called it, lied. Still, she bit back the words she felt teasing the tip of her tongue and turned to Mr. Morrison. "Thank you for a very interesting afternoon, sir. And for suggestions concerning places Miss Mary and I might like to see while we are waiting for our London wardrobes to be delivered to us. I will look forward to a tour of London Tower. I have read of the many important people who have found themselves imprisoned there and . . ."

"And," interrupted Lord Dalreath, drawing her attention away from his cousin, "have you also read about their ghosts?"

"Not ghosts!" The thought brought Mary out of her unwonted shyness. She shuddered. "Oh, no. I would *not* enjoy a visit to such a place! Perhaps we should choose another destination . . ."

"Mary, do not pretend you are afraid of ghosts."

"But Sam, I *am*." Mary's eyes widened in the way they had when she wanted someone to believe her. It didn't matter whether what she said was true or untrue. In this case, however, it *was* the truth. "You *know* I am."

"But not in daylight and not with such stalwart protectors to guide us through the dangerous bits," insisted Lady Samantha, letting her eyes flick toward Lord Dalreath a couple of times.

"Oh, but . . ." Mary's tongue caught up with her friend's hints. "Oh! Oh, yes. Of course, with the gentlemen to protect us we need fear nothing. I will—" She swallowed hard. "—enjoy it of all things!"

But her behavior contradicted her words and made it obvious she spoke mendaciously. James took her hand. "Truly, Miss Pringle, no one visiting the Tower has seen a ghost walk in daylight. However, if you feel you would not care to chance it, then you and I will await the others outside when they explore those places where ghosts are most often known to roam."

"Thank you," said Mary, but turned to look at Lord Dalreath—only to discover he was looking at Lady Samantha. "My lord—" She jerked at his sleeve, forgetting to be tongue-tied. "—you *will* protect us, will you not?" she asked, attempting to draw his attention to herself.

"If there is anything from which you need defending, Miss Pringle, I will be certain to assist James in seeing that you are safe."

Mary was a trifle uncertain that his response was exactly what she'd wished, but she sighed softly, nodded, and, along with Lady Samantha, said all that was proper before going into the house Lord Forsythe had rented for the season.

"You will never attach him that way," said Samantha when they reached the room the girls shared. She tugged on a long hatpin, carefully placed through a thick coil of hair. It seemed determined to remain where it was but, tugging hard, she finally managed to remove it. *And* several pins with it, allowing a coil of autumn-colored hair to drop to her shoulder.

"I haven't a notion what you mean," said Mary, airily. Now his lordship was beyond sight, she could recall only the words she wished to remember and interpret them and his tone in any way she wished. "He has promised to protect me, has he not? He thought me delightful and pretty. That is promising. Perhaps we will not require your love potion after all. That would be quite the best thing, would it not?"

"It most certainly would," retorted Samantha. "I have told you and told you that love potions rarely behave as one would wish them to do, all too often handing a surprise of one sort or another to the hopeful one. Sometimes a good surprise, but all too often *not.*"

"Since it looks as if his lordship has taken a decided fancy to me, then we are unlikely to need it, and that makes everything quite all right," said Mary smugly.

Mary turned to the wardrobe to put away her bonnet and didn't see Samantha's look of confusion, disbelief, and a trace of wonderment that anyone could be so blind or live in such a make-believe world, deluding oneself so thoroughly. When Mary turned back, Samantha, her features once again under control, was busying herself with pinning up her hair.

"You will soon see Wren's monument to the Great Fire," said Rath, his eyes burning into the side of Samantha's head.

He wondered why she kept herself turned from him. If he had believed she was watching the sights, he might understand it, but it seemed to him that she was not so much looking at other things as avoiding looking at him. Miss Mary's admiring stare *should* have compensated for Lady Samantha's lack of interest, but he found it merely irritating.

"Wren designed and built it," he persisted, "between 1671 and 1677. He had, as perhaps you know, great plans for rebuilding the whole of the City of London, of which more than 400 acres were destroyed."

"Nearly a hundred churches and more than 10,000 homes burned before the fire was brought under control," added

James, who had studied Dalreath's newly purchased guidebook at least as thoroughly as Rath had done.

Samantha glanced at him and back toward the shops along the way.

"How terrible," said Miss Mary, never taking her eyes from Lord Dalreath.

Persevering, Rath asked if either young lady would feel like climbing the three hundred and eleven steps to the observation platform at the top of the two-hundred-two-foot-high tower.

"Can one? Climb to the top?" asked Lady Samantha, finally turning to look at him. "Is it truly possible?" she asked, overriding Mary's tiny squeaks and squeals of horror.

"It most certainly is possible." Dalreath felt a certain satisfaction that he had, finally, caught her interest.

"But it is so terrible high!" said Mary rather timidly. "Surely it is not healthy to be so far up in the air?"

"Healthy? Mary, you gudgeon," said Lady Samantha scornfully, "the Alpine regions are known to be excessively salubrious, and they are ever so much higher."

"Is that true?" asked Miss Mary, turning her big eyes on Lord Dalreath. "Have the Alps a healthy climate?"

"I believe they do," he said in solemn tones, but his eyes danced. "However that may be, I've no basis for making any claims for the salubriousness of the climate at the top of the Monument. On the other hand, I've no reason to believe it a danger to one's health either."

Mary was unconvinced. "A greater danger exists, surely. One might grow dizzy and fall . . ."

"The platform, Miss Mary," said James in soothing tones, "is enclosed. It was found necessary to make a sort of cage about the top."

"Necessary? A cage?" asked Lady Samantha.

"There were, er, several distressing incidents," said James repressively.

Lady Samantha turned to Lord Dalreath, her look questioning.

"Suicides, my lady," he explained, having a far better notion of her ability to handle distasteful details.

Mary squealed again.

Samantha looked sad. "How terrible. I am glad they made it impossible for other poor souls to use this particular means of escaping their problems. One should add the number of suicides to those who lost their lives in the fire, should one not?"

"Only nine died in the conflagration, my lady," said James, "and, I believe, no more than six jumped before the tower was closed and the framework installed so it could not happen again." He turned to Mary. "Please do not look so distressed, Miss Mary. We will not climb to the top if it bothers you so dreadfully."

"Mary, surely you are not such a widgeon you would deny the rest of us this treat?" asked Lady Samantha, turning to her friend.

"Yes, I would," said Mary promptly. "All those stairs? I do not believe I *could* do it even if I *wished* to do it and I *don't.*"

"Perhaps you and I can return another day, my lady," said Lord Dalreath, sounding bored, "when your friend is being entertained by something of greater interest to her. We two can then climb to the top of the Tower."

Samantha sighed but nodded. It seemed to her that every time she discovered some means of gaining a trifling bit of exercise here in London, she was prevented from utilizing it. At the rate she had gone on since their arrival, she would forget to what use to put her limbs before she returned to the country and had the whole of two estates open for her pleasure—her father's and Lord Dalreath's, which, since he was rarely in residence, she wandered as freely as she did her father's.

The carriage stopped short of the memorial so they could stare at it, and Mary was more determined than ever that she never set foot inside it. "It *must* be dangerous," she insisted. "So tall and thin. It cannot be safe. Why, it could topple over at any moment!"

That it had *not* in more than a century was not deemed the least bit relevant.

Only a few blocks beyond the monument, Samantha, who had returned to staring over the side of the barouche, gave a gasp and leaned forward. *"No,"* she said.

"What is it, my lady?" asked Dalreath, looking in the same direction. His mouth firmed at what he saw and, instantly, he ordered his driver to stop. Not bothering to open the door and let down the steps, he hopped over the side. James, a trifle slower to see the problem, followed in a more conventional fashion. And Samantha, despite Mary's clutching hands, did likewise.

"Here now," said Dalreath to the inebriated giant who had a well-dressed and obviously distressed young lady in hand. "Let her go."

The huge man laughingly fended off the ineffectual parasol wielded by a tiny gray-haired lady as he clutched the frightened young lady to his side. The laugh cutting off abruptly, he turned toward Dalreath. "Here now yerself," he growled. "I found her. She's mine."

"I think not," said Dalreath.

Samantha gently removed the parasol from the older woman's hand, looked at it, and handed it back. The wispy thing could not possibly do any damage to the villain, who had yet to unhand the girl. She looked around and saw a cart piled with lumber, which she approached with a determined stride. She returned with a nicely trimmed length of wood while Dalreath and the man exchanged insults, their voices escalating and drawing a crowd.

Samantha, returning to a position behind the man, listened for a moment, then grimaced and, lifting her weapon, brought it down, hard, on the man's head. With a great deal of satisfaction, she watched him sink down, nodding her approval when Dalreath, with great presence of mind, grabbed the girl and held her away from the descending behemoth.

Once assured the child was in the arms of the little

woman, she returned her board to those in the cart, and, dusting her hands, came back to where James spoke quietly with the elderly lady.

"Now that is settled, shall we go on?" she asked, looking from Dalreath to James and back.

"I think," said Dalreath, fighting laughter, "that perhaps we should first deliver this lady and her charge to their home, do not you? I doubt the fellow's head is so hard he'll, uhm, *sleep* for long and I doubt—" He sobered. "—he'll be happy when he wakes." He turned to the elderly lady who, with great dignity, thanked him and then Samantha, and then insisted she and her granddaughter would be quite all right. Their carriage was just around the corner and, assuming the gentleman would not mind escorting them to it, then, once they were safely inside, they would be of no further bother to their rescuers.

With one last glance toward Lady Samantha—who James was insisting he help into *their* carriage—the lady, her granddaughter, and Dalreath turned the corner and disappeared. Dalreath soon returned, uncertain whether to feel insulted or succumb to amusement. Never before had he been offered recompense for a trifling favor as had just happened. The woman, a cit's wife, obviously had more wealth than sense—although he knew she was seriously relieved and thankful that her granddaughter was safe.

His attention turned to Lady Samantha when she spoke to him.

"Thank you, sir, for stopping the carriage so expeditiously. I did not feel it my place to do so, but—" Lady Samantha's eyes sparkled. "—very likely I would have demanded we halt if you had not."

Mary sat in her corner looking grumpy. "It was just like you, Sam, to stick your oar in. Lord Dalreath would have seen to the fellow, but no, you had to take part. How could you? How dared you? Oh, you embarrass me half to death with your hoydenish ways. Truly, Lord Dalreath," said Mary earnestly, "she is perfectly sensible *most* of the time. But when she thinks there is an emergency, she will insist only she knows how best to handle it."

Dalreath's brows arched and his eyes twinkled. "But, Miss Pringle, I did not mind. Not in the least." Lord Dalreath grinned. "I will happily admit that I was rather flummoxed as to what I should do. Indulging in fisticuffs in front of ladies is most improper, as I am certain you know, but I doubt there was any other way I could have managed to convince the fellow he must leave the girl alone. He had it in his head—"

James hurrumphed loudly.

"—that he would *not* let his prize go and he had, I fear, drunk just enough he was in that stubborn state where there is no changing a man's mind. Yes, James? You wanted something?" Dalreath turned to his cousin, his brows high.

James's own brows rose and fell as he drew in a deep breath and let it out. "No, cousin," he said dryly. "Nothing at all."

Dalreath, knowing James had thought he'd meant to say something entirely different, something not properly mentioned before ladies, grinned. He'd had, after all, no intention, none at all, of mentioning *why* the man wanted to keep the girl close.

"Lady Samantha, that was a very brave thing you did," said James, ignoring his cousin.

"It was an *unwise* thing," said Dalreath.

Mary nodded her head several times in agreement. "Also," she said, "exceedingly unladylike."

"Foolhardy, more like," said Dalreath, in response to Mary's rather snide comment. "My heart, Lady Samantha, was in my mouth when I realized what you would do. I don't know how I kept from signaling your intention to that great oaf. If he had seen, he would have taken the board from your grasp and very likely *he'd* have hit *you,* my lady."

"I was in no danger at all. You had him completely mesmerized with your, er—" Her eyes danced at the memory. "A fine selection of *words,* and that gave me all the time in the world to see that I did it properly."

"I wonder," mused Dalreath, eyeing her from beneath lowered lids, "just where you learned such a trick."

Samantha laughed. "It is not, my lord, the sort of trick one *learns.* It was merely the most expeditious way of dealing with the situation."

"Hardly gentlemanly," he murmured.

"I am hardly a *gentleman,*" she retorted pertly, drawing a laugh from the two men and a scowl from Mary, who could see no reason at all why either man should encourage Samantha in her wild ways.

Lady Samantha put the whole from her mind and enjoyed their visit to the Tower as if nothing whatsoever had occurred to interfere with their jaunt. She was enthusiastic about the chopping block on Tower Green, listing those famous and infamous people who had met their ends there, and scornful of the dirty, uncared-for royal jewels in the vault, which, for a monetary consideration, was opened by the guard for their viewing. The apartments where a queen had been held prisoner fascinated her, as did several other places where prisoners were once incarcerated. Samantha spoke of Lord George Gordon, the instigator of the Gordon Riots, who had been incarcerated there for eight months as recently as 1780.

"Just think. That was only a little over thirty years ago," she finished, staring around at the stark walls of the small apartment in which he had been held.

Dalreath was both surprised and fascinated by her knowledge. He had meant to hire a guide for the afternoon, but soon discovered that her ladyship knew as much, if not more, than any of the men who scraped a living by the fees they garnered for sharing their information—or, as the case might be, misinformation.

Mary, no scholar, was soon bored. James, noting this, offered to take her to feed the ravens. Soon she grew bored with that as well, and James wondered what might hold her interest until his cousin and Lady Samantha reappeared. In desperation, he asked, "Have you been much occupied with choosing your wardrobe for the Season?"

He had, luckily, recalled that clothes were almost always of prime interest to young ladies, and his gambit proved successful. Long before the others appeared, it was *James* who suffered from boredom, but nevertheless he was pleased he had managed to keep Miss Mary contented, which she obviously was, while relating, in great detail, the tale of her first visit to Lady Forsythe's mantuamaker—without, of course, mentioning that woman's unnecessarily verbose praise of Samantha's form and her lack of interest in Mary's.

The four returned to the Forsythes' residence, and all went in to where Lady Forsythe was pouring tea for herself. The lady instantly put aside her book and ordered a larger pot, along with refreshments of the sort a man would prefer. Once she saw Mary and her daughter settled with Mr. Morrison, she and Lord Dalreath put their heads together concerning such important subjects as Almack's and presentations at royal drawing rooms and the proper decor for ballrooms when introducing young ladies to the *ton*.

That evening, pretending to read while Mary played the pianoforte for her mother and father, Samantha found herself musing over their day. She had been quite surprised to find Dalreath going to the young lady's rescue as he had done and with nary a thought to the size of the man he confronted. She had thought him a care-for-nobody—not a coward, exactly, but overly concerned for the set of his cravat so that the thought of a fight would be unsettling if not actually upsetting. She was chagrined to find she had assumed he was unlikely even to notice that another might be in trouble. She'd been wrong. He had stopped the coach without a single glance at Mary or herself to see if his action had impressed them. She was forced to conclude he was not the here-and-therian she had thought him.

Once they reached the Tower, he not only had listened to

her pronouncements, but had asked interesting questions and joined her in speculation about some of the history, the most interesting, of course, the true cause of the deaths of the two young princes who had died so mysteriously—and so much to the benefit of their guardian!

In fact, she concluded, *he is not quite the total wastrel that I believed him to be. It is too bad one cannot take him in hand and do what one might to reform him . . .*

Then, realizing the direction in which her thoughts were once again trending, she felt the heat of a blush in her throat. Glancing around surreptitiously, she saw that no one was looking her way to notice the revealing color and, sternly, she reminded herself that *Mary* found his lordship interesting, *not* herself.

She determinedly set her mind in order and then set herself to *really* reading her book. If her concentration was not quite all she'd hoped, at least she managed to pass the time agreeably until the tea tray was brought in and it was time to gather up her bed candle and for them to take themselves off to their bed.

The following days were much the same. Mary was soon bored by viewing great edifices, and suggested they go to Somerset House to the Summer Exhibition, where modern artists had the best of their current work on display.

Mary had, almost by accident, nosed out the information that the exhibit was a proper place to see and be seen. She soon discovered other venues where it was wise to present oneself to the view of others. The opera was high on Mary's list, but she lacked proper attire and despaired of ever being able to attend a performance. She was, therefore, ecstatic when appropriate gowns arrived and, prettily—but with determination—she begged Lord Forsythe to hire a box for the evening.

It was, however, Lady Forsythe who convinced his grumbling lordship he must do so.

"Samantha is your last chick," scolded her ladyship. "You were not required to put yourself out for any of the others, so it will not hurt you to do so for this one."

But when it came time to leave and Lady Forsythe saw how her husband was dressed, she groaned, mentally reviewed his wardrobe, and excused him, telling him that on the morrow, without fail, he was to repair to his tailor and, on the *next* occasion when it was proper to wear formal evening gear, he was to have it in his possession.

The implied "or else" hung in the air, and his lordship hurriedly capitulated before her ladyship was forced to put the threat in plain words.

Lady Samantha had no expectations of enjoying the evening. She, as well as Mary, had heard that the opera was no more than an excuse for dressing up in one's best and for showing off one's jewels—and one's daughters—and she did not like the notion of being put on display. She discovered, however, that it was an evening of mixed blessings. The music enthralled her, the performance beyond her wildest dreams. On the other hand, the company which crowded into their box at intermissions was boring in the extreme.

Only Lord Dalreath had a word to say about the music. Only Lord Dalreath told amusing, rather than disgusting, tidbits of gossip. Only Lord Dalreath looked like a prince— or like a prince *should* look—in his tight black coat and white pantaloons, neat black ribbons holding his clocked stockings at the knee, and evening slippers which were polished until she wondered if she might not see her face in them.

In fact, much to Lady Samantha's horror, only Lord Dalreath seemed something other than a fop or a rake or a sot or a gambler. And Lord Dalreath was *Mary's* hope for the future.

Lady Samantha went to bed that night with a tiny ache in the region of her breasts. She feared it was an ache that would grow far larger before it waned and disappeared.

* * *

"Oh, yes. The seventh daughter of a seventh daughter, you know," said Mary airily, happily the center of attention for the first time since coming to London. "Such are always witches, of course." She preened at the interest she generated with her stories of Lady Samantha's ability to read the future in tea leaves and the efficacy of her potions.

"Do you mean to say she actually sees the future?" asked an excited young lady. "Could she tell me if—" The chit looked around and blushed, and then, firming her chin, continued. "—my Harry will ask for my hand?"

"Oh, yes," said Mary, nodding. Then, caution overcoming her exuberance, she added, "Well, no. She cannot tell *who* will ask, if that is your question, but if you ask to know if some *particular* man will, then she can say yes or no."

"And could she tell me if my horse will come in first in the race it is running tomorrow?" asked a young man who was perennially in debt because he was addicted to sport but had no head for it.

"Of course," said Mary. "She is very good."

Lord Dalreath, overhearing, entered the discussion. "Miss Pringle, you must not tease people so. Someone might be so foolish as to take it seriously and, of course, it is all nonsense," he said in scornful tones. "A delightful pastime when one wishes to entertain, but *not* something any *sensible* person would take seriously."

"You don't understand . . ." said Mary, her eyes wide.

"Do I not? *I* think you spout such nonsense in order to make yourself interesting, Miss Mary, but—" He said it in such a teasing way, she could not take offense. "—surely you do not truly wish to make game of your friend?"

"But . . ." sputtered Mary, horrified. "Oh, I never would."

"Ah. Then it is Lady Samantha who wishes it put about that she is"—he appeared to hide a chuckle. "—a witch? When everyone *knows* such creatures do not exist?"

Mary suddenly recalled Samantha's insistence she not

discuss such things, that Samantha did *not* wish it known. She hung her head.

"There, there," said Lord Dalreath in a more kindly voice. "You see what happens when one is carried away by the enthusiasm of the moment. Come along, Miss Mary. I believe they are tuning up for our Sir Roger de Coverly, and we will miss it if we do not find our place."

His grasp on Mary's arm was not exactly gentle, and she glanced up at his expression, which was, as usual, one of boredom. "I'm sorry," she murmured.

"Are you?" he asked politely.

"I didn't mean . . ."

"You didn't, of course, but whatever you may have meant, you have very likely caused difficulties for her ladyship. *Serious* problems," he said when she frowned and shook her head slightly. "We will hope not. Now," he said, bowing, "let us put our best foot forward . . ." and he took the first step of the energetic dance.

Mary, breathless when it was over, stared at Lord Dalreath over her fan as she panted gently, her great eyes shining.

"Are you as much in need of a glass of lemonade as I?" he asked politely.

Lady Samantha, sitting only a few seats away, heard his question and felt as if a part of her broke. "Nonsense," she muttered. "It cannot happen. Hearts do not break. It is merely that one's feelings are bruised."

Mary joined her while waiting for Dalreath to bring her lemonade. As usual she was ecstatic: about her dance with his lordship, about how wonderful he was, how graceful, how well he knew the steps and was not one who found it necessary, as did far too many men, to simply walk through the forms, and about how handsome and how thoughtful . . . and stopped speaking abruptly when he arrived before them followed by a footman holding a tray with three glasses on it.

"Lady Samantha? Will not you too enjoy a glass of lemonade?"

"I told you," said Mary behind her fan. "He is so thoughtful!"

"I believe," he added once the glasses were in hand and each had sipped, "that our waltz is next, my lady?"

Samantha nodded—and could not prevent a small feeling of satisfaction seep into her when she saw a fleeting frown cross Mary's face.

The satisfaction had disappeared long before the evening ended and the two were alone in their room once again. Samantha, drowsy, would have gone straight to sleep—if she'd been allowed to do so.

"Why did he waltz with you? When were you given permission? We have yet to go to Almack's, so I hope you have not ruined yourself . . ." and on and on until Samantha yawned in her friend's face. "Well?" asked Mary. "Have you nothing to say?"

"You have not allowed me room for a single word, have you?" asked Samantha.

Mary flushed. "Now I have. Did you ruin yourself—and me, too, of course—by waltzing without permission?"

"Do you truly think Lord Dalreath would have allowed that to happen?" asked Samantha softly. "Your wonderful, thoughtful, sensitive Dalreath?"

Mary turned pale. "Don't tease me. You know he . . . I . . ." She burst into tears. "Are you ruined? *Are* you?"

"Of course not. I happened to be exchanging civilities with Lady Jersey when Dalreath approached to ask for his dance. She suggested I might like to waltz. Neither his lordship nor I had a thing to do with it, but I assure you, we did have the permission of a patroness."

"Oh. Well. And it was her *ladyship's* notion—" Which proved to Mary's satisfaction that it was not Dalreath's idea. "—so in *that* case . . ."

"May I go to sleep now?" asked Samantha politely. She had discovered that having Mary underfoot all the time was more than a trifle wearing. It was not that she did not love her friend—she did. But she could not help but wish they had separate rooms. Still another disadvantage to being in town was the lack of sufficient rooms, especially bedrooms, in most town houses.

"How can you possibly sleep?" she was asked—and dozed off while Mary prattled on merrily about all her conquests, what so-and-so had said to her and what she had said to so-and-so and, asleep, missed hearing it when Mary, eying her friend to be certain she *was* asleep, let it slip that she had revealed that Samantha was a witch.

"Mother, I assure you, I never once mentioned it to a soul."

"Then, Lord Dalreath? You revealed it?" asked Lady Forsythe turning to the bearer of bad news.

"I did not," said his lordship, frowning. He stared over Mary's shoulder rather than at her. "I have been doing my best to laugh the gossip into nothingness, but I fear it has not sufficed."

"Then how could it possibly—" Her ladyship turned toward Mary, who blushed rosily. "You," she said. "Mary, how could you?"

"I . . . I . . ."

"Mary wouldn't," said Samantha. "She knew I did not want my witchy ways bruited around the *ton*."

"I . . . I . . ." Mary flicked a look toward Lord Dalreath, who still looked at nothing at all. She breathed a sigh of relief when she realized he would not tattle. "Of course I know that," she said.

Lady Forsythe grimaced. "Who, then? Have we neighbors other than yourself in town just now? Could someone perhaps have written the word to someone here and it have got around that way? Or . . . no, I cannot think how it could have happened."

Mary cast another quick glance toward his lordship, saw disappointment in his expression, and almost found the courage to admit her error—but not quite. Mary was afraid she'd be sent home if it were discovered she was the source of the gossip about Sammy. *Dear Sammy,* she thought fondly, aware her friend had guessed, but that she, too, would not give her away.

"I suppose the best we can do is as you've already begun to do, my lord," said her ladyship. "We, too, must simply laugh it off as nonsense."

"After all," said Dalreath silkily, "who in their right mind believes witches exist?"

"Exactly," said her ladyship, but avoided her daughter's lifted eyebrows and steady gaze.

When it became clear no more would be said, Samantha smiled. "If things become too difficult," she said, a sly note creeping into her voice, "we can always go home, which is where I would prefer to be in any case."

"Sammy!"

"Yes, Mary?" asked Samantha, and her voice was very nearly as smooth as Lord Dalreath's had been only moment's earlier.

"You cannot want to go home." Panic made Mary a trifle shrill. "You know . . ." She flicked still another look toward his lordship.

"Do I? I wonder," said Samantha.

"What do you wonder?"

"Shall I," asked Samantha in a voice that, this time, must be called sly, "read your tea leaves?" She stretched her hand toward Mary's empty cup.

Mary glanced toward Lord Dalreath and saw him watching her, frowning slightly. She attempted to laugh, but it sounded quite false even in her own ears, so she stopped abruptly. "Oh, no. It is nothing but nonsense, as Lord Dalreath says. Parlor games. I do not wish you to put yourself out," she added and, seeing Samantha's expression, looked just a trifle frightened.

"Then we will not," said Samantha after a long moment and Mary breathed again.

That is, she breathed easily until she noticed Samantha

picking up her used teacup some minutes later and glancing into it. She was a bundle of nerves until she managed to corner her friend. "What did you see?" she almost hissed.

"The usual. What I've always seen. A long marriage with several children and grandchildren in due course."

Mary relaxed. "That's all right then. Oh, he is so wonderful," she breathed. "How could I not be happy?"

Samantha's eyes narrowed. *I did not say you would be happy,* she thought. She was very slightly soothed by her next thought: *On the other hand, I did not see great unhappiness, either.* She turned away. Something else she had not seen, *could* not see, was the name of Mary's husband, so, just perhaps, it would *not* be his lordship but someone else entirely?

Samantha berated herself for wishful thinking. If his lordship did not soon begin paying her friend more particular attention, Mary would once again demand that love potion—and then what? Samantha was not happy with the notion. Worse, she did not wish his lordship to be *tricked* into loving her friend—not when, more and more, she rather hoped he might find love for *herself* in his heart.

But that was truly nonsense. Who was she that such an eligible leader of the *ton* would look her way? Besides, how could she be so wicked as to hope to attract the man her best friend so badly wanted? That was *not* a proper thought. It was not *nice* to hope to cut Mary out. Samantha did her best to hide a sigh.

"What is it?" asked Dalreath softly, glancing to where Lady Forsythe and Mary were discussing decorations for the girls' ball, which was to be held in a hired ballroom.

It was not what Lady Forsythe had wanted and something she deeply regretted. Her primary irritation was that it had taken her so long to convince Lord Forsythe of the necessity of coming to London that it had been too late to hire a house with a proper ballroom. She would never be so cheeseparing as to throw together the two salons and pretend they were a ballroom, so not only was the girls' introduction to have no particular cachet as to *where* it was held, but it would also be held rather *later* than her ladyship liked, and for no better reason than that Forsythe had balked at coming to London so there had been no ballroom available for rent when she wanted it, because all favorable dates for presentation balls were already taken.

Poor Lord Forsythe had already been made aware he would spend an uncomfortable few years, his dilatory behavior thrown in his face every time the two had the slightest disagreement.

"You do not answer," continued Lord Dalreath. "What is it?" he repeated his question.

"What is what?" asked Samantha. She searched her mind for a response that had nothing to do with her thoughts.

"You sighed."

"I had hoped no one would notice," retorted Samantha softly but spiritedly.

"You would suggest I am ungentlemanly to refer to it— but I wish to know."

She stared at him and saw a warm look in his eyes that made her heart pound. *Is there hope?* she asked herself. And then shook her head.

"I don't wish to know?" he asked, trying for a light note.

"You may wish it," she said when she'd managed to control her rampaging thoughts, "but you'll not have the wish fulfilled."

"Why will you not answer me?"

A mischievous smile touched the corners of Lady Samantha's mouth. "Because, with all this banter, I have forgotten. Should I thank you for lifting my spirits?"

"I do not want your *thanks*," he said, a trifle grim, and turned to the others, making rather terse good-byes before leaving the room without another glance in Lady Samantha's direction

Then, two days later, a friend from Lady Forsythe's own presentation days arrived at an unconscionably early hour of the morning. Lady Forsythe was still in her undress, wearing an old and comfortable sack gown and her hair down around her shoulders. She was, as might be expected, duly annoyed.

"My dear Cecily!" she said. "What can have happened that you arrive on my doorstep at such an hour?" As she spoke, she swept into the salon into which their butler had shown the visitor.

"My dear!" gushed Lady Cecily. "I have just heard the news! Oh! It is so *wonderful!*"

Lady Forsythe's forced smile of welcome faded. Surely one of the girls had not become engaged and she unaware of it! "What is wonderful?"

"That your daughter is a witch, of course."

"Nonsense," said her ladyship firmly.

"No, no. I have it on the best of authority . . ." Lady Cecily's eyes widened. Then her expression turned morose. "Not?" she asked.

"No, of course not," insisted Lady Forsythe.

"But everyone is saying . . ."

"I do not know how these rumors get started," fumed her ladyship.

Lady Cecily's eyes narrowed, and she turned her head slightly to the side, her eyes never leaving Lady Forsythe's face. "But she is the seventh daughter of a seventh daughter," she reminded Lady Forsythe—as if that poor beleaguered woman had not enough to deal with, with all the other visitors who had, curiosity impelling them, visited since Mary's faux pas. Not that her ladyship was aware Mary was the culprit.

"So?"

"Everyone knows the seventh daughter of a seventh daughter is born a witch."

"Then everyone knows more than I do," said her ladyship with something approaching a snarl.

"Oh, Amelia, you are such a jokesmith!" Lady Cecily laughed lightly and then, her eyes narrowing still further, said in a firm voice, "I want her to read tea leaves at my costume ball." She smiled tightly. "Such a coup!"

"No."

There was a brief silence while the two woman attempted to outstare each other. Then, turning slightly away, Lady Cecily said, "Amelia, do you happen to recall an evening at Vauxhall Gardens—oh, perhaps ten years ago?"

"You wouldn't."

Lady Cecily's chin rose a notch. "The competition among London hostesses is fierce, Amelia, and it is known I have ambitions to be counted among the very best. I will do whatever is necessary to assure that I hold the ball of the Season!"

Lady Forsythe twisted her hands in her lap. "You *know* I had had too much to drink. In fact, now I think of it, I am not quite certain but what *you* had a hand in helping me to climb a trifle up into the altitudes."

"Did I?" Cecily pretended to consider. "Perhaps I did. John was so . . . infatuated with you it made me cry to listen to his pain, his hopes, his fears, his threats to do himself an injury . . ."

"Don't attempt to excuse yourself. Your brother was a gazetted rake, dangerous to most any woman, and certainly not to be trusted with one who had been allowed a trifle more wine than she should indulge in."

"But you did indulge and, as I recall, John appeared quite pleased when you returned to our booth after that interesting absence."

"Cecily, why did I ever like you?"

"You still do," countered her ladyship. "You are merely irritated that I have the upper hand. As I recall, you, too, appeared quite pleased."

Lady Forsythe bit her lip. "Cecily, I *cannot* promise that Samantha will cooperate. She has a mind of her own, is very stubborn, and does not *like* to be thought a witch. She will rarely display her, er, talents just because others wish her to do so."

"I am certain that if anyone can convince her, that person is her mother." Cecily rose to her feet. "You will do your *best,* of course." She smiled a tight knowing smile—one that said a great deal more than mere words. "I will expect word later today that she has agreed."

The door closed behind Lady Cynthia, and Lady Forsythe groaned softly.

"I presume," said Samantha, a bite to her tone, "that her fine ladyship can cause you harm if she talks about that evening ten years ago?" She rose to her feet and walked around the high-backed chair in which she'd been sitting and reading when Lady Cecily was shown in. Samantha had never particularly liked her mother's friend and had, reprehensibly, stayed hidden.

"I might have known you'd be where you were not wanted," muttered her mother, two spots of color high in her cheeks.

"Perhaps it is just as well. You will not have to scramble for reasons why I should oblige Lady Cecily. I think, for a tiny piece of revenge, you should wait just as long as you dare before you tell her that I have agreed. And I think you should also tell her that, except that I will dress up as a gypsy and sit in whatever sort of gypsy tent she provides, I agree on one condition only: that she does *not* tell anyone who I am. The family will not, of course, accept an invitation to her ball. It is not at *all* the thing for girls just out to attend costume balls, is it?"

"You may moderate your tone, Samantha. I will certainly tell her you will not oblige her if there is any chance your name will be bandied about—although such things have a way of getting around, willy-nilly." Her ladyship's high color faded. "Thank you for agreeing, child," she added in a far more subdued tone. "I admit I was foolish that evening. I would be devastated if your father were ever to hear of it."

"He would be hurt, would he not?"

"Yes." Her mother headed for the door. "We will never again discuss this," she said, her firm tone indicating she had returned to normal.

Samantha nodded. She knew that tone.

* * *

"Not attend the costume ball? But you know you would enjoy it." James Morrison stared at his cousin. "You always enjoy costume balls!"

"Not this one."

"Why?"

"Because a certain young lady of my acquaintance will not be in attendance, of course."

James relaxed. "I see. Then where *will* she be? What invitation *have* we accepted in place of Lady Cecily's?" He glanced with just a touch of regret at the costume he had painstakingly planned and ordered made up for himself.

"Another invitation? None. Lady Forsythe has decreed a quiet evening at home. She claims the girls have been trotting too hard and will not be in looks if they haven't an evening's rest. Actually, with Lady Cecily holding her ball that evening, there isn't another hostess of note who will attempt to compete, so I suppose you and I will . . . oh, I don't know. Is there a play you wish to see?"

"No." James sighed, his eyes on the costume. It was a glorious notion. There would be no other like it at the ball.

"Then perhaps we can spend the evening at one of our clubs?"

"No." James turned his eyes from the jewel-toned glory spread across his bed. He looked at his cousin. "No, I will attend the ball without you if you do not mean to go."

"Why?" asked Rath, curious.

James went to the bed and picked up the heavy silk shirt, bright red, with overlarge sleeves. He turned, holding it against himself. "Voilà! A pirate!"

"It is well made," said Rath tactfully.

"There will be no other like it."

"There are bound to be a dozen pirates."

"But not like me. You see, I have found a real parrot to sit on my shoulder!"

Rath repressed a smile. "A well-trained parrot?"

"He talks a treat. Says all sorts of things," said James, nodding.

"I wasn't thinking of his *talking,*" muttered Rath. "You really want to go?"

James nodded, casting a hopeful look toward his cousin. "Very well."

"But what will you do for a costume?" asked James, suddenly worried. "It is too late to order one made for you."

"I think I've still that Rom costume from last year. No one knew me in it then. Or no one who would give me away, at least."

"A gypsy?" James frowned. "I was out of town last year, was I not, but I can see you as a gypsy. If you rumple your unruly hair and add an earring to one ear and darken your skin . . ."

"I've still got the dye I used last year, but I'll not try *that* again. I had to leave town for weeks, if you recall. The stuff would *not* wash off."

"So what will you do?"

"I'll think of something . . ."

Samantha looked at herself in the mirror. She had finished with the makeup and now held a false wart on the end of her finger. She tried it on her nose, on her chin . . . and finally attached it not far from her mouth, a little to the left and down a trifle. She turned. "There. Do I look like myself?" she asked Mary.

"Not at all," said Mary, just a trifle awestruck at how *unlike* her friend this gypsy creature looked. "What if it will not wash off properly?"

Samantha turned back to the mirror and adjusted the headscarf. "I practiced. It washes off. Not easily, but it won't stain me permanently." She shook out her skirts and wondered if she truly dared go into public showing quite so much ankle. She stared at her reflection and then frowned. Something wasn't quite right.

"You will need other slippers, Sam. Those are far too new to match your rags!"

"Slippers. That is it." Samantha kicked them off. "There. Now the only problem is that my feet are entirely too clean." She considered and then, grinning, she picked up two of the oily cosmetic sticks and put them in her pocket.

"Sam! You would go barefoot? You cannot!"

"Can I not? But I am only a poor old gypsy hired for the evening for a few pence and some food. Am I not?"

"You will not go without shoes!"

Samantha chuckled. "Not to and from," she agreed, "but while I sit in the tent Lady Cecily means to provide?" Lady Samantha grinned. "I most certainly will. Anyone with the least suspicion of my identity will reconsider when they see I am not wearing shoes and that my feet are so very dirty!"

Lady Samantha, wrapped from head to toe in an old, oversized caped coat belonging to her father, arrived at the party through a gate in the back garden to Lady Cecily's mansion. As arranged, the gate had been left unlocked so that her mother's footman, an older man who had been in the Forsythes' employ since he was a boy, could hold it open for Samantha. He followed her up the path to a door opened for them by Lady Cecily herself.

Her ladyship very nearly pulled Samantha through the door, telling the footman that she herself would see that her ladyship got home safely come morning. Then she shut the door in his face. She leaned back against it and looked Samantha up and down.

"Excellent," she gloated. "Truly, you look the part."

"No one is to know who I am," said Samantha. She wasn't happy when spots of color appeared in Lady Cecily's cheeks and her ladyship would not meet Samantha's steady gaze. Samantha reached for the doorknob.

"No! I have told no one."

Samantha eyed her. "It is merely that you mean to do so."

The color deepened. "Well, how will anyone know what a coup I have achieved if I tell no one at all?"

"I am unlikely to reveal to anyone the whole truth of their future. You'll not find anyone marveling at how good a prognosticator I am."

"But . . ."

Before her ladyship could finish, Samantha asked, "Do you truly wish me to inform some one of your guests his son will engage in a duel on the morrow, or another that I see a long miserable illness and death in his future?"

Lady Cecily blanched. "Oh, but surely . . ."

Samantha sighed "You see why I hate doing this? Why I wished to refuse? Do you think I *enjoy* foreseeing disaster in someone's life?"

"Oh, dear."

"I am quite willing to return home at once."

But Samantha had overplayed her hand. Her ladyship's mouth formed a hard line. "No. I have promised a tea leaf reader, and a reader I will have. Come along. You may wait in a small salon near where I have had the tent put up for your use."

"And you will tell no one who I am?"

Her ladyship sighed. "I'll not tell. If you do not mean to read proper futures—" She held up a hand when Samantha would have spoken. "—and I understand why you will not— in fact, I do not *wish* you to speak of ill fortune—then there is no reason to tell anyone who you are." She pouted. "But I did so look forward to the expression on Lady Fitzroy's face!"

As previously arranged, Samantha had arrived early. A tray of good things to eat awaited her in the sitting room and, after locking the door, she served herself. She took her plate along with one of the books also supplied for her use and seated herself before the fire. Nibbling at the party food, she lost herself in the story.

After reading the first half dozen pages, she tipped the book around, checked the spine, and muttered, "A Lady. Why are books always written by merely A Lady, especially when they are as good as this one?" She turned it back around and continued reading *Sense and Sensibility.*

A knock had Samantha looking up from the book, looking around, blinking and wondering for half a moment where she might be. Then, recollection returning, she reluctantly unlocked the door and Lady Cecily entered, asked if all was well and if Lady Samantha was ready.

Samantha was not and would never be ready, but she merely nodded.

Her ladyship glanced back into the hall and then beckoned. "Come. It's time," she whispered, excitement in her voice.

Samantha sighed. Carefully she closed the book and laid it aside. Then, sighing again, she removed her slippers and held them in her hand. "No one is ever happy with a reading," she said. "You do know that, do you not?"

"It makes no difference. They will still wish to hear what you have to say." Her ladyship beamed. "Besides, your mother told me you never lie, so there should be *some* interesting revelations!"

Samantha's eyes narrowed. "She is correct. I do not lie. However, I rarely tell the whole truth, either. You need not anticipate anything of great interest."

Lady Cecily pouted. Then her eyes narrowed at some thought and she smiled one of those small, untrustworthy smiles. "Oh well, you will see what you see, will you not?"

Samantha's eyes narrowed equally. "If you think that once the evening is over I am likely to tell you juicy bits I've told no one else, you may think again."

This time her ladyship's smile faded quickly. "We'll see," she said, and Samantha heard a threat.

"Perhaps you would care for a private reading, my lady," suggested Samantha softly.

The revealing eyes widened. "A *special* reading? For me alone? With, perhaps, more than you would normally say?"

"I could do that," said Samantha, nodding. "I warn you,

however, that I can rarely tell a person the sort of thing she *wishes* to hear."

Lady Cecily paused for half a moment and then opened her mouth to respond. She shut it. Then she tried again. The third time she opened her mouth, she had made her decision. "I will take my chances," she said. "What, after all, could you possibly see to my disadvantage? Since my life is perfection itself, what could be wrong with it?"

Samantha nodded. "On your head be it," she said.

"Now?" asked her ladyship brightly.

"Tomorrow. When I've rested."

"Rested?" Her ladyship chortled. "You are young and healthy. Why will you need rest?"

Samantha glared. "My lady, have you no conception of what you have asked of me? Of what powers I must call upon? Of how tiring it will be? How exhausting?"

"Fiddle. It is a game, nothing else."

"I hope you feel that way when I have given you your reading," said Samantha. She cast a wistful glance at the book and then, for the third time, sighed. "Let us go. Perhaps I will be lucky and there will be nothing to fear . . ."

"Fear?" asked Lady Cecily, once again slightly apprehensive.

"Do you think I dislike doing this merely to be contrary?" Samantha's lips pressed into a fine line. "Oh, the devil take it! You've no understanding and no wish to understand. Let us go."

"Understand? I understand very well. You are a mere child who would dramatize yourself." Lady Cecily glared. "Come along now and behave yourself."

Samantha went—but whether she behaved or not was a question that would be decided by what the evening brought.

The tent was made up of brightly colored silks. Inside was a low table and lots of cushions. Samantha hid her shoes under one of them, took out her dark cosmetics and rubbed them over her feet, and then settled herself to await her first customer. There were lamps turned low hanging from the tent roof so that she was not without light, but it was very dim.

Too dim? She hoped it would be bright enough for her work.

She felt the teapot and nodded. It was quite hot and was sitting on a trivet above a small fat candle so that it would stay hot. She had been told that, whenever she needed more, she was to set the teapot outside the tent entry and another would be put in its place.

She was ready. Or as ready as she could ever be when faced with what the next hours would bring. She hoped she would not become overtired. All too often when doing a witch's work, she found herself growing weary and had wondered if this was normal or if it was lack of practice and would be easier if she did it more often . . . but, since she could not bring herself to test that latter thought, she assumed she would never know.

Samantha truly did not like drawing on her talents as a witch!

The evening progressed just as she'd foreseen—and she had required no tea leaf reading to make *that* particular prediction. For the young girls who entered her tent, she had only good things to say. Most readings *were* good, in the sense that there was nothing particularly bad to report in the near future. But when an older woman or gentleman entered her tent, she found herself searching for the positive and trying very hard to ignore what was not.

Only once did she lift her head quickly to look at the sitter. Her gaze met wise old eyes. It was an elderly lady, who smiled, although it was not a particularly pleasant smile. "Well, my child? Will you not tell me what you see?" She held up her hand when Samantha would have spoken. "The *truth? Just* as you see it."

Samantha's gaze was held firmly. Finally, reluctantly, she nodded. "It is not good, my lady."

"No. I do not expect it to be good. Can you see how . . . soon?"

"A week. Perhaps less."

A regal nod of the head and the old eyes closed tightly. "We have had over fifty years together. I should not repine."

"Of course you should!" said Samantha.

Her tone drew a brief chuckle from the elderly lady. "It is true then?" she asked.

"That I am a witch?" asked Samantha.

"Yes. You use the accents of a countrywoman when talking to everyone else. Why have you allowed me to know you?"

"You would not have been fooled."

"No, but it surprises me you did not try."

"Would *you* have done so in my place?"

Another soft chuckle. "Then you know?"

"Do we not always know one another?" retorted Samantha.

The elderly lady nodded. "Oh, yes. When we have lived a bit of life. You are young to have discovered that particular ability."

"Thank you."

"I don't know that it was a compliment."

The elderly woman rose, with difficulty, to her feet. She stared down at Samantha, her eyes sad. "I had hoped you would give me a different reading."

Samantha shook her head. "You wanted the truth. You merely hoped my truth was different from that you had seen for yourself."

"You are perceptive, child. Shall I read your leaves?"

Samantha straightened. She'd have backed away if it had been possible, but she was seated on a low stool and it was not. "No," she said in an abrupt tone. "No, I've no desire to see my future," she added in an apologetic voice.

The woman nodded. "Very sensible. I wish you great happiness, child." She smiled a truly glorious smile and added, "Quite as much as I have known."

"Then, if what I saw of your past is true, I would be a very lucky woman indeed. Thank you."

The elderly woman lifted the tent flap high rather than

ducking under it as most did, and Samantha caught a glimpse of two well-known gentlemen. "No," she muttered. "Please, no . . ."

She hadn't a notion if it was a prayer or something else, but whatever, her request was not granted. James Morrison pushed at the flap and ducked in, peering around in the dimness. "Lady Cecily managed quite a good atmosphere, did she not?" he asked as he settled himself across from Samantha, who kept her head ducked low, her outrageously messed hair drawn partially across her forehead and face.

"Well, here we are," said James nervously. "Er, what do I do?"

Samantha lifted a clean cup and saucer to the table before her. She picked up the teapot and swirled it, swinging it slowly in three circles above the cup. Then she poured. And, silently, offered it to James.

"I'm to drink it?"

"First," she said softly in the voice as unlike her own as she could make it, "you swirl the cup as I did the pot." As he did so she added, "And then you drink, quickly, and, when you finish, turn the cup over into the saucer."

"It is all such nonsense, is it not?" he asked as he awkwardly turned the cup in wide circles. She didn't respond and he followed the rest of her directions.

Samantha pulled cup and saucer nearer. She lifted the cup and noted that two leaves had fallen into the saucer. She stared at them. Then she turned the cup right side up and stared down into it. At one point she glanced at James, a quick wondering look, but then she shook her head.

"Well, madam? Do you see anything of interest?" asked James.

"There is a strong possibility you will wed before summer's leaves turn brown and fall to earth," she whispered. "I see sons in your future, one of whom will make you very proud, one of whom will make you very happy, and one of whom will hold your heart for worry of him."

James laughed awkwardly. "Well, a good thing I'm to

wed, is it not? Wouldn't want all those sons if I didn't have a wife! Not that I will, of course. All nonsense."

She pursed her lips.

"Of course it is nonsense." There was a touch of bluster in his tone. "Not about to wed anyone. No intention of wedding. Ever."

"I know," she said.

He cast her a startled look. "You do?"

She nodded.

"Oh." He shifted uncomfortably on the stool across from hers. "Well . . . if that is all?"

"Is that not enough?"

"Don't suppose you saw when I'll die and where?" he asked, attempting a jesting tone that did not quite come across as it was supposed to do.

She stilled. "I never give that information to anyone," she said very softly. "No one *really* wishes to know."

He stared down at her. Finally, baffled, he shrugged and left the tent.

Samantha braced herself. She hated that she had promised Mary to tell Lord Dalreath enough so he would believe himself fated to wed soon and to wed Mary in particular.

Lord Dalreath seated himself with easy grace. "Do I cross your palm with silver?" he asked lightly.

"My palm has been crossed for all," said Samantha in her false voice. "You will swirl your cup thrice before drinking," she said as she swirled the pot and poured. "You will turn your cup over and pass it back."

Without looking up, Samantha pushed cup and saucer across the table. She didn't watch as he turned the cup or as he drank, but she tipped her eyes up and watched him set his upside-down cup in his saucer and, fascinated as a bird facing a snake, she watched it as he pushed it toward her.

Samantha could not have said why she hesitated. Oh, she knew what she did not want to *do*, which was to give him a false reading, but why would she not wish to see his real future? Why did it bother her to lift the cup, look into it, read what was there and then . . . well, it was obvious, the rest of it. She had promised to lie to him, and lies were bad.

"Well?" he asked gently.

Samantha forced herself to look. Nothing in the saucer. That was good. And in the cup?

She stilled, her eyes widening. "This . . ." she began before she recalled she was to change her voice to that of a countrywoman . . . "cannot be. What has happened here?"

"That is what you are to tell me."

Samantha raised horrified eyes to meet his steady, faintly ironic gaze. His eyebrows arched and, feeling a blush climb her cheeks, she looked down. *At least,* she thought, *he'll not see the blush for the makeup.*

Dalreath tapped the top of her head, but she continued to stare into the cup. "Well?" he asked.

Finally she peered up at him, raising only her eyes, not her head. His brow quirked and he grinned a knowing grin.

Samantha looked back down. Surely she was mistaken. The leaves, however, continued to read exactly as they had done the first time. If what she saw was true, then Mary . . .

"Mary," she mouthed silently, having up to that moment had her friend and her promise to that friend driven from her mind. Under no circumstances could she reveal what she saw. Not *exactly* what she saw. Not when she'd made that promise to Mary.

"You are supposed to tell me what you see," he said gently, breaking into her thoughts.

Samantha drew in a deep breath. "You love a small woman," she said. "Someone hailing from near your estate."

"How nice for me," he said and chuckled softly.

Samantha didn't allow herself to wonder at it. She wanted this done and him gone. "She is blonde."

"She is not," he retorted.

Samantha, still staring into the cup, blinked.

Rath stared down at the bent head and smiled a warm sort of smile, one that would have amazed Samantha no end if she'd seen it. It seemed to him a very long while ago that he'd fallen in love with his Sam.

And I suppose, he mused, *I assumed it was years yet before I need think about wooing her, wedding her, and bedding her. Ah, but the years have passed more quickly than I thought!*

Rath considered his options even as he laughed quietly and exited the tent.

Samantha lifted her head and stared after him—and, once he moved farther away, she moved as well, dropping the entrance cover over the opening. Using a slit at the back that her ladyship had shown her, Samantha escaped through it and through a door hidden behind the tent.

And then she paced—perhaps one might say stalked—the room beyond the door. What she had seen in the cup roused such contradictory emotions she could not make a single thought stand still long enough to examine it. So much was revealed. He *did* mean to wed. He would wed *soon.* And he *would* wed a neighbor. But—something, some tension, shattered at the memory of his comment and it seemed as if she could breathe again—*that neighbor was not blonde!*

There was what she'd seen and there was his comment. A wedding. To a neighbor. But not a blonde? What did it mean? What could he have meant? Samantha's thoughts swirled and then jumped as another thought pricked her emotions. He'd not been at all shocked or surprised by her words. He had not objected—as had his cousin—to the notion he would wed. That in itself was rare among the male of the species. When told he was about to settle down to married life, most men denied it—but Dalreath had not!

Samantha paced back and forth, from one side of the room to the other and back again and then began again and still again—until Lady Cecily, frowning, arrived.

"What are you doing? Why are you not in the tent? Everyone is asking for you."

"I warned you that what I do tires me. I had to stop for a

time." Samantha hoped her ladyship would accept her excuse and not pursue the question.

Lady Cecily tipped her head slightly. "Tired? And yet you are pacing?"

"It is a change, and the tired feeling is in my head and emotions. Perhaps you have never had that problem?" Samantha realized her tone had, perhaps, not been quite all it should have been. She glanced at Lady Cecily and away.

Her ladyship was silent so long that Samantha, finally, looked up again. She lifted her chin at what she saw and Lady Cecily, who had obviously been about to say something nasty, which both would have regretted, relaxed.

"Come along," said her ladyship. "You have rested long enough."

Samantha, reluctantly, went.

That night, when she finally fell into the bed her ladyship provided her, she slipped so deeply into the arms of Morpheus that the next morning the maid had to try twice in order to rouse her sufficiently so she could dress and go home.

And once home, Samantha returned to bed and to sleep and slept the rest of the day—until suddenly, abruptly, she awakened. She stilled, her eyes closed. What was it? What had roused her? She cracked open one eye the tiniest bit.

Mary stood beside the bed, silently crying. While Samantha secretly watched, the girl just stood there, obviously impatient, but obviously not doing anything which would wake the sleeper. Samantha wondered what it was that had brought her from her sleep. It was not the crying, she was certain, which was of the sort that made no sound. And she was very nearly certain Mary had not touched her, so . . .

"Oh, no. Not again," she muttered.

"What? What? Oh, Sammy, what did you *do?*" asked Mary and began sobbing more loudly. "Why did you forget your promise?"

"I refuse," muttered Samantha, ignoring her friend, who continued to rant. "I will not have it. I cannot bear it . . ."

"But you must! Nothing else has worked," insisted Mary.

"No. It stopped. It must stop again. I will not let it happen all over again . . ."

"Again?" squeaked Mary. "But you haven't done it at all!"

"Nonsense. Obviously I did it." When Mary looked confused, Samantha added, "Something inside me woke me. There was a time a few years ago when the least sort of emotion anywhere near me would echo through me, oftentimes very loudly. Sometimes it was a good emotion, but more often it was pain or anger or—but it stopped. I'll not have it start again, that is all. What do *you* think I am talking about?"

"I don't understand a word you are saying and haven't a notion as to what you refer, but *I* am speaking of Lord Dalreath. What did you *do?* He won't even talk to me!"

Samantha rubbed her eyes. "Won't talk to you? But that must be nonsense. He is a gentleman. He would not ignore you."

"It is *worse*. He snubbed me. The cut direct!"

Samantha blinked. She was still half asleep and could not understand what her friend meant. "Dalreath? Cut you?"

Mary nodded and scrubbed at the tears still streaking down her cheeks. "We were walking along Piccadilly, my maid and I—oh, Samantha, I was wearing that new bonnet, the one . . ." She saw her friend frown and caught herself. "He was driving the other way and he *snubbed* me!"

"Mary, did he *see* you?"

"I'm sure he did." Mary looked bewildered. "How could he not have done?"

Samantha stared at her friend. "He was driving?"

Mary nodded, new tears leaving more damp tracks, which, impatiently, she rubbed away.

"There was traffic?"

"It was *Piccadilly*," said Mary, scorn for a moment interrupting the watering-pot shower of tears.

"It was Piccadilly and busy as it is always busy and you ask how he cannot have seen you?"

Mary's shoulders fell from their hunched position. She thought about it. "Oh."

"There was no opportunity for him to speak with you."

"No."

"He did not snub you, did he?"

Mary shook her head.

"Then why are you crying?"

"I thought . . ."

"What?"

"I thought he would come this morning." She scowled. "At least, assuming you told him . . ."

"I told him," said Samantha, and frowned, recalling the part of that little scene she most wished to understand. *Not a blonde, he said* . . . and then she forgot his enigmatic statement when she recalled that she had, for the first time in a very long time, experienced another person's pain. Mary's pain. Mary was truly in pain. Only if the pain were real would she have felt it to the extent that it would waken her from an exhausted sleep.

"Mary, do you love him so very much?" asked Samantha. She had not believed it—had not wanted to believe it?—had believed Mary merely infatuated with the idea of marriage. Especially marriage to a rich and personable peer.

"I must," said Mary, the tears once again spurting. "I was so unhappy until you explained why he ignor—no! Why he didn't see me this morning."

"Unhappy . . ."

But unhappy because she'd thought herself *deliberately* ignored, not because she thought her *one and only love* had ignored her?

Samantha wondered at herself. She was grasping at straws, as the expression went, and to what end? Surely she had not been so ridiculous as to fall in love with the man Mary wanted above all others. It would be outside of enough if that were the case . . . *but only if Mary truly loved the man!*

"No," she muttered.

"No—what?" asked Mary. "How can you say no when I have not yet asked you!"

"Haven't . . ."

Mary adopted a stubborn look. "You have to."

"Mary, are you making sense?"

"Of course I am. You have to do it."

Sam merely frowned.

"The *love potion,* Sam. I have to have it. Time is growing far too short. If he were in love with me, he would have known I was there. *Somehow* he would have *known.*"

Samantha wondered if Mary truly believed such nonsense.

"He would have seen me. He would not have driven right by without at least a wave and a smile."

"Mary . . ."

"Yes, I know. You insist they don't work. But they *do,* Sam. If they did not," she asked naively, "then why would anyone ever want one? Why would I ever have heard of such a thing?"

"Mary . . ."

"I know you say they always go wrong. But they *don't.* I'm sure they don't."

"You have to do it *exactly* right. You put the dose in his drink and then the last drops into your own, and the two of you have to drink at the exact same moment. And *something* always prevents one from doing exactly what one must at the exact instant it must be done in order for it to work. *It doesn't work,* Mary."

"I'll be careful. Very careful. Truly I will."

Samantha sighed. She yawned, wishing she had not been awakened so abruptly. Her mind felt fuzzy, and she knew she should not make a decision when feeling so odd.

"Sam? Please?"

Samantha yawned still more widely—but somewhere inside, unwanted, she felt the intensity of a new feeling flowing from her friend. It was a sensation of need.

"Say yes," offered Mary, "and I'll go away and you can

sleep some more. Although why you need to sleep when you haven't done anything . . ."

Samantha, thinking of the stresses and strains of the evening before, the funny sort of energy required to do what she'd been asked to do, growled softly.

"Why will you not?"

"Because when it all goes wrong you will blame me, that is why."

"I won't. I promise. But truly, Sam, nothing will go wrong!"

Samantha could take no more—neither the emotions flowing from Mary into herself, nor Mary's water-on-stone determination to get her way. "Oh, all right," she growled—and yawned again. "Now do go away."

"Oh, Samantha, you are the most wonderful friend!"

"Just keep on thinking that when the potion does its usual mischievous thing," grumbled Samantha.

"Oh, go back to sleep. Maybe you won't be so pessimistic when you are feeling more the thing."

"Don't expect me to change. I have said the same thing for years, so why would I tell a different story now?"

"But you'll do it?" demanded Mary.

"I said I would," said Samantha and turned her back on her friend, pulling the coverlet high up around her ears.

And she did do it. But not at once. Not the instant she arose and Mary pounced on her, wanting her to go immediately to the kitchens, where she could make up the dose. Samantha, insisting secrecy was a necessity, waited for a night when her mother left for an evening of cards, leaving the girls to go to bed early to recoup their looks—although Mary rather pettishly insisted that the previous two late nights in a row were not enough to do *her* looks any harm.

Samantha was waiting for her mother's departure when Lady Cecily arrived for her private reading. Lady Sam, called to the small salon, found the lady pacing the floor. Unobserved herself, Samantha eyed her ladyship and—unwanted—again was privy to another person's emotions. There was pain. There was a feeling of bewilderment. There was an odd mixture of fear and anger. Samantha sighed softly, dreading what she might see in the tea leaves of a lady so upset as this one was revealed to be.

The sigh, soft as it was, caught Lady Cecily's attention and she swung around, the tiny train at the back of her gown ruffling across the floor. "Lady Samantha," said Lady Cecily, smiling overly brightly. "As you see," she continued, admitting to her agitation, "I am much in need of your reading." She frowned, her chin jutting slightly. "And it is to be a true reading. Do you understand? I'll not have you making up bits or leaving pieces out. I want the truth."

"My lady," said Samantha softly, "I thought you did not believe. You said it is merely a pastime, did you not? A game. A . . ."

Lady Cecily flushed hotly. Her head rose. "I lied. I have always believed. There was an old lady in my village where I grew up. She knew. She *always* knew . . ." Cecily's skin paled and her hand rose to her throat. "She told me . . ."

"Yes?" asked Samantha when her ladyship's voice trailed off.

Cecily shook her head. "No. I'll give you no hints. You are young. You cannot have had a great deal of experience. If I give you the least hint, then you will use that to see what I expect you to see, and I'll not have it!"

Her voice rose on the last, and Samantha muttered some soothing words, a phrase her governess had taught her. Lady Cecily instantly relaxed. "If you are certain?" asked Samantha. "Very often it is better *not* to know. Sometimes I think a person brings about what happens merely because he has been told it will and if he had not expected it, he might have avoided it."

"Surely knowing what to expect makes one better able to avoid a thing!"

Samantha nodded. *"Sometimes* it works that way—if the reading is ambiguous."

Cecily flounced around, her back to Samantha. After a moment she turned again to face her. "Order the tea. I will drink."

Samantha bit her lip, wondering if there was any way out. Then, shrugging, she went to the door. Her favorite footman stood without, awaiting orders, and she asked him to bring up the tray she'd ordered the moment she knew of Lady Cecily's arrival.

"It is not too late," she told her visitor once the door was shut behind the footman and the teapot gently steaming on the low table set between a pair of sofas placed to face each other. She touched the pot, the heat moving into her palm, up her arm, and into her center. *These leaves will give a clear reading,* she thought—and wished very much they would not.

"Pour."

"If you insist."

"I insist."

Samantha closed her eyes and said a brief prayer. She hated giving bad news to anyone, even someone as unpleasant as Lady Cecily. "Very well," she said and, after swirling the pot three times, poured. She asked Lady Cecily to turn the cup three times and to drink quickly, turning her cup over in her saucer when she'd finished.

Lady Cecily did as requested and, after only the briefest of hesitations, handed the cup and saucer back to Samantha.

Samantha set them down in front of her and bent over them. She had discovered long years earlier that hiding her face as she first looked into the cup was a wise move, since she could not always control her first reaction to what she saw. "There is some bad and some good," she said.

"Tell me the worst first."

"He is gone."

There was silence for a long moment. "Gone . . . dead?"

"No. Merely gone. He will not return." Samantha had heard no word that her ladyship's husband had left her . . . and then she kicked herself for her naïveté. The man in question was not her husband, of course.

"Thank God," breathed her ladyship, falling back against the cushions. "Not dead." After a moment, she asked, "Is that all the bad?"

"It appears to be the worst. There is something odd about the child you bear."

Her ladyship sat up, obviously startled. Her hand went to her stomach. "Child?"

Samantha nodded. "A girl child."

Lady Cecily relaxed. "A girl. Good."

Samantha guessed it was not her husband's, but his lordship was not likely to deny a girl child as he might a boy who might, even if there were older boys, become his heir.

"What else?"

Samantha hid a grimace. It was not a request, but a demand, and she did not like demands. "You will travel. Soon. But not where you wish to go."

"I don't *wish* to go anywhere," said Lady Cecily harshly. "It is the middle of the Season!"

"Nevertheless, I see great turmoil. It is immediate. You will travel."

"Nonsense!"

Samantha shrugged.

"Is that all?"

"That is all the bad. I see love. Contentment. Even a degree of happiness. But not for some time. Perhaps years. It is neither certain nor soon."

It was her ladyship's turn to shrug. "What comes, comes. But—" A mulish look hardened Lady Cecily's features. "—I will not leave London before the end of the Season!"

"I am very sorry, but you will. There is no question."

Cecily rose to her feet. "I am warned. I will discover a way around it." She swept from the room.

Samantha leaned back and closed her eyes. She had not had to reveal the very worst of all. The child—something was very wrong with the child. Poor Lady Cecily.

But why, demanded Samantha, *must the child be pun-*

ished for her ladyship's sins? Her question remained unanswered—not that she had expected a response, of course.

Before leaving that evening, Lady Forsythe looked from one girl to the other. She shook her finger at Samantha, who lolled on the sofa in an exceedingly unladylike manner. "You will go to bed. Early," said her ladyship. She turned her glare on Mary. "An early night will harm neither of you," she said as she pulled a glove up over one elbow. She turned back to Samantha, a tiny frown between her brows. As she drew up the other glove, she said, "I am told Cecily was here just an hour ago. Why was I not informed?"

"She wanted a private reading," said Samantha and yawned.

"You don't do those."

"I did this time," said Sam a trifle grimly.

"Early to bed," said her ladyship firmly. "Your looks have suffered with all you've done. You need rest." She nodded and left the room.

"Why do we need rest when the Season passes by so quickly?" groused Mary. "I do not understand."

"You know there is nowhere special one might go tonight," said Samantha and yawned. "If we must rest, then tonight of all nights is one for resting."

Mary pouted. "I know. But it is two nights this week I have had to remain home. First it was the night of the Lady Cecily's costume ball, when you were allowed to go and stayed away the whole of the night. It isn't at all fair that I must pretend we were both at home so that no one will know you were not. You had all the fun, while I was bored to tears."

"Fun!" Samantha looked at her friend. Mary really and truly had no understanding of how tiring was her evening at Lady Cecily's. She sighed. "I only wish it had been fun." Mary gave her a disbelieving look and Samantha did not try, again, to explain the truth. She changed the subject. "Besides, you want that potion. That Mother is gone is a beginning, but we must wait until Cook has gone to bed. She was hired here in London and doesn't know me. She would never understand."

Mary giggled. "Word would be all over London that you are a witch."

Samantha gave Mary a straight look and Mary, recalling that she herself had let that particular cat out of the bag, had the grace to blush. But then spoiled it by blustering, "But no one *believes* it, Sam."

"And if they did believe you?"

"But they did not, so can you not forget that I spoke when I should not?"

"No, that is impossible," said Samantha firmly. Then she sighed when her friend looked abjectly sorry and, knowing Mary, very likely was. "What I can do is cease teasing you about it." She moved to a table where she had, earlier, set a closed basket. She set herself to sorting through her supply of herbs, checking each one, making certain that there was nothing *but* the herb she required among a particular bunch of dried leaves or, in some cases, entangled with a root.

"You didn't forget anything, did you?" asked Mary anxiously.

"No. Now you must be silent, Mary. My mind must be properly in tune with the ley lines." Samantha frowned.

"Ley lines? What are they?"

"Sources of power. They run through the earth from place to place. They are particularly strong at Forsythe Place, but here they are weaker than those I'm used to, and it is difficult. They are not nearly so easily tapped as at home. I hope all goes well."

"Will you know?"

"Yes, of course.

"But . . ."

"Shush."

"But will you be very careful to do it properly?"

"I have *told* you I will do it and having said I will, you should know that I will do it properly." Samantha dropped her hands and rolled her eyes. "Now, if you cannot keep silent you must go away."

Mary subsided, pouting. She opened her mouth to speak, met Samantha's glare, and sighed. Softly. And then fiddled with her ribbons, and then squirmed, and then sighed again, and, finally, whispering that she had better go to their room since it was difficult not to speak, she left Samantha in peace.

It was another hour before Samantha dared tiptoe down into the kitchen. The first time she peeked, the cook was rocking in a chair near the dying fire and humming a song. Lord Dalreath would have recognized it as an exceedingly bawdy tune, but Sam had no way of knowing that. She was merely irritated the woman had yet to go to bed.

Another trip to the kitchen half an hour later and she breathed a sigh of relief upon finding it empty. Moving from place to place quickly but quietly, she collected the equipment necessary to her work, stirred up the coals and added a few more that would catch while she did the weighing and grinding and mixing. And then, with the ingredients all laid out, the everyday sort of kitchen staples measured and waiting, she straightened and closed her eyes.

Sometimes it was difficult, finding that place inside, that center from which her powers flowed, and this was one of them. Only when all was finally right within did she begin the work without.

Much later everything was cleaned, put away, and the fire once again banked against going out. She looked around and, except for a mildly medicinal odor left over from grinding the herbs, no one would have known she'd been there. By morning even the scent would have dissipated and all would be well. She picked up the corked vial she'd laid on the table, looked around once more, nodded, and quickly left the room.

Mary would have her potion.

She would have it, yes, but Samantha, staring at it, wondered what would go wrong this time. Somewhere deep inside was the knowledge that the potion would do its work in an unexpected manner—but whether for good or evil, she could not determine.

"Almack's!" breathed Mary.

Samantha glanced at her friend's shining eyes and awestruck expression and hid a grimace behind the fan her mother had insisted she carry. A grimace which was, thanks to it, hidden from two of the starchiest of the patronesses who, standing near the door, looked down aristocratic noses at their entrance. She curtsied with her usual grace, received a wintery smile from Princess Esterhazy and a nod of approval from Countess Lieven, and, the proprieties attended to, the Forsythe party entered the long, low-ceilinged room.

"Where are they?" whispered Mary.

Lord Dalreath and his cousin had promised to arrive early but were nowhere in sight.

"Surely," fussed Marry, "they have not forgotten."

This time Samantha's grimace, barely hidden, was due to Mary's lack of understanding of a man's honor. The cousins had promised. Therefore they would come. And Mary would, somehow, do what she had come to do. The two men would arrive and, sometime in the evening, Mary would hand Dalreath a drink with the love potion poured into it. Samantha's heart fell all the way to her neat slippers, which, by the end of the evening's dancing, would likely be in shreds.

"What is it?" asked Mary. "Do you too think they have forgotten?"

"They will not forget," said Samantha. "Hush. Here come Lord Leigh-Martin and Lord Sothingham."

Mary's expression changed instantly from a frown to beaming smiles. She gracefully granted the men's requests for dances and turned toward Mr. Holden, who followed on their heels. Mary had not found herself quite the belle she was in their home region, but she never lacked partners at a ball.

Samantha absently agreed to dance after dance—except for the waltzes. Although she had been permitted by Lady Jersey to participate in the provocative dance, she had discovered, the one time she'd danced it, that she felt exceedingly odd while engaged in it. Held in Lord Dalreath's arms, feeling the warmth of him, whirling about the floor to a lilting rhythm . . . it was all very unsettling. Unlike most of her friends, she had decided it was *not* a dance she could enjoy.

When Lord Dalreath and Mr. Morrison approached, she was shocked to discover she'd no remaining dances. She had filled in names along the ivory sticks of her fan for all the contra- and country dances. Lord Dalreath gently removed the fan from her grasp, glanced at it, and grinned. Without asking, he wrote his name in for two of the waltzes and, shocking her, pretended to write along a third stick.

When she looked down, she realized he had tricked her, and when she met his eyes, she found them laughing at her. He tugged at the end of the closed fan and asked, "Shall I do it after all?"

She glared.

He pretended a soulful sigh and then, speaking softly so the others would not hear, asked, "Ah, but you will dance the waltz with no one else, so why should we not?"

"You are a rogue," she whispered. "And unkind to tease me so, putting me to the blush. You well know why you must not."

He tipped his head studying her features. "But you are not blushing."

"Am I not?" She was surprised. "I feel as if I am."

He chuckled, took Mary's fan and scribbled his name along one of the sticks and then, before either could say a word, he walked off, joining several of his cronies who were propping up the wall and doing their best to emulate Lord Byron's glowering look of ennui. Not that any of them would have done so if his lordship had been in attendance, but, unable to dance because of his clubfoot, Byron almost never made an appearance at Almack's.

"Let me see." Mary, made suspicious by Lord Dalreath's long conversation with her friend, slipped Samantha's fan from her relaxed grip. She stared. "No!"

"Not so loud!"

Mary glared.

"What is it?" whispered Samantha, wondering what she had done now.

"You gave him two dances and they are *waltzes.*"

"I didn't *give* him any. He took two."

The easy tears that Mary could produce very nearly on demand glistened in her eyes. "He only took one of mine. Another Roger de Coverley." She grimaced.

"But that is good," said Samantha, thinking quickly.

"How is it good?" Mary's damp glower dared Samantha to come up with an acceptable reason.

"Of course it is good. In the first place, you are very nearly the only young lady in London just now who can dance the whole thing faultlessly, even when the pace picks up at the end. In the second place, it is a thirst-making dance, and you will have the perfect excuse to demand he take you into the supper room for lemonade or orgeat."

Mary's frown gradually lightened. Then she smiled. "Samantha, I should never doubt you. You are always right."

"If you thought me always right, you'd throw that potion into that potted palm and forget the whole thing."

The stubborn look appeared that all who knew Mary dreaded. "I love him," she said in a soft but determined tone . . .

. . . but Samantha saw her friend's eyes flick toward James Morrison with a faintly wistful look in the soft gleam, and she wondered if Mary loved his lordship or if Mary was merely too stubborn to recognize that she had changed her mind as well as the object of her devotion. Her own gaze went toward Lord Dalreath's. She discovered he was looking at her in return, and this time she knew she blushed. She lowered her gaze to her fan.

The evening progressed as such evenings always do. Mary joined enthusiastically into every dance. Samantha played her part but, her mind on those waltzes his lordship had claimed, she was, she feared, a less than sparkling partner.

"My dance, I think," said Lord Dalreath.

Samantha found her heart beating more rapidly. It shouldn't. This was the man her friend meant to wed. The man for whom she had concocted a potion that would turn his heart and mind in Mary's direction. The man she had angered when she was only a child and then again, later, when almost a woman. The man she should hate for his hunting, for his long negligence of his estate and tenants. She sighed.

"Are you tired? Would you prefer to sit this out?"

Samantha heard what she was certain was a hopeful note in that and, perversely, decided to dance. And then, once in his arms, wished she had not.

"You are lovely," he whispered.

She cast a frowning look up into his face and then dropped her gaze to the beautifully tied glaringly white cravat that was framed by the deep midnight blue of his vest and the slightly lighter blue of his coat. "You shouldn't cast the hammer around so easily," she said. "Someone might get hurt."

"You?"

"Another."

He bent her elbow and, using one finger, forced her chin to rise. His steady gaze met and trapped hers. "My only concern is that I not hurt you," he said softly.

She felt the blood leaving her head. Why, oh why, had she made that potion for Mary?

"You do not respond. Does that mean you do not care?" he asked.

Was this the mischief? Would he drink and feel a change of heart? Find himself in love with Mary when he . . . when he what? What did his words imply? Did she dare to believe it was what she wished it to be?

"Sam, Lady Samantha, has—" His brows quirked into a quizzical look but there was a watchful expression in his eyes. "—the cat stolen your tongue?"

"I cannot answer you," she muttered, dropping her chin when he released it.

"Have I not made it clear to you how I feel about you?" he asked softly.

A vision of that tiny vial nestling in Mary's reticule filled Samantha's mind. "Now is not the time for this conversation!"

"Can you tell me a better time?"

"Tomorrow?" she asked flicking him a look. "By tomorrow . . ." She shook her head, took a huge breath, and let it out. She could not warn him. She dared not interfere. Determined to do what she must and do it with grace, she said, "If, on the morrow, you wish to continue this conversation, I will speak with you." She forced herself to meet his eyes.

His frowned. "What is it, Sam?" This time he did not correct himself and Samantha wondered if that was the way he thought of her.

"Tomorrow."

His lips compressed. "Very well. Tomorrow."

When it was time for their second waltz, Samantha disappeared into the lady's retiring room and did not come out until the music had ended. She could not bear to be so near to him knowing that after the next dance—Mary's Roger de Coverley—he would no longer wish to speak to her . . . at least not in the fashion he'd *implied* he wished to speak.

She maneuvered her partner so that they joined a set well beyond the one in which Mary and Dalreath danced. Twice she saw him looking at her, but the dance was too energetic to allow for either talk or much in the way of flirtation—especially between people in different sets! When the dance ended, she watched Mary speaking quickly, watched Dalreath offer his arm, watched them walk off toward the supper room.

Her heart heavy, she forced a smile for her next partner . . . and discovered it was James Morrison. She sighed softly.

The evening was not progressing well. Here she was with James while those not so subtle hints that Lord Dalreath just might be feeling for her what she wished he'd feel rang in her ears. She was with James and must give up all hope of his cousin, who was meant for her friend. Her friend, who just might have fallen, without knowing it, in love with James!

No, however one looked at it, it was not a good evening.

Mary accepted her glass and wondered how she was to introduce the potion into the two of them. Some friends of his lordship entered just then, and he set down his drink as they approached. Mary moved quickly, hiding what she did behind her skirts. It took only moments to pour the potion into his glass, drop the remaining dribble into her own, and then, turning a bright smile on his friends, hand him his glass.

But he merely stood there talking, holding it. Mary wished she dared drink. She was so very thirsty. Why was he not? Had he not experienced, as she had, the thirst-making consequences of the dance? Oh, why did he not drink?

As thoughts of a like nature swirled through her head, she half listened to the laughing conversation, was more than half bored that she hadn't a notion who the people were to whom Dalreath and his friends referred, and was about, in despair, to drink her drink without his cooperation, when he turned to her, took her glass from her and set the two on a convenient table.

"I am remiss," he said. "Are you acquainted with Lord Harry and Miss Tribble?" His brows rose when she shook her head and he quickly made the introductions.

Miss Tribble, a kindhearted young woman, drew Mary aside and asked her about her Season, how she was enjoying it, and what she had done. Mary, her eye on his lordship for fear he'd pick up that precious glass, answered somewhat at random, giving Miss Tribble an odd notion of her intelligence. Mary was pleased when, shortly thereafter, Samantha arrived on James's arm.

James veered off to get lemonade and Samantha joined the others. She noted the two full glasses on the table and looked at Mary. Mary grimaced. Somewhere inside Samantha something loosened. Perhaps he would *not* drink. Perhaps it would not happen. Perhaps . . . just perhaps . . . he would come on the morrow to complete that conversation and there would be no fault on her part if she were to answer him honestly. She had, after all, warned Mary that love potions were mischievous things and did not behave as one wished or expected them to do.

Samantha, suddenly feeling quite lively, joined in the conversation, chuckled twice at something said to her, realized James had set their drinks down beside Mary's and Lord Dalreath's, and suddenly felt a great thirst. Nevertheless, she waited until Lord Harry and Miss Tribble moved away before she reached for her glass. In fact all four reached for glasses. All four drank deeply. James and Mary set their goblets back on the table.

Samantha glanced at the glasses and looked over at Mary and James, who were talking volubly, laughing, as they walked off, arm in arm, toward the ballroom and their second dance of the evening. She turned back to look, warily, up at Dalreath and found him looking down at her. Suddenly her heart seemed to shrivel inside her, seemed to tighten into a tiny ball—and then, quickly, to expand to huge aching proportions.

Which glasses had held the potion?

Then, his gaze holding hers, she felt the warmth in him, a glowing look that grew out of all proportion to anything she had said or done. Dalreath reached for her glass, setting the goblets on the table. He turned back to her and reached for her hand. Holding her firmly, he gazed deeply into her eyes.

Oh dear, oh dear, which glasses had held that potion?

With a quick glance to assure himself the room was

empty, he ducked his head and dropped a soft, tantalizing kiss upon her wondering lips.

Samantha's heart sank. He had kissed her, but . . .

In which glasses was that potion?

. . . if it were because he and she had gotten the potion— the mischievous magic going awry in the worst possible way—then she did not want him. Not if his love was a trick of her witchery. Not if he didn't, from a whole heart, love her for herself, for who and what she was. Oh, if only she had not come this evening. If only she had not made that potion. If only . . . if only . . . if only . . .

If only I could go home, she wailed silently.

Going home when the evening finally ended was, in some ways, worse. Mary would not stop going on and on about James Morrison, how thoughtful, how nice, how manly, how handsome in a quiet comfortable way, how . . . how . . . how . . . until Samantha thought she would scream. Again, she wished she and Mary were not forced to share a room. She had not shared a bed with anyone since she was a very small child, and she was quite certain she never wished to do so ever again. Especially not with someone who would not stop talking long enough to fall asleep.

Especially when she only wanted to think about that kiss. Oh, such a faint hint of what a kiss should be. Would she ever experience the real thing? Ever know . . .

And yet, even that merest touching of lips, which should not have affected her in any particular way, had been entrancing. She *should* have felt nothing. She should *not* have wanted him to deepen it, not have wanted him to pull her into his embrace, not wanted to rest there safely forever and ever . . .

Instead, thought Samantha, the thought writhing within her overwrought mind, *what I should want is for all of us to leave London and go home. Immediately.*

* * *

Finally, much later that night, ensconced in their favorite chairs in Dalreath's rooms, James and his lordship each held a final glass of wine. James looked over the rim of his at his oldest friend, looked down into his wine, drew in a deep breath, and opened his mouth to speak . . .

"She's all I ever hoped," said Dalreath dreamily.

"Mary?" asked James a trifle sharply.

"Who? No, of course not. Why would you think any such thing?"

"She has shown her preference for you in every way a lady may do and remain a lady," grumbled James—but then remembered that at Almack's that evening, things had been somewhat different. His mood lightened.

"Mary? *Only* in those ways a lady may use?" Dalreath chuckled. "Now my Sam is not so reticent. She would never let a little thing like propriety stop her. Not if she wanted something badly." Dalreath's smile faded as a sense of horror filled him. He sat up rigidly straight. *"Does that mean she does not want me as much as I want her?"*

James ignored his reference to Lady Samantha. "Miss Mary is a lady," he said. "She is exactly the sort of woman I have dreamed I'd someday win." He frowned. "But if she is in love with you . . ."

"Is she? My Sam? Do you think so?"

"Will you stop harping on Lady Samantha?"

Dalreath blinked. James's sour tone jerked him from the haze in which he'd drifted ever since he'd given in to that uncontrollable urge to kiss Samantha. Not that it had been the sort of kiss he'd wanted to give her . . . but something was the matter with James. "James?"

James sighed. "I have done what I swore I'd never do."

"You have?" asked Dalreath cautiously, his mind going over all the things James had ever said he'd never do. Duel, for instance. Surely he had not somehow managed to become mixed up in a duel?

"I realized it in an instant," said James—and in turn was

lost in that dreamy state in which lovers spend so much of their time.

"Realized what?" asked Dalreath, overly blunt in his determination to discover what, exactly, his cousin meant, since so far he was completely in the dark.

"Love."

"Love?"

"Mary."

"Love Mary?"

Dalreath cogitated. He was certain he'd not drunk so much wine that evening that his logical facility was impaired, but James was not making sense. Unless . . .

"You?"

"Rath, all in an instant I knew."

"Knew what?"

James cast his cousin a disgusted look. "Have you not been listening? I am in love with Mary. Only this evening did I recognize it. But—" He lost that blissful look and scowled. "—if she is still yearning after you, then all is lost and I might as well put a pistol to my head!"

"Mary Pringle was infatuated with my title and my fortune. She has never yearned after *me.*"

James thought about that. "You sure?" he asked cautiously.

Dalreath chuckled. "James, how often have we known some young thing to think herself in love with me when she was merely in love with the idea of being my countess rather than my wife?"

"Mary wouldn't," said James stubbornly. "She would never be so shallow."

Dalreath, thinking over what Mary had, time and again, revealed concerning her conventional upbringing and predictable behavior, almost decided to debate that point. Then, with a look at his cousin's mulish expression, he recalled that James was a rather conventional sort himself. The two might suit very well.

"Very well," he said pacifically, "but I am quite certain she was never *in love* with me."

James considered that. "No. Perhaps it was merely that you look like one of those old Greeks. *You* know. The ones who are all sleek muscle and bearing a noble countenance? Girls can't help themselves yearning after that—until they discover there are more important things in life."

Dalreath laughed uncomfortably. He was always uncomfortable when someone referred to his more than adequate physique and overly handsome features. "Yes. Definitely there are more important things. James, wish me luck," he said, coming to the decision toward which he'd been edging all evening. Tomorrow he would visit Lord Forsythe and formally ask for Samantha's hand.

"Wish you luck?" asked James. He was already falling back into his dream world and responded more or less at random. "You are always lucky, Rath."

"Not always," said his lordship, thinking of the harsh and greedy man who had been his guardian for too many years.

The blood kinship between Dalreath and his guardian had softened the man not one whit. There was even a time before Dalreath had been sent to school when he'd wondered if an accident he'd suffered had truly been an accident.

"There have been occasions in my life when I was very unlucky indeed," he explained, "so please wish me luck."

His uncle was dead now. He could forget the man ever existed. Dalreath drew in a deep breath and, for the last time, put such old history where it belonged: well into the past.

James nodded agreement but, frankly, he hadn't a notion what it was to which Rath referred. And just then, dreaming of his Mary, of a future with her, he didn't wish to delve into the whys and wherefores of it.

Samantha looked at the closed door to the ground floor room her father had chosen for his own. She paced the hall in both directions until she decided it was too crowded—there were, after all, a footman standing at attention near the stairs and a maid polishing a table near the door on which rested the salver for cards left by visitors. Samantha went into the salon, where she found not people but far too much furniture for pacing.

"I want to go *home*," she muttered, longing for the wide acres where she could roam for hours, striding along with a rather mannish stride, and not worrying about what might or might not be in her way.

"Home? Nonsense," said Mary, looking up from her embroidery. "Why would anyone wish to return to the country in the middle of the Season?"

"Dalreath is with my father," said Samantha and wrung her hands.

Mary rose to her feet, the handkerchief falling to the floor. "Are you certain?"

"Yes. I was at the top of the stairs and I heard him ask for Father. I waited there and heard the footman return for him and take him into Father's room."

"Then he has come to . . ." Mary's mother's lecture on the duties of wifehood filled her head with disturbing pictures and her eyes widened. Suddenly she, too, was wringing her hands. "But I don't want . . . I didn't think . . . no!"

Samantha stopped short and swung around. "What are you talking about?"

"I was *wrong*. Samantha, I do *not* want to wed him. I *don't*. Isn't there something you can do? Can you not undo the spell? Make everything right again? Oh dear, I do not think I can bear it. Sam, I have discovered it is *James* I want! What am I to do?"

Samantha's eyes widened. "You think Dalreath is asking my father for your hand?"

"What else could it be?"

But he kissed me. Just last night his lips touched mine. It had been a sweetly drugging moment in which she had realized just how dreadfully deeply she had fallen in love with the man. But if he had kissed her merely because he had drunk of that potion . . .

"Mary, why do you think he is asking for *your* hand?"

"But what else can it be?" repeated Mary, bewildered. "We drank at exactly the same time. Just as it was supposed to happen. You were there, Sam. In Almack's refreshment room. You *saw* it happen."

Samantha frowned and tucked a fingernail between her front teeth. "But, Mary . . ."

"Sam, please. You must know a way to undo the damage!"

"Mary . . ."

"Please?" Mary wheedled. She moved nearer and grasped Samantha's hands. "You can, can you not? It is possible?"

"Mary . . . are you absolutely certain?"

"You were there."

Samantha nodded, her heart thudding. She had been there and she was as *uncertain* as one could be. She hadn't a notion which glass went to which person. Had she and Dalreath drunk the potion? Could Mary be *partially* correct? Or could *Mary* have gotten one glass . . . *and James the other?*

Oh, but if that were the case, why did Dalreath kiss me? Samantha was more confused than ever.

"Sam, you will fix everything? Make it right again? You will, will you not?"

"I warned you love potions were mischievous things and that we could not predict what would happen. And now something has happened and we don't know what it is."

"What *do* you mean?" Bewildered, Mary backed away.

"Mary, which of us drank from the glasses in which you put the potion?"

"I put it in for Lord Dalreath and myself. So of course . . ." She frowned. Mary was a bit of a slowtop—but not *that* slow! "Samantha, are you saying the glasses became mixed?"

"I don't know. I fear I got one of them and Dalreath the other."

"You? And Dalreath?" Mary brightened. "Oh, but that is perfect. Just perfect. James hinted he might come visit this afternoon. I must go change my gown . . ." And, again all smiles, she ran lightly from the room.

"*Perfect?*" Samantha's heart sped up once again. "No. Not perfect. In fact all wrong. I will not have a man who requires magic to make him love me. I will not!"

Not when I fell so deeply in love with him long before drinking a potion of any sort . . . assuming I did drink of the potion . . .

Samantha's mind continued to race in circles, matching those she was wearing into the carpet. It occurred to her to wonder just when she had fallen in love with Dalreath and, after another couple of circles, concluded it had been long years ago. Perhaps when she had faced him after interfering with his birds and he had been in that magnificent temper?

A tap at the door and the footman entered and handed Lady Sam a note. She perused it, shrugged, and tossed the tear-blotched and blotted note into the fire. She already knew Lady Cecily must leave London. Why the lady had thought it necessary to inform her it had happened, she did not know.

Or care. What she cared about was that she *loved* Lord Dalreath. She loved *only* him and ever would but—

She stopped short and stared sightlessly in horror at the wall.

—what if he *had* come to ask for *Mary's* hand? What if *that* was the potion's mischief? That now she knew that she loved *him,* he had discovered he loved another?

Oh dear, what could she do?

But maybe she worried for nothing. Perhaps he had only come to discuss politics. Or mutual problems on their estates. Or the war or investments or . . . anything and everything but what she hoped they discussed: the settlements that must be arranged before they would be allowed to wed.

Whoever it was he wished to wed.

And if it were herself? Her heart beat like a bird fluttering against the bars of a cage, and she pressed her hands to her breast. She wanted him. But she could not wed him if his love were a result of the potion. Samantha, her mind whirling from the good to the bad to the good and back again, thought and fretted and dreamed . . . until, after another tap, the door opened yet again.

Samantha swung around and faced the footman. "Yes?"

"Your presence is requested in your father's study, Lady Samantha."

A handful of moments later, when she'd rushed in and leaned back against the door, Lord Forsythe spoke solemnly. "My dear," he intoned, "you have been accorded a great honor."

Samantha felt herself blushing, but was unsure if it were due to embarrassment or anger at her father's attitude. Perhaps both? She turned a questioning look toward Dalreath. He quirked a brow in such a self-deriding way her anger dissipated in a wish to chuckle.

"I will leave you now. As is proper," said Lord Forsythe— but the last was enunciated with such a questioning tone that Samantha's desire to laugh was accentuated. This time she did not dare to look at Dalreath in case he, too, felt the same and she couldn't contain her chuckles. "Well. Yes. Very well." Lord Forsythe sidled around his lordship, faced his daughter, opened his mouth to speak . . . and closed it. He shook his head and, that same head bowed, one fisted hand tucked behind his back, he left the room, closing the door behind him.

"I suspect I have upset him, although I do not quite know why," said Dalreath.

"My sisters' engagements were achieved in a much less formal manner."

"Are we engaged, then?" he asked softly.

Samantha stilled.

"Ah. We are not."

He sighed and opened his arms. Samantha, without thinking, walked into them and was enclosed in a comfortable and comforting hug. Too comforting? Too comfortable?

Samantha inserted her arms between them and pushed him away.

"Will you wed me?" he asked when she had crossed the room and turned, straight of back, to stare at him.

"Yes." And then she shook her head. "But only if you promise to give up your hunting!"

Dalreath pursed his lips, his eyelids drooping ever so slightly.

"Well—at least the fox hunting?" she asked in a voice less sure of itself.

His lips tightened.

Samantha sighed and fiddled with her ribbons. He moved across the room and, gently, untangled her fingers, drawing her again into a loose embrace. Sam fiddled with a button on his vest, instead.

"You don't really want to wed me," she said so softly Dalreath had to bend his head to hear her.

"I do not?"

"No. It was the love potion. It was supposed to be for you and Mary, but the glasses must have gotten mixed up."

"They were. Miss Mary and James drank what I got for Miss Mary and myself."

Samantha's head jerked up, her startled gaze tangling with his. *He had not drunk of the potion.* Somewhere inside her a huge knot unraveled and left her feeling whole again.

"I think," he said, staring broodingly into her eyes, "that I have loved you ever since you stole that fox. You were such a charmingly determined brat, were you not?" His eyes narrowed, twinkled, his mouth quirking up on one side. "That was, since you do not appear to know it, my last fox hunt. I've not been out since."

"The birds?" she asked, hopeful.

"Don't expect too much, minx." They stared at each other. "Well? Will you?"

"Wed you?"

"Hmm." He touched her cheek with one finger, outlined her left brow, fingered her earlobe . . .

"Well . . . maybe."

Dalreath sobered. He set her aside and, in turn, crossed the room, turning to stare at her. "Because I won't promise to give up hunting altogether?"

"No." She moved her hand in a dismissive gesture. "Of course not. If you had, I would not have believed you and I definitely would *not* marry you. I'll not begin married life with a lie between us."

He prowled back and pulled her close again. "Then?" he asked.

Sam returned to fiddling with the button.

Rath gently removed her fingers and held them. "You'll have it off."

She sighed. "Oh well. I suppose I must."

"Must!"

"It was in the tea leaves. One cannot go against what is in the tea leaves."

He grinned. "You mean that night at Lady Cecily's ball?"

"You did recognize me."

He nodded.

"I thought so."

"It was your eyes, brat." He touched the end of her nose. "You haven't changed so very much from when, nose in the air, you ordered me to leave the poor innocent birds alone. *My* birds. And then, along with your parents and older sisters, you ate what I brought your cook for your family's table."

Sam blushed. "Yes. I am a trifle hypocritical, am I not?"

One brow quirked. "But *not* so hypocritical you'll say me nay when you want to say me yea?"

She bit her bottom lip and looked down. She poked at the button but refrained from twisting it.

"Careful," he said softly, insinuatingly. "You'll make your mouth all rosy and I'll not be able to forego kissing it."

Lady Sam disentangled herself and went to the door. She opened it, looked out, and seeing her favorite footman was on duty, beckoned to him. "A tea tray, please. At once."

When the door closed and Sam leaned against it as she had when she first entered the room, Rath crossed his arms. "I see. My fate rests on what the tea leaves tell you once you've drunk your tea?"

She nodded.

"I wonder," he said, thoughtfully. *"You've* forbidden *me* to hunt and I will do so except for what will go nicely on our table. Perhaps since I have agreed to so much, then *I* should forbid *you* to read the leaves."

Samantha looked at him, her eyes widening. Hope rose within her.

"Yes." He nodded. "I think I will do that. I cannot bear to think what you might see in the leaves over the years. Think of the problems that could arise and cause serious problems between us if you were to believe such nonsense."

"It isn't nonsense."

"Still worse."

"Are you forbidding it?"

His jaw firmed and he looked more stern than she had ever seen him. She waited, more hopeful yet. "Yes," he said after a moment's thought. The word was uncompromisingly firm. "I am."

Lady Sam smiled. The smile grew absolutely brilliant. *"I'll wed you."*

Rath's brows arched.

She sighed a gusty, half humorous, half serious, sigh. "You don't know how often I've given in and given a reading and *not* wanted to see what I see in the leaves. How often I've read something terrible and had to pretend otherwise and then had to wait in silence for the awful thing to happen. Now I've the excuse I need for saying no to anyone who requests a reading. You have forbidden it."

His brows came down, clashing above his nose. "If that is the only reason you mean to wed me . . ."

"That," she said lightly, turning on him a coquettish look from under her lashes, "and the fact that, despite myself, I have fallen in love with you. I think," she said musingly, "it must have happened when you were berating me for frightening your game birds into behaving more like silly geese."

Rath whooped, gathered her close, and kissed her so soundly neither heard the door open—and quickly close. The footman, grinning broadly, nodded to the butler, who immediately went to tell the housekeeper, who told my lady's dresser, who let the news fall to Lord Forsythe's valet and, inadvertently, to the head housemaid, who overheard and who then whispered the news to the tweeny, who told the upstairs maid—and so on.

In fact, the whole household was aware of the engagement between Lady Sam and Rath long before Lord and Lady Forsythe were apprised of it.

Only Mary had no interest in the news when, later, Samantha rather hesitantly informed her of it. "That's good," she said as she looked from the forget-me-not trimmed bonnet in her right hand to the chip straw with the rosebuds in her left. "James has invited me to drive in the park at the hour of the promenade, and I don't know which hat to wear. Which would you wear, Sammy?"

Miss Mary fretted over which bonnet most became her and whether it went with her fanciest parasol and if it did *not,* had she time to go out and buy a new one?

Samantha, who had feared her old friend would be devastated, recalled the love potion. This time, it seemed, the mischievous magic had gone wrong in such a way as to bring about a truly happy ending. James and Mary would, thought Sam, suit each other right down to the ground—leaving her free to enjoy, guiltlessly, the long and happy marriage between Rath and herself that she'd seen in the leaves that night at Lady Cecily's.

And, not *best* of all but very good indeed, she would never again have to read the tea leaves. The *best,* of course, was that Lord Dalreath loved her as she loved him and *not* because of that pernicious love potion!

Historical Romance from
Jo Ann Ferguson

SINK YOUR TEETH INTO VAMPIRE ROMANCES FROM SHANNON DRAKE